POISON IVY

POISON IVY

A MARTHA'S VINEYARD MYSTERY

CYNTHIA RIGGS

MINOTAUR BOOKS
A THOMAS DUNNE BOOK
NEW YORK

This is a work of fiction. All of the characters, organizations, and events portrayed in this novel are either products of the author's imagination or are used fictitiously.

A THOMAS DUNNE BOOK FOR MINOTAUR BOOKS.
An imprint of St. Martin's Publishing Group.

www.thomasdunnebooks.com
www.minotaurbooks.com

Library of Congress Cataloging-in-Publication Data

Riggs, Cynthia.
    Poison ivy : a Martha's Vineyard mystery / Cynthia Riggs.—First edition.
        pages   cm.   (Martha's Vineyard mystery ; 11)
    "A Thomas Dunne Book."
    ISBN 978-1-250-05867-6 (hardcover)
    ISBN 978-1-4668-6308-8 (e-book)
    1. Trumbull, Victoria (Fictitious character)—Fiction.   2. Women detectives—Massachusetts—Martha's Vineyard—Fiction.   3. Serial murder investigation—Fiction.   4. Martha's Vineyard (Mass.)—Fiction.   I. Title.
    PS3618.I394P65 2015
    813'.6—dc23

                                                                    2014042140

Minotaur books may be purchased for educational, business, or promotional use. For information on bulk purchases, please contact the Macmillan Corporate and Premium Sales Department at 1-800-221-7945, extension 5442, or write to special markets@macmillan.com.

First published in 2013 by Cleveland House Books

First Minotaur Books Edition: April 2015

10 9 8 7 6 5 4 3 2 1

FOR
DIONIS COFFIN RIGGS,
POET
1898–1997

POISON IVY

—

CHAPTER 1

The season was still too new to be considered fall, but the sky was that brilliant autumnal blue, the air was crisp and smelled of the salt sea, and this was a fine day for Victoria Trumbull. At ninety-two, she was about to launch a new career as adjunct professor. She had been invited to teach a course in poetry at Ivy Green College.

Adjunct professor, she thought, smoothing her hair. A fine title, a peaceful occupation, and she intended to show her colleagues and students that experience mattered.

She had dressed carefully in her green plaid suit and soft white blouse with its self-bow at the neck, had clipped on the earrings that matched the suit, and had even dabbed on a touch of lipstick.

She stowed the papers she'd worked on for the past several weeks—a syllabus, a reading list, lecture notes, and her own and others' poetry—in her cloth bag along with the baseball hat she always carried.

Gold stitching across the front of the hat read WEST TISBURY POLICE, DEPUTY. Victoria had earned the hat and the title.

Elizabeth, Victoria's granddaughter, drove her to the campus of Ivy Green College, a few blocks from the Vineyard Haven library. The college consisted of three buildings: two former houses and between them, a two-car garage. One house served as the administration building, the second as the classroom building, and the garage had been enlarged into a lecture hall.

The founder of the college greeted her. "Delighted to have you on our faculty, Mrs. Trumbull."

"Thank you, Thackery," said Victoria, shaking his extended hand.

Thackery Wilson was in his early sixties now, his eyes almost hidden by thick lenses in a heavy tortoiseshell frame. He was tall and lean, just as he'd been as a fourteen-year-old. Victoria could remember when he'd played summer softball in the field behind the Grange Hall. Over the years he'd assumed an air of dignity overlain with superiority that didn't entirely suit him. Nevertheless, she'd always admired Thackery. And the fact that he was bringing higher education to the Island was certainly in his favor.

"We'll have an orientation for new faculty members this morning, Mrs. Trumbull. Classes begin after lunch. I see you're all ready." A nod to her bulging cloth bag.

He looked off to his left and scowled. A pear-shaped man, also in his sixties, was rolling, rather than walking, toward them. He was short with narrow shoulders, a round belly, and plump buttocks. He had stringy gray hair, gray face, stained gray cotton trousers, gray work shirt. Even his shoes were gray.

"You know Walter our groundskeeper, of course," said Thackery.

"Good morning." Victoria shifted her cloth bag to her left hand and extended her right. "Nice to see you, Walter."

"You teachin'?" Walter said, jerking his head toward the former garage.

Thackery answered. "Yes. She'll have a class of eleven in Catbriar Hall in an hour and a half. Have you set up the seats?"

"There's only one of me," said Walter, who'd ignored Victoria's extended hand. "Want me to drop everything?"

"If you would, please." A muscle in Thackery's jaw twitched. "I want to show Professor Trumbull her classroom. Is the door unlocked?"

Walter withdrew a long chain with a ring of a dozen keys from some pocket, and with a deep sigh rolled his way toward the new lecture hall.

Thackery said to Victoria, "I'll provide you with a list of your students, Mrs. Trumbull. You'll find you know many of them." He walked slowly, apparently to let Walter get far enough ahead to open the door.

Walter, for his part, had stepped up onto the wide porch and was fumbling with the keys, searching through the jangling key ring, apparently to let Thackery know that he wasn't about to be told what to do.

That meant that when Walter eventually opened the door, all three of them were treated to the stench that poured out of the building in a nauseating cloud.

Victoria stepped away from the door and waved her hand in front of her great nose.

"Walter," said Thackery, his face taut. "What have you done now?"

"Obeying orders," muttered Walter. "Mice. You told me to get rid of them."

"Surely dead mice can't smell that horrid," said Victoria, holding a napkin that she'd hurriedly fished out of her pocket to her nose.

"Drop everything, and clean up this place. Immediately," said Thackery.

Walter unlatched his ring of keys and the long chain connected to them from his belt and tossed them onto the porch flooring. "I can only do so much. Do this. Do that. Set up chairs. Take them down. Clean up the mice yourself, you want them cleaned up."

"You can't quit again," said Thackery. "Not now."

"Oh no?"

"Professor Trumbull has a class to teach."

Walter set his feet apart and folded his arms over his belly, his mouth in a tight pout.

"We can sit under the trees, if Walter doesn't mind setting chairs out there," Victoria said.

"What do you expect from me, Walter? An apology for asking you to do your job?" Thackery stretched himself to his full height, thinning like a rubber band. "You, the janitor? Well, you won't get it."

"That's it," said Walter, leaving the keys and chain where he'd dropped them. He waddled away toward home, across the street from the college.

"It's fine, Thackery," said Victoria, her voice muffled by the napkin. "We can sit on the grass under the trees." She lowered the napkin. "But Thackery, I know how dead mice smell, and I don't believe that stench is dead mice. You'd better call the police."

They turned away from the odor funneling out of the open door and headed toward the administration building.

"You've got to keep people from entering the building until the police get here," said Victoria.

"Mrs. Trumbull," said Thackery with studied patience, "this is not a matter for the police. It is a matter for a competent janitor, and since we don't have one, I shall call Kerry Scott's cleaning service. We do not need police to clean up dead mice." He took a steel pocket watch out of his watch pocket and opened it. "Classes start in a little more than an hour."

"Do you have a cell phone?" Victoria asked.

"Of course not." Thackery strode toward the building with its discrete black-and-gold sign, WOODBINE HALL. Victoria followed.

"I assure you, the smell is not mice," she said, slightly out of breath from trying to match his stride. "I need to make that call."

Without replying, Thackery climbed the steps to the front porch and opened the door. Stained-glass panels, a relic of the building's past life as someone's home, framed the door. The late morning light cast blurry purple-and-green images of fruiting grapevines on the entry hall's scuffed wooden floor.

"Where's Linda?" asked Victoria, glancing around the room for Thackery's assistant, Linda Bacon.

"Out sick again," said Thackery. He made his call to the cleaning service. When he was off the line, Victoria dialed her boss, West Tisbury's police chief, Mary Kathleen O'Neill.

4

"Casey," said Victoria, when the chief answered. "I'm at Ivy Green College and there's a dead body in the old garage." Before Casey had time to respond, Victoria went on. "I know this is state police business, but since I'm your deputy, I thought I should tell you first."

"Have you seen it?"

"I smelled it."

"Oh Lord!" said Casey. "That means it's been there a while. I'll call the state guys and the Tisbury cops and get there as soon as I can." Before she disconnected, she asked, "You okay?"

"Certainly." Victoria hung up and turned to Thackery. "I'm sorry Linda is sick. I hope it's not serious."

"It's an advanced case of hypochondria," said Thackery. "She'll be in tomorrow morning. Late, naturally, because she'll be weak having spent two days in bed. Once she smells the dead mice, she'll leave immediately, feeling faint."

"Her grandmother was the same way," said Victoria, sympathetically.

"I'd get rid of her, but no one else would work for what I can pay her. When she is here, she's an excellent worker."

The two-person cleaning crew arrived within a few minutes and Thackery led them to the garage, now labeled CATBRIAR HALL.

"Phew-eee, mister," said the stout Brazilian woman who seemed to be in charge. "You said dead mice? Not dead mice. Big animal. We don't do dead animals. You want animal control." The cleaners left, waving the stink away from their nostrils.

Thackery smacked the side of his head with the palm of his hand. His once-thick dark hair curled around his head in a sort of gray tonsure. "We have less than an hour until classes begin."

"The police are on their way," said Victoria. They were standing well off to one side of the former garage. "There's no need to cancel classes. It's appropriate for poets to meet under the trees. The other classes were to meet in the other house anyway."

"Honeysuckle Hall," said Thackery.

Victoria glanced up as a state police car pulled up in the parking area.

"Most embarrassing," said Thackery.

"Morning, Mrs. Trumbull," said Sergeant Smalley. "Morning, Thackery. What do we have here?"

"I hope it's a false alarm," said President Thackery Wilson, lifting his nose.

"It's in the garage," said Victoria.

"Catbriar Hall," corrected Thackery.

"Let's see what you've got," said Smalley.

"You'll be able to smell it," said Victoria.

"If you'll excuse me, I have a college to run," said its president, and left.

Victoria led Smalley and Tim Eldredge, one of the state troopers, to the open door of the lecture hall.

"Hmm," said Smalley, covering his mouth and nose with a handkerchief. "When was the building last used?"

"I don't know. I would guess late August when Thackery had a forum on symbolism in fiction."

"Two weeks." Smalley beckoned to the trooper, who was keeping his distance. "Tim, get Thackery back here. He needs to answer a few questions."

"I have faculty arriving," protested the president when Tim returned with him.

"That can wait, Thackery," said Smalley. "Since the hall was last used in late August, has it been locked?"

"Walter was supposed to keep it locked."

"Is he your caretaker?"

"Barely." Thackery folded his arms over his narrow chest, chin up, nose in the air. "If you're here to clean out the dead mice, I suggest you get busy so we can begin to educate our students."

"Before we allow anyone to step inside," said Smalley politely,

"I'll be calling in the forensics team from the mainland. No one's to enter the building."

"Oh, for God's sake!" said Thackery, tugging at the curl of hair that had plastered itself to his sweaty forehead.

CHAPTER 2

"I'm so excited, Mrs. Trumbull," cried Honesty Norton. "I've read all your books." Honesty's long blond ringlets framed a face dwarfed by enormous brown eyes

The class of eleven, ten young women and one young man, settled down under the large oaks behind the three buildings, away from the activity around the lecture hall. Simon Mayhew, the sole male student, found a green resin lawn chair behind the administration building for Victoria.

"Why are the police here, Mrs. Trumbull?" he asked.

"There's a problem in the lecture hall," said Victoria. "Let's introduce ourselves."

"Well, I'm Brittany Silva?" said the dark-haired girl to Victoria's right, ending her sentence in a question. "And I've been writing poems since I was, like, eight?" Brittany tossed her long hair behind her shoulders with a shrug. Victoria had difficulty thinking of these young people as men and women. "I brought some of my poems with me." Brittany's slender tanned legs were stretched out in front of her and she leaned forward in expectation.

"Wonderful, Brittany," said Victoria. "We'd like to hear some of your poems in a later session. Next?"

"I'm Jodi Paloni," the next student said. "What stinks, Mrs. Trumbull?" She, too, was dark-haired, but her hair was cropped close in a buzz cut. The tattoos on her upper arms were circles of vines or snakes, Victoria couldn't tell for sure. She had gold rings in her eyebrows and a gold stud in her nose. Victoria imagined how it must hurt when she had a cold and had to blow her nose.

"Are you related to the Paloni children on New Lane?" Victoria asked. "Their sister, perhaps?"

"I'm their mother," said the girl.

Victoria was momentarily stumped. "Sandy is your son?"

"My youngest. What *is* that smell?"

"That's why we're out here instead of in Catbriar Hall," said Victoria, mulling over the fact that Jodi looked fifteen and her youngest of at least four sons was eight. "They're cleaning up something."

"The police?" asked Simon. "Cleaning up something?"

"Yes," said Victoria. "Simon, tell us why you're taking this course."

The two-hour class flew by. Victoria memorized the names and faces and after her students left wrote down the clues that would help her remember them for the next class meeting on Thursday. Rule Britannia for Brittany, with her ruler-straight hair. Her large eyes gave Honesty an honest expression. Simon says for Simon. And so forth.

Yes, it was a corpse, dead at least two weeks, possibly more, found in the crawl space under the garage. The space had been excavated when the garage was expanded, and was accessible only through a hatch in the closet floor of the new section. A man. It wouldn't be easy to identify him, especially since he'd carried no identification.

Toby, the undertaker, removed the corpse after Doc Jeffers, this week's medical examiner, declared the man officially dead, and the off Island forensics team had vacuumed up every bit of possible evidence.

Kerry Scott's cleaning service returned with disinfectant, bleach, and scrubbing brushes, and in a short time, Catbriar Hall, the erstwhile garage, was almost habitable again, although there was still a faint unpleasant odor that overlay the cleaning scents.

———

The following day, Walter lumbered through the front door of Woodbine Hall, the administration building. President Thackery Wilson was at his desk, poring over a stack of papers.

Linda, his assistant, had called in sick again.

Walter cleared his throat.

Thackery looked up over his glasses. "Is there something I can do for you, Walter?"

"You can apologize, that's what you can do."

"Apologize!" sputtered Thackery. "After you walked out on the job leaving a ninety-two-year-old great-grandmother to do your work?" He slapped his pen down on the papers and stood.

Walter drew up a chair and plunked himself down on it. "I want an apology, and I want my job back."

"I didn't fire you. You quit." Thackery took a deep, deep breath, let it out slowly, and sat down again. "Walter, this is the third time you've walked off the job over the past year."

"With reason, every time." Walter leaned back in the chair and clasped his hands over his belly.

"I can't have this."

At this point, Victoria Trumbull came into the office, which looked much like an unfurnished living room. "I hope I'm not interrupting."

"Not in the least," said Thackery, standing again.

Walter continued to sit, his chin lowered, his lower lip stuck out so its purplish inner surface showed.

"I was passing by and wanted to leave off yesterday's attendance record," said Victoria. "I won't disturb you."

"Please, have a seat, Professor Trumbull," said Thackery. "Walter has come to request his job back." Once Victoria was seated, Thackery sat.

"All I want is an apology," said Walter.

Victoria glanced from one angry face to another. "I'm not sure I understand."

"I had asked Walter to clean up Catbriar Hall, and it turned out to be a larger problem than we expected."

"A simple apology," said Walter.

"A long-dead corpse does require specialized attention," said Victoria. "Not something Walter could be expected to do. I think we can safely apologize."

"That's right," said Walter, nodding.

"Why don't we agree that Walter deserves an apology for having been expected to do an almost impossible task, and you, Thackery, deserve an apology from Walter, who walked off the job at a critical time."

"He apologizes first," said Walter.

"Thackery?" warned Victoria.

"Dammit, I apologize," said Thackery.

"Then I apologize, too," said Walter, hoisting himself out of the chair. "I'll be on the job first thing in the morning, Mrs. Trumbull." With that, Walter nodded to Victoria, ignored Thackery, and left.

"Jeesus Kee-rist," said Thackery. "I hoped we'd finally gotten rid of him."

On the porch of Alley's Store in West Tisbury (Dealers in Almost Everything), Sarah Germaine was sitting on the bench with her back to the sign that read CANNED PEAS. As usual, Joe the plumber was leaning against one of the posts that held up the porch roof, his cheek puffed out with a wad of something.

"Hope this weather holds," said Joe, leaning off to one side to spit a stream of brown juice away from the step.

"Thanks for not smoking," said Sarah, smiling sweetly. She had stopped, as usual, on her way home from Tribal Headquarters, where she worked. This afternoon she was wearing a turquoise sweatshirt with WAMPANOAG TRIBE OF GAY HEAD (AQUINNAH) emblazoned on it in reddish-orange letters that vibrated against the turquoise background.

"You being funny or something?" said Joe, wiping his mouth on his sleeve.

Before Sarah could answer, a silver Porsche pulled up against the granite blocks that edged the walkway and a young man in pressed jeans and ironed plaid shirt got out.

Sarah and Joe stopped talking and watched.

The young man locked the car door.

"Locked it!" exclaimed Sarah.

"New Yorker," said Joe.

The driver walked around the front of the car, strolled across the walkway, and mounted the steps up onto the porch. He nodded to Sarah and Joe, opened the screen door, and stepped inside.

"Well," said Sarah. "La de dah."

"Know who that is?" said Joe.

"No idea. Not from around here, that's for sure."

"Hollywood," said Joe.

"Oh?"

"He's in that teevee series, *Family Riot*. You know."

"No, I never watch that stuff," said Sarah.

"Name's Bruce something. Steinbicker."

"Well," said Sarah. "Oh, my." She tugged the sleeves of her sweatshirt over her knuckles. "Even I've heard of him. What's he doing here?"

"Playground of the rich and famous, dahlin'. Wants to be seen consorting with the natives."

"You heard what Mrs. Trumbull is up to now, didn't you?" asked Sarah, changing the subject abruptly.

"Now what's the old lady doing?"

"She's teaching, but that's not what I meant. She found a dead body yesterday at the college."

"No shit," said Joe, shifting the wad inconspicuously to his other cheek. "Whose body is it?"

13

"They can't tell. Dr. Wilson thought it was dead mice. Mrs. Trumbull called the cops."

"Smelled that bad?"

"Kerry Scott's cleaners refused to clean the place."

The screen door opened again, and the man who looked like Bruce Steinbicker stepped down onto the porch carrying a *Wall Street Journal*. Sarah turned to stare at him. Joe gazed across the road at his truck, where Taffy, his golden retriever, was sitting in the driver's seat.

"Nice day," said the stranger, nodding at Sarah. His voice was mellow. His hair, a light brown, was rumpled artistically.

"Ahh . . ." said Sarah.

The stranger strode across the porch, stepped down onto the walkway, unlocked the driver's side door of his Porsche, got in, started the engine, made a U-turn in front of Joe's truck, and drove off.

"Cat got your tongue?" asked Joe.

After a week, the Island's excitement over the unidentified dead man faded somewhat. Victoria's class had already formed an identity of its own. Even these blasé children had been impressed by her knowing and remembering their names, and Victoria felt quite satisfied with herself. They continued to meet under the trees during the early weeks of the Island's golden September.

Linda, Thackery's assistant, a skinny woman with a massive tangle of curly light brown hair, had returned to work from her sickbed.

Walter went about setting up chairs, un-setting them, mowing the grass, cleaning the kitchen, and generally grumbling, but grumbling with a degree of caution.

Victoria was packing up her papers at the end of the fifth class session, a Tuesday, when Jodi, the teenage-looking mother of the four Paloni boys, spoke to her.

14

"You got a minute, Mrs. T?"

"Of course, Jodi. I'm impressed with the work you've shown me."

"Yeah, well." Jodi glanced down at her bare feet. "I'm working on a project, Mrs. T, and I need your advice."

"Of course. Poetry?"

"No, ma'am. Island history. Sociology, actually."

"Sit down and tell me about it."

She plopped onto the grass, her cutoff shorts barely covering what was necessary. "You know about the hearing impaired community in Chilmark?"

"I remember as a child meeting Chilmarkers who spoke only with sign language."

"That's exactly what I mean, Mrs. T." Jodi was more vivacious than Victoria had seen her in the previous two weeks. "I'm working on my master's degree . . ."

"You're what?" Victoria interrupted. "Your master's?"

"Yes, ma'am. Dr. Wilson got permission from Cape Cod University for me to work on my MA in sociology under Professor Roberta Chadwick."

"She lives on the Vineyard, doesn't she?"

"Yes, ma'am. Oak Bluffs. She teaches at the university and commutes to Woods Hole."

"As well as teaching here at Ivy Green College?"

"She doesn't teach here, just at CCU. She's up for tenure next year. She needs to publish stuff and needs credit for community service." Jodi pointed a thumb at her chest and smiled. "That's me."

"How many Island students does she have?"

"She's working individually with me and two other grad students, I think. I haven't met them."

"Have you decided on a thesis topic?"

"Signing." Jodi drew her feet up under her. "My grandmother was deaf. She taught me signing. I want to do legal signing, you know, for court cases. Trials, depositions, witness interviews. You know."

"I didn't realize there was such a career," said Victoria. "This is wonderful. How can I help you?"

"I'd like to interview you, Mrs. T, for my thesis on the Chilmark deaf-mutes. What you remember or knew firsthand about the community, any descendants you know of that I could talk to. That sort of stuff."

"Certainly. A few people are still around who remember them. You're welcome to come to my house."

"Thanks. I go past your place all the time."

"Tomorrow morning would be convenient for me," said Victoria. "I have some papers and books you may borrow."

"I'll be there as soon as I get the kids off to school. Around nine-thirty?"

CHAPTER 3

Thackery was in his office going over his paperwork when Victoria dropped by after class. She handed him more papers, covered in her loopy backhand writing.

"Linda's left for the day. She can record your attendance records tomorrow."

"She seems to be fairly casual about her work," said Victoria, sitting in the chair next to Thackery's desk.

Thackery rubbed the back of his neck. "She doesn't really need the job. Her husband's in the merchant marine and is away from home weeks at a time. This job is so she has something to do."

"No children?"

He shook his head. "How is the poetry course?"

"We're discussing formal poetry." Victoria brushed off bits of grass from her green plaid skirt. "Villanelles, sonnets, triolets, and sestinas."

Katydids were singing their late-summer mating song in the trees behind the building. Thackery's window was open and rich scents of approaching autumn drifted into the room. "I've given them six words to work into a sestina."

"Fine, fine," Thackery said. "Whenever you're ready to move indoors, I believe Catbriar Hall is habitable. It's been two weeks since . . ." He didn't finish.

"We enjoy meeting outside. It's a lovely spot with that magic circle of lush grass." Victoria smoothed her skirt. She really should get another ensemble now that she was an adjunct professor. "One of my students, Jodi Paloni, tells me she's working on her master's degree."

"She's quite a promising scholar," said Thackery, "improbable though her appearance is. She has a good mind."

"What you've accomplished is remarkable, Thackery."

He looked down at his desk and moved his desk calendar a half inch to the left.

"There must have been some formidable obstacles in setting up the college."

"Quite so. With such a small student body, only a half-dozen students are likely to enroll in any particular course we might offer." He dropped Victoria's attendance records into a wire tray and pushed his glasses back into place. "In our favor, a number of distinguished academicians have retired here. I believed, rightly, that many would welcome the opportunity to teach again."

"Teaching a small class must be appealing."

"Precisely," said Thackery. "A change after facing a lecture hall of five hundred students, half dozing, half texting on their electronic devices."

Victoria heard the honking of Canada geese overhead. A nostalgic sound. When she was a child, that meant geese heading south for the winter. Now they circled the Island's ponds and wintered here.

Thackery said, "At Ivy Green, professors can make eye contact with five or six students, all eager to learn."

"I'm surprised you're able to offer college credit."

"We worked out a compromise with Cape Cod University in order to award credit." Thackery lined up his pens. "The university and teachers' union made concessions and they set up an oversight committee to keep tabs on us. So here we are." He held up his hands. "Some at the university feel we're offering mere training courses. But our students need college credit in such utilitarian fields as education, criminal justice, and social services."

"Jodi's goal of getting a master's in sociology is certainly academically worthy."

"Her work will be a significant milestone for us. Perhaps the most important since our alliance with the university. That is, if she's able to carry through."

"Do you have any doubts?" asked Victoria. "She's a determined young woman."

"Let's hope she's as strong as she seems. The academic world is not easy."

"When does the oversight committee next meet? I should think they would be interested in Jodi's progress."

"Sometime in the next two weeks." Thackery sighed. "I must tell you, Mrs. Trumbull, I dread their visit."

"Why so? Look how much you've accomplished in ten short years with very little in the way of resources." Victoria indicated the faded wallpaper, the mismatched chairs, the scuffed wooden floor.

Thackery sat back, his hands folded over his flat stomach. "A slim majority of the committee supports what we're doing, namely providing higher education for everyone. The minority believes only a select few should be offered higher education." He sighed again. "With the discovery of a long-dead body in the cellar of our lecture hall, I'm afraid we'll lose what lukewarm support we have."

"How ridiculous."

He nodded. "I couldn't agree more."

"You're providing a new life for some of your students. Jodi could never hope to go to college off Island with her four boys to worry about."

Thackery stood and walked toward the cracked window that looked out over the campus. He clasped his hands behind his back and stared out. "Fortunately, I have a strong champion on the committee, Harlan Bliss, a philosophy professor. He was instrumental in setting up our criminal justice program."

"His name is familiar."

"He's not only a well-respected academic, he's also a Beacon Hill Bliss, heir to a sizable fortune."

"Ah," said Victoria.

"With his support, we may be able to swing the minority three members to his way of thinking."

"What motive would anyone have to oppose the college?"

"Academic politics. Power, egos, small-mindedness, envy." He turned to Victoria, hands still clasped behind his back. "I thought a small college would never have to deal with academic politics. It seems we haven't escaped." Thackery shrugged and returned to his seat. "I've never been able to sort out the underlying politics of the oversight committee members." He looked over at her, his eyes magnified by the thick lenses.

Victoria nodded.

Thackery continued. "The disagreement over our curriculum has nothing to do with the college. Yet, we're likely to be a victim. Pointless."

"Who are your advocates, besides Professor Bliss?"

Thackery shuffled through the papers he'd straightened and drew one out and read from it. "There's an engineering professor, Dedie Wieler; a geology professor, Journeyman Cash; and a professor of African-American studies, Noah Sutterfield."

"With the advocacy of those three and Professor Bliss, it sounds as though you needn't worry," said Victoria.

He forced a smile. "Professor Cash, the geologist, misses numerous oversight committee meetings because of fieldwork. He missed the August meeting, for example." He leaned back in his chair. "I can't imagine where his work took him. His field courses are in Death Valley, usually scheduled in winter when the temperatures are bearable."

"And Professor Sutterfield?"

"A quiet man. Doesn't speak up often." Thackery swiveled the chair. "It's critical to have the committee's support. They go over every faculty appointment, course offering, student application, the facilities, our grading." He pushed back from his desk and faced Victoria. "Professor Bliss has indicated that he might help us financially, once he's sure we're firmly established."

"Surely ten years is enough to convince the most skeptical."

"I wish that were so."

"What about Professor Wieler?"

"She's up for tenure next year, and therefore has to be cautious about what she says and who she offends by voicing her opinions."

"I thought universities prided themselves on their respect for academic freedom."

"There is no academic freedom before tenure," he said.

Early the next morning, Victoria called Casey. The line was busy, so she hiked the quarter mile to the police station on this perfect day. Jodi was scheduled to meet with her later, but she needed to talk to the police chief. When she reached New Lane she saw Jodi's four children at the bus stop, stiff in their new school clothes.

"Good morning, boys."

"Morning, ma'am," they chorused.

"You must be proud of your mother and her schoolwork. I'm meeting with her later this morning."

"Yes, ma'am," said Caleb, the eldest, a lanky boy with flaming red hair.

The yellow bus approached. The boys picked up their backpacks. The bus stopped. The red lights flashed. The boys, who'd been silent during the brief exchange, waved at Victoria and scrambled aboard.

After the bus left, Victoria crossed the road and continued on, swinging the lilac wood stick Elizabeth had cut for her. She didn't really need the stick, but it pleased Elizabeth to see her use it. Along with the stick, she carried a paper bag of stale bread for the ducks and geese that hung around the police station.

As she walked she breathed in the scent of wild grapes and sun-warmed pine and the ever-present salt-sea smell. Earlier this morning, while the dew was still sparkling on the grass and spiderwebs were spread out like linen drying, she'd picked a bouquet of goldenrod and Queen Anne's lace for an arrangement on the dining room table.

When she reached the station's oyster shell parking area, she shook the stale bread from her paper bag. Resting fowl rose to their feet, shimmied their tails, and waddled toward her, quacking and hissing. She tucked the folded-up bag into her pocket and climbed the outside steps to Casey's office.

The office door was open and fine weather poured into the one-room station house. Casey was on the phone. She finished the call and greeted Victoria. Her coppery hair shone in the sunlight. Casey was in her forties, a single mother with a nine-year-old son named Patrick. She'd wanted Patrick to grow up with a sense of community she hadn't felt in Brockton. She found it in West Tisbury.

"You're up early."

"This is a quick visit," said Victoria. "I've got a full day ahead of me."

"You should have called."

"The line was busy. Is there any news of the body at Ivy Green College?"

Casey nodded at the phone. "That was Sergeant Smalley. They've identified the victim."

Victoria sat in the wooden armchair in front of Casey's desk. Through the windows on the west side she could see a pair of swans sailing regally on the Mill Pond.

Casey glanced at her notes. "The victim was a tenured professor at Cape Cod University named Harlan Bliss."

Victoria half rose. "Oh, no!"

"Did you know him?"

"He was on the oversight committee for the college. A strong supporter of Thackery's."

"What was he doing here?" asked Casey.

"Probably attending the August committee meeting. You'd think his family would have missed him."

"He's divorced, no children," said Casey. "Smalley is trying to locate next of kin."

"I suppose his colleagues assumed he was on vacation after the meeting. Has the cause of death been determined?"

"Strangulation. The forensics scientists found fibers."

Victoria shook her head in dismay.

"He wasn't killed in the cellar where the body was found," Casey said. "The killer apparently wrapped him in a sheet and carried him through that small opening in the closet floor. Not easy."

"What a strange place to leave a body."

Casey shrugged. "Who knows what's in a killer's mind."

"Perhaps he—or she—thought it would be dry there and the body would mummify. Then we had an unusually rainy August. What happened to the sheet he was wrapped in?"

"It wasn't with the body. The forensics guys found other fibers on him consistent with a bedsheet."

Victoria sat forward and leaned her hands on her stick. "The first thing we'll need to do is—"

Casey held up her hand. "Not 'we,' Victoria. The state police. If they ask for assistance, of course we'll help."

Victoria looked at her watch and stood up. "I'd better get moving. One of my students is coming over this morning to discuss a paper she's writing." At the open door she turned. "I'm so sorry about Professor Bliss's death. It's going to be especially hard on Thackery and his dream of an ivy-covered college."

CHAPTER 4

A blue Jeep was parked under the Norway maple and Jodi was sitting on the sun-warmed stone steps when Victoria walked up her drive. Victoria had been thinking about the death of Professor Harlan Bliss and what it would mean for the fragile state of the college.

"Morning, Mrs. T. I'm early." Jodi was stroking McCavity, who had curled up next to her, paws tucked under him, purring. "You look kind of down."

"I've had some unpleasant news." She didn't want to talk about it and changed the subject. "McCavity's not usually that docile."

"I love cats," said Jodi. "We've got four, one for each of the boys."

They went into the library. Victoria produced a three-volume Island history and a number of articles she had clipped out of the *Island Enquirer* over the years, then sat on the stiff couch, a twin to the one in the parlor. Jodi pulled up a chair next to her.

"These are Islanders who might have heard family stories about the Chilmarkers." Victoria handed Jodi a list. "I remember riding in the horse-drawn truck wagon that delivered groceries up-Island. We stopped for lunch at someone's home. As a child, I was struck by how quiet the couple was. Both husband and wife were what we called deaf-and-dumb." She regaled Jodi with stories of her childhood contact with the community. "At one time about one in twenty-five Chilmarkers were deaf. Nobody ever thought they were different from anyone else."

"Firsthand accounts. Awesome," said Jodi. "I mean, it's like ancient history, and you lived it. Wow!"

Over the past weeks, Victoria had warmed to Jodi despite her off-putting tattoos and body piercings.

Jodi closed her notebook. "Thanks, Mrs. T."

"How do you like your graduate advisor?" Victoria asked after Jodi had stowed books and notes into her backpack and was about to leave.

"Professor Chadwick? She's great. I call her Roberta now. You know her, don't you, Mrs. T?"

"By reputation only. I've never met her."

"She's never married. She says her students are her children."

"I saw your boys this morning at the school bus stop. They have lovely manners."

"Thanks. Jonah can be kind of strict with them, but he wants them to grow up right." She buckled the straps on the backpack. "Roberta is just wonderful. She's interested in my research on signing, and asks lots of questions that get me thinking in new directions."

"I'm glad she's giving you that kind of support."

"It's exciting, Mrs. T. You know, I dropped out of school in eighth grade, got into drugs, married a loser, had three kids, got divorced, got clean, met Jonah, and had Matthew. Jonah made me get my high school equivalency."

"I'm not sure I could pass the test."

"It was pretty hard. Then Dr. Wilson, Thackery Wilson, encouraged me to get my degree at Ivy Green College, and"—she flung out her arms—"Ta, dah! The rest is history. Here I am. Thinking graduate degree and a future."

"Wonderful," said Victoria. "Thackery Wilson tells me you're setting an example for the college, a pioneer."

"Well, anyway. Roberta Chadwick. I just love her. She's almost like a big sister." Jodi hoisted her heavy backpack onto her shoulder. "I gotta go. And let you get back to work. Again, thanks a million, Mrs. T."

The day after the decomposed body was identified as Professor Harlan Bliss, the Ivy Green College Oversight Committee convened an emergency session to appoint a new member to replace the deceased professor.

Five of the six remaining members of the committee, known as IGCOC, had come over on the eleven-thirty ferry from Woods Hole. On the ferry, they discussed, at length and with no consensus, the meaning to them of the untimely death of Professor Bliss. They were now walking the short distance from the ferry dock to the Ivy Green campus.

Hammermill Jones and Dedie Wieler, both brisk walkers, had outdistanced the other three professors.

"It's good to get away from the university for a few hours," said Dedie Wieler, assistant professor of engineering and the lone female on the oversight committee, which she privately called BIG-COCK.

"Frankly, Dedie," said Hammermill Jones, professor of business administration, "this college is a joke. A waste of our valuable time."

Hammermill was a thickset man, six foot one, a former linebacker for the University of Arkansas Razorbacks. Dedie, also six foot one, had been a rower at Williams College. Unlike Hammermill, she had kept herself in shape.

"It seems to me, Hammermill, this college is doing exactly what I, for one, dreamed of when I went into teaching. Making higher education available to everyone."

"At the risk of sounding politically incorrect, my dear Dedie, not everyone deserves a higher education. This so-called college"—he gestured in the direction they were walking—"Ivy Green whatever, is wasting your time, my time, and your 'everyone's' time and money. Raising unrealistic expectations."

Because she had less than one year to go before facing the dreaded tenure committee, Dedie said nothing further. Hammermill might be on that committee, she couldn't be sure. She had already alienated two of the six men in the engineering department, both of whom had dismissed her teaching as being populist. Over the past six years her students had awarded her the highest marks the Division of Engineering Science had ever recorded.

Dedie was so intent on Hammermill's attempt to out-walk her, that she didn't pay much attention to the view of the harbor to their right. The golden September day had brought out a fleet of boats ranging from day sailors to schooners, white butterflies on the brilliant blue harbor.

At the outskirts of town, a road led off to their left. Hammermill sucked in his gut. Dedie assumed to catch his breath. "We take a left here on Greenleaf," he stated.

"Yes, I know, Hammermill." Dedie turned and looked back. The others were lagging behind a full two blocks. "Let's wait for them." Despite her feelings for Hammermill, she didn't want him to have a heart attack on her account.

"They know the way." Hammermill held up a hand to an SUV that was heading toward West Chop, and when the vehicle stopped, strode across in front of it. The driver beckoned to Dedie as well. She waved thanks and hurried across, embarrassed and annoyed that Hammermill had halted traffic, namely a lone car, for his own convenience.

When they reached the other side of the street she said, "I was thinking we should present a united front to Dr. Wilson, the college president."

Hammermill snorted. But he stopped, sighed as though it was Dedie who needed the rest stop, folded his massive arms across his chest, crossed one thick ankle over the other, and leaned on a nearby stone wall.

The three laggards eventually caught up.

The slight man with a pencil-thin white mustache who was in the lead said, with a touch of sarcasm, "Thank you for waiting." He was Professor Phillip Bigelow, chair of IGCOC and a tenured professor of American military history. "You two taking a power walk?"

"Something like that," said Dedie.

The full committee hiked the remaining block to the college at a more sensible pace.

Thackery was waiting for them on the porch of Catbriar Hall. "Nice to see you again, Professor Bigelow." They shook hands, and Thackery nodded to the other committee members. He wore a tweed jacket with leather elbow patches over a black turtleneck, collegiate looking, but too warm for the summery weather. "Sorry it's under such unfortunate circumstances."

"You remember the other members of the committee, of course," said Professor Bigelow. "Dedie Wieler is with the engineering department, Dr. Hammermill Jones is professor of business administration, Dr. Noah Sutterfield is associate professor with the department of African-American studies, and Dr. Cosimo Perrini is professor of romance languages."

Dedie stepped forward and stuck out her hand. "I'm Dr. Wieler, Dr. Wilson. "Assistant professor of engineering. We met last month at the August IGCOC meeting." She'd almost put the *B* in front of the acronym.

Thackery said, "Shall we go into Catbriar Hall? A light lunch is laid out. Sandwich makings and fruit."

"We don't have a great deal of time," said Professor Bigelow, checking his watch. He stepped up onto the wide porch and the others joined him. "Why don't you give us a quick report on the unfortunate circumstances of Professor Bliss's demise before we go inside."

"There's not a great deal to say," said Thackery. "Professor Bliss had been dead for some time."

"My understanding is that his death was dated to around the time of our last meeting," said Professor Bigelow. "Mid-August."

"Correct," said Thackery. "His body was found in the cellar under the new part of this building."

"I assume the police are working on the case?"

Thackery nodded. "The state police want to interview the committee members today."

"Please ask them to get here as soon as possible." Professor Bigelow darted his small pointed tongue out and in again. "We'd like to leave no later than the three-forty-five ferry. Earlier, if possible."

Thackery glanced around to see if there was someone to whom he could delegate the summoning of the police, but Linda was out sick again and the only class that was meeting now was Mrs. Trumbull's. She was sitting in a green resin lawn chair and her class was gathered around her on that singular patch of green grass. He heard a burst of laughter, then another.

"We'll be discussing the appointment of Professor Bliss's replacement on the committee," said Professor Bigelow. "You needn't be present, Thackery. After that, we'll call on you to give us a full report on the new semester, your faculty, your courses, and your facilities."

Thackery flushed at the polite dismissal. He took out his blue-bordered handkerchief and dabbed at his forehead. "Before I call the police, I'll go in with you to make sure everything is in order, then I'll let you have your privacy."

He opened the door. A faint unpleasant odor that the cleaners hadn't been able to eradicate hung in the air. Professor Bigelow wrinkled his nose. "If you don't mind, Thackery, we'd prefer to meet in a different venue."

Thackery led the IGCOC committee to Woodbine Hall where he made his call to the police, fussed around a bit, finding chairs and setting up a card table.

"Walter will bring the luncheon here to Woodbine Hall. Actually, this will be more convenient as this building has kitchen facilities. Is there anything else you need?"

The group of five stood awkwardly in the middle of the former living room.

"Thank you, Thackery, that will be all," said Professor Bigelow.

Feeling more like servant than college president, Thackery bowed slightly, marched with dignity to the front door, and closed it gently behind him.

CHAPTER 5

Hammermill was first to speak. "They call this a college? We're supposed to waste our time overseeing this?" He waved a hammy hand around the room with its wallpaper of faded pink roses on a pale blue background, the stained ceiling, the cracked windowpane.

Professor Noah Sutterfield, a tall man with cropped white hair, a white mustache, and ebony-black skin, spoke up. "Many of our leaders were educated in one-room schools, Hammermill. I endorse Dr. Wilson's efforts to bring higher education to those who couldn't otherwise afford it."

Professor Bigelow rapped his knuckles with an ineffectual thump on the padded plastic surface of the card table. "Your attention, please. We're not discussing the merits of this educational institution. Cape Cod University appointed our committee to provide oversight. Period. Academic standards, faculty credentials, student qualifications, and facilities condition." He pulled up one of the mismatched chairs and sat down. "Be seated, please."

"Where is Professor Cash?" asked Dedie. "He missed the August meeting, too."

"He's teaching a field course," said Hammermill Jones.

"His field course is in Death Valley," said Dedie. "He'd hardly take a class into Death Valley in August and September. That's why it's called Death Valley."

Hammermill puffed up slightly, and turned away. "My dear Dedie . . ." he said and didn't finish.

Professor Bigelow slapped his hands on the tabletop again. "We can't waste time discussing nonessentials. We have a quorum and we need to name a replacement for Professor Bliss."

Cosimo Perrini, a shy, pale man with rimless glasses, crossed himself. "Bless him," he murmured. He was wearing sandals and a blue seersucker suit over a white T-shirt.

"Thank you, Cosimo," said Professor Bigelow. "Any suggestions as to a successor?"

Dedie Wieler piped up immediately. "Dr. Petrinia Paulinia Kralich, mathematics."

The tip of Professor Bigelow's tongue protruded as he noted the name on the white pad in front of him. "Other suggestions?" He glanced around.

"Ms. Kralich is a mathematician. No experience in overseeing anything," snorted Hammermill Jones.

"*Dr.* Kralich," Dedie corrected.

"We are listing names at this point, Hammermill," said Professor Bigelow. "We'll go over qualifications once we've done that. Any other suggestions?"

"Dr. Kamil Chatterjee of the sociology department," said Noah Sutterfield.

Bigelow noted that and looked up again. "Others?"

"Ron Smith of the Department of Psychology."

This went on until Professor Bigelow had a list of eight names. "If there are no other nominations, we'll go down the list and discuss the qualifications of each.

The list was narrowed down to Dr. Petrinia Paulinia Kralich and Dr. Kamil Chatterjee.

"We already have one female on the committee," said Hammermill. "And one black."

"Dr. Chatterjee is not black," said Professor Sutterfield. "He's a person of color."

Dedie stood up and leaned both hands on the rickety card table.

34

"One female! If we're going by quotas, the committee should have three of us, at the very least."

"Please," said Professor Bigelow, patting the table. "We are looking for qualified persons regardless of gender, race, religion, or sexual preference."

"Baloney," said Dedie. "One token female. One token black." Her voice was louder than she'd intended.

Professor Sutterfield held his hand up to his mouth so only Dedie could hear. "Tenure," he whispered.

"Oh, shit," said Dedie and sat down.

Victoria was still sitting in the green resin chair making notes when Jodi approached. Victoria looked up. "Hello, Jodi. I didn't realize you were still here."

"Yeah, well, I should've thought of this before."

Today Jodi was wearing cut-off jeans with ragged legs that stopped above her knees. Her midriff T-shirt exposed yet another gold ring in her navel, and the missing sleeves gave Victoria an opportunity to examine the tattoos.

Jodi continued, "I got back to the parking lot and I thought, you know, I go right by your house on my way to the college. I can, like, give you a lift to class, if you don't mind riding in my Jeep."

She crossed her arms, and a colorful corn snake writhed around a vine. Or possibly a coral snake. The two had similar markings.

"Thank you," said Victoria, looking away from the tattoos. "That would be wonderful."

"Thackery," said Professor Bigelow after the committee invited him back to the meeting. "The police have not yet arrived, and we're running out of time." He looked at his watch. "We have a major issue we are concerned about, and that is your choice of Dr. Wellborn Price as adjunct professor of economics."

"What conceivably can be wrong with him?" asked Thackery,

still upset at his dismissal a couple of hours earlier. "Dr. Price is a Nobel Prize–winning economist."

"True, but we question his teaching skills."

"What?!" sputtered Thackery.

"We care about *teaching* at Cape Cod University," said Bigelow, licking his lips.

"He taught at Stanford, Harvard, and Princeton. His Ph.D. is from Yale. He has honorary doctorates from Berkeley, University of Washington, Wellesley, Oxford, and Trent University. How can you possibly question his credentials?"

"He hasn't taught for five years."

"He retired to the Vineyard five years ago, for God's sake." Thackery was quite worked up. "During that time he's published two books on economic theory and more than a dozen papers in peer-reviewed journals."

"Dr. Wilson, we are simply doing our duty." Professor Bigelow pushed his chair away from the table and stood. Cosimo Perrini righted the table as it started to topple over. "Cape Cod University has its standards for faculty appointments. If you wish to have your courses accredited by the university, you abide by the rules and standards that have been set up. High standards, I am happy to say." Professor Bigelow sat again.

Thackery took a deep breath and pulled up another chair to the card table. "What must we do in order to have his courses approved by Cape Cod University?"

"Dr. Price hasn't taught during those five years of retirement," said Professor Bigelow.

Thackery stood again. "He's been teaching a regular elementary economics course at the high school every year of those five years and . . ."

"High school." Bigelow looked down at the papers on the table.

"It's not merely high school," said Thackery. "He's been teaching a series of adult ed courses on macroeconomics theory."

"You don't seem to understand, Dr. Wilson. Adult ed courses are not good enough for the university."

"What do you require, then?" Thackery, with effort, kept his voice under control.

"Cape Cod University offers a course in principles and practices of education for those planning to go into the teaching field. We believe it would be helpful for him to take that course as a refresher . . ."

"An introductory-level course?" Thackery couldn't help showing his astonishment. "Dr. Price could teach that course."

Dedie Wieler smiled.

"We're not hearing impaired, Dr. Wilson," said Bigelow. "If he's had as much experience as you claim"—he held up a hand as Thackery was about to say more—"then it will be a simple requirement for him to fulfill."

Thackery, defeated, sat again.

After the IGCOC meeting broke up, Dedie Wieler beckoned Thackery aside. "A word with you, Dr. Wilson."

Thackery, not sure where the next blow was coming from, remained standing next to his desk. He placed the fingertips of his right hand on the desktop and leaned on them. He scowled at Professor Wieler and said nothing.

"Is the kitchen fairly private?" she asked.

"I doubt if Professor Bigelow will interrupt us there," said Thackery, lifting his nose in the air.

They moved from Thackery's living room office through Linda's dining room office, through a pocket door into the kitchen, which was a standard 1950s remodeled kitchen with pink refrigerator and stove.

"What do you want of me?" asked Thackery, leaning back against the refrigerator.

"I thought you might be interested in knowing the history of Professor Bigelow and your Dr. Price."

A dog barked. There was a noisy scuffling in dry leaves. Dedie went to the high window over the maroon sink. "Can't see from here what that's all about."

Thackery adjusted his glasses, which kept slipping down his nose. "I suspect Walter's mongrel got loose again. I've lost patience with him and his dog." He folded his arms across his chest.

Dedie turned from the window and set her papers on the chrome-legged table. The tabletop was pink vinyl with yellow boomerangs. She was wearing jeans, a blue-and-white-striped man's shirt, and sandals. At six foot one, Dedie was almost as tall as Thackery, and he found it disconcerting to speak eye-to-eye with a woman. "Dr. Price was on Professor Bigelow's tenure committee at Stanford."

"Oh?" said Thackery, beginning to understand. "Wellborn Price voted against him for tenure?"

The dog whined.

"That's right," said Dedie. "Dr. Price, as you so rightly pointed out, was and is a powerful, influential economist. Even at the time Professor Bigelow came up for tenure review, Wellborn Price had influence. He convinced the other members of the committee to turn down Professor Bigelow's tenure application."

"And why, if I may ask?"

"From what I understand, ten years earlier, when Dr. Price was up for tenure, Professor Bigelow's father was on the tenure com-mittee. He blackballed Wellborn."

Leaves rustled, a scratching sound as though the dog was dig-ging.

Despite his intent to remain aloof from gossip, Thackery was drawn in. "Blackballed him?"

Dedie nodded. "Price was an associate professor or whatever they called it at the time. He seduced and impregnated papa Big-elow's daughter, our Professor Bigelow's sister."

"Seduced her," repeated Thackery.

"Thaaat's right," said Dedie. "His kid sister Laurel, who was eighteen at the time. She kept the baby who's now in his thirties. The baby was named Price Bigelow. When the sister married, the new hubby adopted him."

"Let me understand this. Dr. Wellborn Price, the Nobel Prize winner, as a graduate student impregnated his tenure professor's daughter."

"Not a smart thing for a supposedly bright man to do," said Dedie. "He wanted to marry the girl, but papa put his foot down. She eventually married someone else, but that's another story."

"Wellborn was refused tenure?"

"Yup. He appealed and overturned the decision. An unusual thing to happen, but," Dedie shrugged, "Wellborn Price was a star." She ran her hand down the front of the pink refrigerator. "This was some color scheme. Pink, maroon, and gray. This kitchen is a real antique."

"Hardly antique," said Thackery, slightly offended. His fifties childhood didn't seem to warrant the term.

"To finish the story, papa Bigelow's son Phillip came up for tenure a decade later. Dr. Wellborn Price was on the tenure committee." She held out her hands. "There you have it. You can't fight academic politics."

"The indignity, the humiliation of Dr. Wellborn Price being told he must take a freshman-level course from a lowly Cape Cod institution."

"Ah!" said Dedie, holding up a finger. "This is why I wanted to talk to you. A colleague of mine teaches that freshman ed course. I guarantee, if you'll get Dr. Price to agree to give a lecture to the class on whatever he wants to talk about, she'll give him an A-plus and a certificate of completion of the course."

"I understand you're up for tenure," said Thackery.

She shrugged. "I face the committee next year. The pressure is building and I'm ready to quit. To hell with it all. I wanted to teach. I don't want to fight all this adolescent-boy bullshit, if you'll pardon the expression."

"Bigelow's revenge," murmured Thackery.

"You could say that." Dedie smiled. "Took him a quarter century."

"What happened to our Bigelow's nephew? Wellborn's son?"

"Price Bigelow? Our IGCOC leader, spelled with a capital *B*, has never had anything to do with his sister's son." She looked at her watch. "Gotta run if I'm going to catch that three-forty-five ferry."

A dog barked.

Thackery walked her to the front door. "I'm calling the police about Walter's loose mutt."

On their way home from the college that afternoon in Jodi's Jeep, Victoria tried to maintain her dignity. After all, she was an adjunct professor.

Her student chatted amiably. "That's really something, Mrs. T, about that body you found turning out to be a professor at CCU. Did you know him?"

"That was before my time," said Professor Trumbull.

"That first day of class, you were really cool, Mrs. T. We were all wondering what the cops were doing here. And about the stink."

Victoria allowed herself a smile. She was cool.

Jodi was driving the back way, on the road that went past the old waterworks. Through the trees, Lake Tashmoo sparkled below them in the afternoon light.

After a respectful silence, Jodi said, "You know, Mrs. T, I've been interviewing the families you suggested, and I've got awesome material. All original. They have the most amazing stories. No one ever interviewed them before."

"We never considered Chilmarkers handicapped," said Victoria. "They were like people with different hair or eye colors. Chilmark was five miles from my house. A great distance in those days. How's your thesis coming along?"

"Great. Original material no one's ever written about. Dr. Wilson knows a couple of scholarly book publishers who might be interested in looking at my finished work."

"Professor Chadwick must be delighted."

"She is. Definitely. She wants me to prepare a short paper based on my thesis, and she'll help me get it published." Jodi looked away from the road briefly. "You can't imagine how much this means to me."

"Yes, I can. I'm proud of you, Jodi."

Victoria heard her phone ringing as she got out of the car. She waved thanks to Jodi, hurried inside, and lifted the receiver before the answering machine kicked in.

"Hello?" she said, out of breath.

"Good afternoon, Victoria," said Casey, "although I'm not sure how good it is."

"Oh?"

"I hate to tell you this, but they've found another body at Ivy Green."

"Who is it this time?"

"No identification as yet."

Victoria took a deep breath. "Where was it found?"

"Behind the administration building."

"I'll need to get back to the college, right away," said Victoria. "In my teaching capacity, not as your deputy. Will you give me a ride?"

"I'll be right there," said Casey. "No need to ask."

CHAPTER 6

When they arrived at the college, two state police cars, a Tisbury Police cruiser, and the hearse from the funeral parlor were parked in the space reserved for faculty. Casey slipped the police Bronco between the hearse and a Harley-Davidson and they got out.

As she sidled around the motorcycle, Victoria patted the leather seat. She'd never ridden on a motorcycle. This, she knew, belonged to Doc Jeffers, who must be this week's medical examiner.

Sergeant Smalley greeted them. "Not pleasant, Mrs. Trumbull, Chief. The victim's been dead a while. Doc Jeffers is at the site."

"Who found the body?" Victoria asked.

"Walter's dog, Brownie, unearthed him."

"Is the victim another man?" asked Casey.

"We're assuming male because of his clothing and hair. Doc Jeffers can tell for sure."

"Murder," said Casey.

"Again, we're assuming so. We won't know for certain until they do the autopsy."

"Is Thackery here?" asked Victoria.

"He's in his office. He'd called us to complain about the dog being loose."

"He called the state police?" Casey laughed and hitched up her belt with its assortment of tools. "Mind if we take a look?"

"Not much crime scene to disturb after all this time," said Smalley. "But I've called forensics. They'll do what they can. The body is on the far side of the building."

They walked from where the vehicles were parked, stepping over stones that delineated the parking area, past tall, sweeping forsythia bushes showing a touch of autumn gold, under an arbor draped with vines heavy with ripening grapes, to the back of the house, now known as Woodbine Hall. They crossed a stretch of grass to the far side of the building, an area Victoria hadn't been to before.

A small crowd had gathered to watch Doc Jeffers work. The crowd included Toby the undertaker and his assistant, Tisbury police officers, two state troopers, and a few passersby that the Tisbury police were asking politely to keep their distance.

Victoria was so intent on watching Doc Jeffers she didn't even notice the magnificent vine that covered the side of the building.

Casey looked up at it. "Guess that's why Thackery calls the place Woodbine Hall."

Doc Jeffers was crouched over the remains the troopers had finished unearthing after Brownie's discovery. The body had been covered with less than a foot of sandy soil, and the soil had then been topped with dead leaves from around the base of the vine, the accumulation of many years.

"Can't tell much from this," Doc Jeffers said, waving a latex-gloved hand at the pile of clothes in the shallow trench. "It's a man, that's about it. At a guess, he was between forty and sixty." The doctor stood up and snapped off his gloves. He was wearing leather trousers and motorcycle boots festooned with chains. A green scrub shirt exposed a V of white chest hair. "We'll know more after the autopsy." He looked around and spotted Smalley who was standing off to one side. "Toby can take him away now."

Toby, the undertaker, would transport the corpse off Island on the ferry for autopsy. There was not much left of the person to identify, except by dental records.

The Steamship Authority would require a passenger ticket for the corpse, even one in this condition.

———

44

"Was the victim buried around the same time Professor Harlan Bliss was killed?" Victoria asked Doc Jeffers. "That was the man whose body was in the old garage."

Doc Jeffers tossed his used gloves into a red metal box marked HazMat and latched the lid. "At a rough guess, I'd say this burial was a month or so earlier."

Casey had been crouched over with her hands on her knees, studying the remains. She straightened up. "Wonder why Brownie didn't discover the body sooner?"

"Walter keeps the dog in a fenced yard. It got out," said Smalley. "Not much the forensics people can find after so long a time, but who knows."

"Forensics has entomologists on staff who can date the burial pretty closely by examining insect activity," said Doc Jeffers. "Larvae, eggs, that sort of thing." He picked up the HazMat box and his black leather bag. "See you around." A motorcycle started up a few minutes later.

Casey and Victoria stood back a respectful distance while Toby and his assistant maneuvered the corpse into a body bag, zipped it up, and left. Victoria heard Toby mutter, "And I'm expected to pay for a passenger ticket on the goddamned ferry."

After the remains were taken away, Casey, Victoria, and Smalley stood together. No one spoke.

The neighbors who'd been standing around left.

Victoria pondered on the two deaths, both on the Ivy Green campus, one a Cape Cod University professor, the other as yet unidentified. This second murder had to be related to the first. Actually, this was probably the first murder, considering the condition of the corpses.

The troopers who'd dug up the ground to expose the corpse, Tim Eldredge and Ben Athearn, were sitting on the stone wall that marked the boundary of Ivy Green College campus. Tim was absently scratching his forearm.

Casey glanced again at the vine that clambered up the side of Woodbine Hall. Shiny scarlet leaves framed every window, bunches of delicate white berries hung from it. "Wish I could get my ivy to climb like that."

"Give it time," said Victoria. She looked up at the vine and stared at it in awe. She had never seen such a lush growth. The hairy base of the vine was as thick as the trunk of a sapling. The scarlet leaves glowed. Odd she hadn't noticed it right away. But her attention had been on the corpse, not the vine.

"Spectacular, isn't it?" Smalley had seen what they were looking at. "When we're done here I'll ask Thackery if he minds if I cut a bunch of it for my wife. She makes wreaths that she sells at the farmers' market." He reached out a hand to touch the pretty leaves.

"No!" Victoria knocked his hand away. "That's not woodbine, it's poison ivy."

Smalley withdrew his hand as though the vine had shot poison darts into him. Casey opened and shut her mouth.

"The dead leaves." Smalley sounded like a fifth-grade schoolboy learning about the horrors of sex and girls. "Are they . . ." He stopped. "My guys dug through piles of dead leaves at the base of the vine to uncover the corpse."

"The oil that causes the rash is quite long lived," said Victoria. "It can be active for several years, even on clothing or gloves. You'd better send your men home to take showers, now, right away."

"Tim, Ben!" shouted Smalley. "Get over here. Mrs. Trumbull has something to tell you."

Victoria said, "You probably were exposed to poison ivy oil when you dug in the leaves. You need to take a cool shower with plenty of soap. Don't use hot water. Get the oil off your skin." She leaned on her stick. "Hot water opens pores and allows oil to get into one's system. Launder your clothing. It won't hurt to launder it twice."

"Report back as soon as you can," Smalley ordered.

Victoria looked up at the menacing vine with its shiny bright red leaves. "It's really quite beautiful, isn't it?"

Thackery appeared while Smalley was giving instructions to his troopers.

"What seems to be the problem, Sergeant?"

"We've found another body."

"You already informed me of that. Why are you sending your men home? Surely they haven't finished."

Smalley indicated the vine-covered side of the house. "That's poison ivy, according to Mrs. Trumbull. My men need to get home to clean up."

"Nonsense," said Thackery. "People who don't know plants frequently mistake woodbine for poison ivy." Before Victoria could stop him, he reached out and plucked off a stem with its three glistening leaves.

Victoria, miffed at having her knowledge of plants impugned, felt a mild glow of satisfaction, immediately replaced with concern.

"Thackery, I hope you're not sensitive to . . ."

At this point Walter came around the side of the building, his bedraggled mutt trailing after him. The mutt was gray, like his master, had patchy wiry hair that partly covered his eyes and muzzle, and was soaking wet.

"Where have you been, Walter?" Thackery demanded, ignoring Victoria.

"Giving Brownie a bath."

"Woodbine," said Thackery, crushing in his fingers the three leaves he'd picked. Before Victoria could stop him, he held them up to his nose.

Victoria, herself, was not particularly susceptible to poison ivy. She'd occasionally get a few blisters that she liked to scratch.

That was about it. She hoped the same was true for Thackery. Otherwise . . . Her thoughts trailed off.

"Think it's woodbine, do you?" said Walter. "Won't get me to touch your woodbine like you're doing."

Brownie shook himself, sending a spray of doggy water toward Thackery's pressed khaki trousers.

"Walter!" warned Thackery, dropping his leaves.

Smalley returned from sending his troopers off. He'd apparently heard the poison ivy exchange between the campus caretaker and the college president. "You knew it was poison ivy?" he asked Walter.

Thackery brushed at his pants with a blue-bordered handkerchief. "Control that dog, will you?"

"'Course I knew it was poison ivy. Everyone knows poison ivy," said Walter.

"My men spaded up that area." Smalley gestured at the disturbed heap of dead leaves.

Brownie sat on his haunches and scratched an ear.

"I had better sense than to rake up them leaves."

"Why didn't you tell them it was poison ivy?" snapped Smalley.

"They didn't ask," said Walter.

Brownie turned around in a circle, lay down, yawned hugely, broke wind, and closed his eyes.

"Take that animal away," said Thackery. "Immediately!"

"Thackery," said Victoria, "I really think you'd better wash your hands thoroughly with soap and water, and right away. Even if it's woodbine, it won't hurt to wash."

Walter smirked, showing stubby gray teeth. "It's most likely too late."

The Island grapevine is one of the most efficient communications systems known.

Joe the plumber and Sarah were in their usual places on the porch at Alley's Store the next afternoon.

"You hear about the case of the poison ivy?" asked Joe.

"What are you talking about?" asked Sarah. Today's garb was a pale green sweater with a knitted pattern of black and white and red feathers around the neck and sleeves.

Joe laughed. "That mutt of Walter's got loose and dug up another corpse buried in poison ivy."

"What!?"

"You know Walter."

"The caretaker at Ivy Green College. Sure."

"You know Thackery Wilson named that house he's using for an office 'Woodbine Hall.'"

"Yeah? So?"

"Not woodbine." Joe cackled. "Poison ivy. The state cops finished digging where Walter's dog started."

"Eee-yew!" Sarah lifted her sweater and scratched her stomach.

While Jodi, Victoria's chauffeur, was running errands after class the following Tuesday, Victoria walked over to Woodbine Hall to turn in her attendance records.

Thackery was sitting at his desk with his handkerchief held up to his nose. Both hands were covered with a dried pink paste that crumbled onto the papers on his desk when he moved.

Calamine lotion. Victoria refrained from saying anything.

Linda sat at her desk in what was formerly the dining room separated from the living room by a gracious archway.

Victoria handed her the attendance records. "Good afternoon, Linda. How are you?"

"Thank you for asking, Mrs. Trumbull. I had an awful spell of stomach trouble last night. I had supper at my sister's. I should have known better. I was up all night with diarrhea and vomiting and—"

"I'm so sorry," said Victoria, interrupting her. "I hope you've recovered." She retreated quickly to Thackery.

"You don't want to catch what she's got," Thackery muttered under his breath.

"You're right," Victoria said.

Thackery nodded at the seat next to his desk. "I owe you an apology."

"Oh?" Victoria seated herself.

"I was sure that was woodbine. When I first saw it ten years ago it was already covering the side of the hall."

"I don't suppose you'll want to rename the building," Victoria said, and immediately realized her smart remark was less than tactful.

"With your police connections, have you heard any indication of the latest victim's identity?" asked Thackery, brushing a pink flake off his desk.

"It will take a while." Victoria settled back in her chair. "Has the oversight committee appointed a new member to replace Professor Bliss?"

"I'm afraid so. They discussed Professor Petrinia Paulinia Kralich and Professor Kamil Chatterjee, both of whom would have been good choices from my point of view, but because the committee members couldn't agree, they decided on someone who's a complete unknown to me, a Reverend Bob White, professor of theology."

"As a theologist, perhaps he'll do the right thing," said Victoria.

"I doubt it," muttered Thackery, shuffling papers aimlessly on his desk. Every time he moved, a small shower of dried calamine lotion dusted his desk. "When I was called back in to give my report, the committee questioned my appointing Wellborn Price as adjunct professor."

"Good heavens! That man has been awarded more honors than I can name."

"Apparently this is the result of a longtime feud between Dr.

Price and Professor Bigelow. Price was on Bigelow's tenure committee and made sure his tenure was denied. Bigelow, as I suppose you know, is head of the oversight committee." He sighed. "Ivy Green College will be the one to suffer in this squabble."

There was nothing Victoria could say.

Thackery ran his hand over the back of his neck. "I hope Journeyman Cash returns from the field soon. He's missed two of the oversight committee meetings. We need his support. Desperately."

CHAPTER 7

On the following Thursday, before the second body was identified, Brownie, Walter's dog, got loose again. From his office window Thackery saw the dog trot across the street, his head and tail both up in a perky, irritating manner. Thackery heaved himself out of his chair, straightened his tie, covered the papers on his desk with his big desk calendar, and started to go after the dog. Before he reached the door, he decided he'd better first call the police and the animal control officer.

"I want to file charges against Walter and that mongrel," Thackery told Tim Eldredge, the state trooper who'd answered the phone.

"Yes, sir. That's really a Tisbury Police matter," said Tim. "You can file charges at the police station near the Steamship Authority terminal. But I'll be happy to dispatch a state trooper, sir," Tim said, with a smirk in his voice, "just in case, you know, maybe the dog found another . . ."

"That's not amusing," said Thackery and slammed down the phone.

He shrugged into his tweed jacket, still a bit warm for this unseasonably mild fall day, and went after the dog himself.

It took him a few minutes to find Brownie, who was chasing his tail in the center of what Thackery thought of as Professor Trumbull's al fresco classroom, a circle of grass in the dappled shade of the big oak trees.

The entire scene remained with Thackery for some time after. Brownie squatted. His head was slightly tilted. He lifted a back leg and scratched an ear. Mrs. Trumbull's green lawn chair was off to one side. Brownie lay down, yawned, and closed his eyes. His ears twitched. Suddenly, abruptly, he leapt to his feet, trembling, and started to dig.

"Hey, hey!" shouted Thackery. "Stop that! Get away!"

Brownie paid no attention.

Thackery looked around for a stick to deter the dog, but when he got close, Brownie looked up and snarled. His eyes were red, his mouth dripped saliva, his moth-eaten fur stood straight up. Thackery backed off and Brownie returned to his dig. Dirt and green grass flew. Thackery retreated to his office and called the animal control officer, the state police, the Tisbury Police, Walter, and because he was shaking with anger and couldn't think of who else to call, he called Victoria Trumbull, who said she was leaving shortly for her class.

Thackery tugged his steel watch out of his pocket and looked at it. Not yet one o'clock. He put his watch back into his pocket.

By the time the state police arrived, Brownie had uncovered a bone. Actually several bones. Not really a corpse, since it was no more than a skeleton. He'd dug up the middle of the magic circle, that tidy oasis of lush grass that Walter had kept mown like a putting green.

The state police surrounded the once-grassy circle with yellow crime scene tape. Thackery stood outside the taped-off area, hands behind his back. He turned, scowling, at Victoria's approach with her class trailing behind her.

"You may as well cancel your class, Professor Trumbull. I don't believe any of us can accomplish anything here today."

"What happened?" asked Victoria. "That was such a lovely spot."

Thackery sighed. "That dog of Walter's dug it up."

Victoria leaned on her stick. "Ah."

"He found bones."

"Not ones he'd buried?"

Thackery shook his head, disgusted. "Human bones." He rubbed the back of his neck. "You might as well dismiss your class. Not much we can do here."

"We don't want to waste such a lovely day," said Victoria. "I'll take my class on a field trip."

Three hours later, the skeleton had been disinterred and was lying on a plastic sheet next to the excavation. All that remained besides bones were a few scraps of clothing, a few buttons, a belt buckle, and boating shoes. No socks.

"A man, from the looks of the belt buckle and size twelve shoes," Smalley said to Thackery, who hadn't gone near the grave after Brownie's discovery. Sergeant Smalley had called in Doc Jeffers, who thought the body had been in the ground for six to eight months. Hard to tell.

The off-Island forensics team returned to the Island.

"How about renting us a permanent place, Thackery, old boy?" said the head of the team, whose name was Joel Killdeer. "In between your corpses, we can go fishin'." Killdeer was a tall slender man in his forties with skin the color of black coffee and a shiny shaved head.

"That's hardly amusing." Thackery turned his back on Killdeer and saw Victoria to his left, returning from her field trip with Jodi next to her. And to his right, Walter was dragging Brownie along with a clothesline looped around his neck.

Thackery, more upset than he cared to show, called to Walter, "Can't you control that wretched dog of yours?"

Walter didn't answer. Brownie made a half-circle at the end of his rope toward Thackery and sniffed his leg. "Get away from me!" shouted Thackery as Brownie lifted a leg.

Walter hauled in on the clothesline and Brownie, tongue out, backed reluctantly toward his master.

"He the dog that found the body?" asked Joel Killdeer, the forensics boss.

"Yes, sir," said Walter.

"Found the other corpse, too, right?"

"Yes, sir," said Walter.

Victoria stopped next to Thackery.

"How was the field trip?" asked Thackery.

Killdeer said, "We could use a corpse-sniffing dog on this case."

"The field trip will result in some wonderful poetry, Thackery. The surf was dramatic." She turned to Walter. "Brownie must have an unusually sensitive sense of smell."

Walter said to Killdeer, "You pay the dog for sniffing out corpses?"

"Absolutely."

"Hourly rates?"

"Flat rate per case."

"What if he gets hurt?" asked Walter.

"Dog gets killed in the course of duty, he gets buried with honors."

Victoria bent over and patted Brownie, who looked up at her with sad eyes. His tongue hung out, he was panting, and the clothesline seemed awfully tight around his neck. Victoria loosened it.

"Third body," said Walter thoughtfully to Killdeer. He studied the dug-up patch of once-green lawn.

Killdeer ran a hand over his smooth scalp. "Could be more."

"Certainly not, Dr. Killdeer," said Thackery.

"With the crazies running this place you never can tell," said Walter.

"Walter," warned Thackery. "Dr. Killdeer has—"

"How about we borrow your dog for a couple days, Walter?" asked Killdeer, snapping his chewing gum.

Walter stuck out his purplish lower lip. "For pay?"

"'Course," said Killdeer. "Who knows what your pup might sniff out?"

———

"You seemed a bit downcast today, Jodi," Victoria said as they were driving home after the remains had been taken away. "This business of dead bodies on campus must be terribly distressing to you."

"No, it's not that."

"How is your thesis research coming along?"

Jodi, hands high up on the steering wheel, looked straight ahead. "Okay, I guess."

They were driving home along the shady road that skirted Tashmoo. Jodi braked to let a flock of wild turkeys strut across the road. They reached the waterworks before either spoke again.

"You know that paper Roberta wanted me to write?"

Victoria felt a surge of anxiety at the tone of Jodi's voice. "For a professional journal, you said. That would be a feather in your cap."

"Yeah, well."

They reached the stop sign at State Road.

"What is it, Jodi? Something's bothering you."

Jodi turned, pulled into the overlook, and shut off the engine. Victoria waited for her to say what was on her mind.

The view spread out before them. The end-of-September day was unnaturally clear, so clear Victoria could make out the water tower, houses, and trees on the mainland, four miles away. Today was what her sea captain grandfather would have called a weather breeder. No wonder the surf had been so heavy at Quansoo. Foul weather was brewing, and would be here in a day or two.

She turned to Jodi and waited. Something was wrong in the life of the bright, gutsy, too-young mother of four boys, the body-pierced and tattooed rebel, the scholar testing the waters of graduate school.

"I finished that journal article, Mrs. T. I was so excited about it." Jodi wiped a wrist across her eyes. Victoria handed her a paper napkin she'd kept from her lunch at the senior center and Jodi dabbed at her tears. "I think the article was pretty good."

"Was?" asked Victoria.

"Yeah, well." Jodi made a fist, squeezing the napkin. "Roberta said it needed editing. I figured she knows best. She changed it all around and it doesn't sound like my work anymore."

"She was probably editing it to meet the standards of a particular journal."

"Yeah. Well, I thought okay, she knows best. She's helping me. You know how interested she is in my research."

"You've been quite enthusiastic about her."

A tour bus pulled in behind them, and Victoria could hear the driver's voice over the loudspeaker describing the summer homes of various celebrities. The bus left after a few minutes, trailing diesel fumes.

"I don't know what to think," said Jodi. The bus geared up the hill and disappeared around a bend in the road. "She's putting her name on my paper."

Victoria said, "It's standard academic practice for an advisor to put his name on a student's paper as junior author. It gives an unpublished student credibility."

"Yeah, well." Jodi had draped both arms over the steering wheel and was staring straight ahead in the direction the bus had taken. "She said, since she'd done so much work on it and she didn't, Mrs. T." Jodi glanced at Victoria. "She maybe changed my words around, but she didn't add any stuff—she said she was putting her name on my paper as senior author. In other words, she's taking credit for all the work I did."

"Have you spoken to her about it?"

Jodi shook her head. "I don't want to rock the boat. I need that degree."

"Would you like me to talk to her?"

Jodi glanced back at Victoria. "Omigod, no, Mrs. T! That would be the kiss of death for sure."

Late that afternoon, Victoria was on her kneeler, weeding the squash and bean rows. Robert Springer, who helped her occasionally with yard work, was mowing her grass, the last cutting of the year.

She felt a sudden chill. Clouds had moved across the sun, high broken clouds that looked like fish scales, a mackerel sky. Weather was on its way, and soon.

She tossed the pulled weeds into the garden cart and hoisted herself to her feet with the handles of her kneeler. She'd done enough work for now.

Robert pulled up to her on the lawn tractor. "Want me to dump those on the compost heap?"

"Yes. Thank you, Robert."

He got off the tractor with a sigh. He was a short man with a two-day growth of beard, not the stylish kind boys the age of her grandchildren affected, but more like a street person's. One of his ubiquitous hand-rolled cigarettes was dangling off his lower lip, the smoke curling up past his nose into his red-rimmed eyes.

"Going to have some rain, looks like," he said when he returned with the empty cart. "The garden can use it."

"I believe you're right," said Victoria.

Early this morning, before her class, she'd hung laundry on the line to dry in the good southwest wind. Now the wind had backed around to the southeast. By tomorrow it would be northeast, bringing two or three days of rain. The surf pounded on the south shore, a steady rumble that she could feel through her feet. She needed to bring in the laundry before the storm broke.

She unpinned the sweet-smelling sheets, folding them right off the line, carried the basket of clean laundry into the house, and set it on the washer in the downstairs bathroom. Elizabeth would put it away when she got home.

She decided to write a sonnet inspired by Jodi's initial delight and enthusiasm changing into such abject misery. She would title the poem "Weather Breeder."

Chapter 8

Victoria was taking her typewriter out of its case when a silver Honda she didn't recognize stopped in the drive. A tall, nicely built young man with bright red, almost orange, hair got out and headed toward the house. She met him at the entry door.

"Mrs. Trumbull? I'm Christopher Wrentham. I'd like to talk to you, if I may. Is this a bad time?"

Victoria wasn't sure whether this was a bad time or not. She was in the throes of composing her sonnet, but she was curious about this young man's mission. Now that he was up close she could see his dark eyes and fine large nose.

"What is it you need to speak to me about?"

"A professor at Cape Cod University, Roberta Chadwick."

"Ah," said Victoria. "Come in." She ushered him into the cookroom and he waited politely for her to sit, then took a chair at right angles to hers.

"This must seem presumptuous of me, but, well, I was told you're a professor at Ivy Green College."

Victoria smoothed her hair. "Yes, adjunct professor."

He nodded. "I was also told you're apprised of a certain situation."

Victoria folded her hands on the table. "Having to do with Professor Chadwick?"

"Yes."

When he looked at her she realized his dark eyes had golden flecks. "Why don't you tell me about it?"

He rubbed his hands on his thighs. "I'm enrolled in a master's program at Cape Cod University." He glanced at Victoria, who nodded. "Since I live on the Island and Professor Chadwick does, too, the university agreed to let her be my thesis advisor, working together here on the Island, saving both of us time and expense."

"You're one of the three Island students she's mentoring, then."

"Yes. Jodi Paloni is the only one enrolled in Ivy Green College, the other two of us are with Cape Cod University. I did my course work off Island, just need to have my thesis approved."

"Did Professor Chadwick recommend that you submit a paper based on your thesis to a professional journal?"

He nodded.

Victoria absently picked up her pen and drew a few arrows on the back of her notes. "What is the subject of your thesis?"

"The intermarriage of European settlers and the Wampanoags of Martha's Vineyard in the early nineteenth century."

Victoria drew a few more arrows until she'd sketched what looked like a picket fence. "I'm almost afraid to ask the next question."

A few dry leaves fluttered across the drive. The wind was picking up.

"I think you know where this is going," said Christopher. "I can't begin to tell you how angry I am."

Victoria set down her pen and folded her hands on the table. She could see a muscle twitch in his jaw. Under normal circumstances, he must be a pleasant looking man. What were probably laugh lines ran from his cheekbones to his jaw. Now they were deeply incised and he looked hard. The freckles across his nose and cheeks looked green on his fair skin. He probably sunburned and didn't tan.

"Professor Chadwick has put her name on my paper, claiming that's academic practice. Otherwise I wouldn't be able to publish under my own name."

"I see," said Victoria.

"I did the research. Interviewed more than thirty people with Wampanoag ancestors." He set both hands flat on the table. "I taped dozens and dozens of interviews, heard family stories that had never been told publicly."

A few drops of rain slatted on the windowpanes.

"I wrote what I considered a great article. Roberta said in order to ensure that my paper would be accepted by the journal, she needed to include her name as author." He dropped his hands into his lap. "Well, I figured. Okay. The paper is authored by me, and she's on there as my advisor."

Victoria shoved her notes aside.

"Instead, she listed herself as senior author. Then somehow, my name got left off entirely." He lifted his hands and brought them together with a slap.

"You heard she's done the same thing to Jodi?"

"That's why I'm here." He leaned back in his chair, arms folded over his chest.

Victoria was about to warn him not to lean in the chair, when she heard a snap.

He stood up. "My gosh, I'm so sorry! My grandmother was always warning me."

Victoria scowled. "You should have listened to your grandmother."

He checked the chair leg. "I'll fix it."

"It won't be the first time that chair has been repaired. Take another seat." Victoria went on with their discussion. "Jodi doesn't plan to take any action. She claims she'll never get a position in her field if she does. Is that your situation, too?"

"No." He leaned his elbows on the table. "I have my own software company. Has nothing to do with my interest in Wampanoag culture. I don't depend on the whim of some goddamned untenured professor who's got to publish or perish, excuse my language." He pinched his thumb and forefinger together. "I'm that close to taking care of the perish part."

A lock of Christopher's hair had fallen over his forehead. His eyes, with those glittery gold flecks and those deep, hard creases down his face, made him look a bit frightening at the moment.

"Furthermore, I already have a Ph.D. in computer science, and taught long enough to know how wicked academia can be. This was an opportunity to explore a subject I'm interested in and know a lot about, and this goddamned bitch stole my work. Sorry, Mrs. Trumbull."

"Quite understandable."

They were both silent after that. Victoria tapped her fingers on the checked tablecloth. Christopher stared out the window.

The guinea fowl were making their rounds, four adults and a dozen keets, uttering soft chucking sounds. They stopped next to the silver poplar stump where Victoria had scattered birdseed. The keets were about three weeks old now. One after another, they hopped onto the stump and extended stubby wings to flutter from the foot-high perch. The four adults had protected them, so far, from hawks, skunks, raccoons, and automobiles.

They watched until the guineas herded their babies across the drive and into the west pasture.

Victoria was the first to speak. "What made you decide on your research topic?"

"My great-great-grandmother was a Wampanoag."

"Jodi's grandmother was deaf and that spurred her interest in a career in signing for the hearing impaired. Who else is that woman robbing of both credit and incentive?" Victoria stood and headed into the kitchen. "I think we could use a cup of tea."

While the water was heating, the sky had darkened. Raindrops raised small fountains of dust in the drive. Victoria returned to her seat. "Have you spoken to the other graduate student working under Professor Chadwick?"

"No. I thought I was Roberta's only Island student until I met Jodi at a baseball game one of her boys and my daughter were playing in. We got to talking."

Victoria nodded.

"Learned she was working on her master's. I was, too. Sociology, me, too. Advisor, Professor Chadwick? Yup."

The teakettle whistled and Victoria stood.

"I'll take care of that, Mrs. Trumbull."

"Next time," said Victoria, already in the kitchen.

"Roberta submitted the abstract of my paper to the journal." He turned to the kitchen while she was brewing the tea. "I have to tell you, Mrs. Trumbull, I feel positively murderous toward that woman."

Victoria carried the teapot into the cookroom and poured tea into mugs. "I assume you've come to see me for a reason, not simply to complain about the situation." She handed a mug to him. "Do you take anything in your tea?"

"Black is fine." He leaned forward. "I need your help, Mrs. Trumbull. Between us I think we can make a small dent in an outrageous practice."

Victoria held her own mug in both hands. "Have you tried going through the university's grievance channels?"

"Yeah." He snorted. "Good ole buddy network. They closed ranks. I'm just a student, after all. They're tenured professors, and Chadwick is up for tenure review."

"Do you have a suggestion as to how I can help?"

"Have you met Chadwick?"

Victoria shook her head. "I've only heard about her. Jodi was quite enthusiastic about her at first."

"She puts on a good act. Comes across as warm and fuzzy." He sipped his tea and set his mug down. "She thinks of herself as a big sister to her students. A lot of crap."

"If you think it would help, I'll speak to her."

Christopher ran his hand through his bright hair. "It wouldn't hurt for you to get to know her. Then you can decide what to do."

"If anything," said Victoria. "Jodi insists that I not get involved. I think I can meet with Professor Chadwick on a professor-to-professor basis." Victoria set her mug on her envelope. "If there's some other way I can help, let me know. Her appropriation of your papers is far beyond what academia ought to accept."

Christopher stood up. "Thanks, Mrs. Trumbull." He glanced out of the window. "Really coming down hard."

"Someone left an umbrella in the entry. You're welcome to take it. It's been there at least a year."

"I'll bring it back," he said. "Give me an excuse to call on you again."

Victoria smiled.

CHAPTER 9

After Christopher Wrentham left, Victoria watched as rain poured over the edge of her gutters. She'd have to have them cleaned out, which meant Robert, who seemed willing to do anything, getting up there with a long ladder.

She didn't intend to get deeply involved in this particular dispute between students and a faculty member. However, she decided it wouldn't hurt to invite Roberta Chadwick for lunch.

"What about tomorrow?" she asked after Professor Chadwick accepted with alacrity.

"Tomorrow is fine. I've heard so much about you, Mrs. Trumbull. I look forward to meeting you."

The following day, wind howled and shrieked and whipped brittle branches off the maple trees. The nor'easter had set in to stay. There'd be plenty of kindling for her evening fires. Horizontal sheets of rain rippled across the drive, now a muddy river.

An ancient Volkswagen surged through the puddles and parked away from the falling branches. The driver shoved the car door open against the wind and hunched out, tugging the hood of her yellow oilskin over her head. She wore black rubber boots that came up almost to her knees.

Victoria greeted her at the entry door. "I picked a fine day for our luncheon, Professor Chadwick. You can leave your boots and slicker out here and dry off inside."

Roberta Chadwick tossed her hood back and grinned, a gaptoothed grin that made her look quite young. "I love storms, and always have." She kicked off her boots, exposing socks with a pattern of pink kittens on a lime-green background. She hung her wet jacket on a nail in the entry. Underneath the jacket she wore a pink sweatshirt over a white turtleneck and jeans, wet in front from her knees to midthigh where her jacket and boots hadn't protected her from the deluge.

"Can I get you a towel to dry off a bit?" Victoria asked.

"I'm fine. My jeans didn't get really wet." The professor held out her hand. "It's a pleasure to meet you, Mrs. Trumbull."

Victoria hadn't planned to like this woman, but she couldn't help herself. A free spirit who appreciated weather. She held the kitchen door open with one hand and shook the professor's hand with the other. "Please, come in."

Roberta Chadwick was not at all what Victoria had expected. She was comfortably plump, her brown hair was short and tightly curled. She projected an image of complete trustworthiness. In her pink sweatshirt with chickadees printed on it and her green-and-pink socks, she was the image of niceness. Victoria remembered Jodi's initial enthusiasm for this almost-like-a-sister teacher, and reminded herself to be careful.

Before they went into the cookroom, she said, "I think a glass of wine might help brighten a day like this. I have some chilled Chardonnay. Would you care for a glass?"

"That sounds wonderful. Can I help?"

Victoria handed her the unopened bottle and a corkscrew and the professor set to work.

"Um, I think this is a screw-top, Mrs. Trumbull. I've just punctured the cap."

"Never mind, I have a spare bottle cap." Victoria smiled. "I think screw-tops make more sense than corks. The only problem is they make one think inferior wine."

"Not anymore, Mrs. Trumbull."

They took their glasses and the bottle into the cookroom, where Victoria had laid two place settings.

She poured and lifted her glass. "To your successful tenure application, Professor Chadwick."

"Please, keep your fingers crossed on that tenure bit, and I'm Roberta. That's what my students call me."

They touched glasses.

"You said when you called, Mrs. Trumbull, that you wanted some advice from me. I can't imagine what."

Victoria nodded.

The professor continued. "I'm not the one to be giving you advice. It's the other way around. You have so much more experience than I do."

This was not the way Victoria had planned the conversation. "I have very little experience in the academic world."

"I'm in awe of your publishing credentials." Roberta's cheeks were shiny and rosy. Her eyes were a pleasing shade of blue-gray.

"Poetry publishing is quite different from academic publishing."

"Different, but I understand poetry is extremely difficult to publish. It's hard enough to publish academic work."

This was the opening Victoria had hoped for. "Must you publish a certain number of papers in order to get tenure? We're all aware of the phrase 'publish or perish.' "

Roberta ran her fingers over her short hair. "I'm expected to publish three to five peer-reviewed papers in each academic year. It's unbelievably stressful."

"I can imagine." Victoria produced a sympathetic look. "One paper a semester would be a challenge." She set her own glass down after taking a sip of wine. "I don't see how you can possibly meet that kind of goal. And you're expected to do community work as well as teaching, I understand."

Roberta looked up at the baskets that hung from the exposed

rafters, at the green waxy vine that twined partway around the wall, at the bookcases that took up a large part of the small space. Then she looked out of the window, away from Victoria's deep-set dark eyes. "I'm advising three Island students. You know, of course, my student Jodi Paloni, who's taking your wonderful poetry course. Advising counts as community service."

"Jodi is delighted with your support of her work." Victoria paused a moment. "I should think your schedule wouldn't leave you much time to do your own research."

"It's not easy, Mrs. Trumbull." Roberta glanced up. "This is such a pleasant place."

Victoria frowned at the sudden change in subject, but said, "In my childhood, this was the summer cookroom, and we've always called it that even though we no longer cook here." She leaned forward, elbows on the table. "I'm interested in your research, Roberta. What is your field?"

"As you know, it's sociology." Roberta smiled and turned her wineglass around. "It's a broad area."

"I should have said your specialty."

Roberta blushed. "Oh, sorry. It's the social structure of communities."

"No wonder you've been able to give Jodi so much help. You must be interested in her work on the deaf-mutes of Chilmark. As I'm sure she told you, I've given her quite a bit of firsthand information." Victoria stopped and looked out of the window. The steady rain rattled against the small panes. Wind flattened the leaves of the lilac bushes. A gull swept by overhead.

Roberta sat still.

Victoria reminisced. "I remember many of the families of the Chilmark community and have kept in touch with their children and grandchildren."

Roberta looked down at her wineglass.

"Jodi has a great deal of original information that no one's ever tapped before. She's thrilled that you're making it possible for her to publish it."

"What has Jodi been saying to you, Mrs. Trumbull?" Roberta finally met Victoria's eyes.

Victoria realized she'd gone too far. She hadn't meant to invoke Jodi's name. "She's very fond of you and talks about you constantly, how supportive you've been, how generous with your time, and your enthusiasm about all the work she's done." Victoria hoped this had taken the conversation in a different direction. "She's excited about the paper, her first academic triumph. I'll have you both over to celebrate when her paper is published."

Roberta looked down at her hands again. "She didn't tell you that her name won't be on that paper? I'm the author."

Victoria avoided her eyes. "You've been a wonderful advisor to her. Surely you won't let the journal make such an egregious mistake?"

"It's not a mistake, Mrs. Trumbull. Jodi can't possibly publish under her own name." Roberta cleared her throat and looked out at the gray sky and the pouring rain. "I invested a huge amount of time on that paper."

Victoria said, "I understand it's common practice for a thesis advisor to list one's name as junior author. I've never heard of an academic policy that sanctions a professor taking credit for a student's work." Victoria folded her hands on the table. She was afraid she'd done exactly what Jodi had warned her against. Well, too late now.

"Mrs. Trumbull, it's a fact of life. Jodi has to learn the way I had to learn. This is how the academic world operates."

"You've made a difference in Jodi's life with your encouragement," said Victoria. "You've turned her around from a young woman with no hope of a successful career to an enthusiastic scholar with dreams of making a difference. She trusted you." Victoria hesitated.

"Mrs. Trumbull . . ." Roberta blurted. "You don't understand.

I am under a huge amount of pressure, both on Jodi's behalf and on my own. It's critical for me, as it will be for Jodi later on, to publish."

Victoria looked up. "I would drop out of a university that allowed me to steal a student's work."

"Mrs. Trumbull, it's not stealing. This is the way things are done in the academic world."

Victoria felt her face get hot. "It's plagiarism and it's thievery."

Roberta shoved her wineglass to one side. "That's a terrible thing to say to me. I've worked hard with Jodi. I have a legitimate claim on publication of that paper. I assure you, she would never be published under her own name."

"But you're leaving her name off entirely."

"I've given her credit in the acknowledgments."

"She's spent more than a hundred hours interviewing families. Don't you think that deserves more than an acknowledgment? I can't see that you will suffer by having the name of the true researcher on the paper as senior author. I can see some justification for an advisor being listed as junior author."

Roberta stood. "I can't take any more pressure, Mrs. Trumbull. I'm getting it from the university, from my department head, from the tenure committee chair, from my fellow academics, from my students, and now from you. I came here thinking we could talk as fellow professors, and instead, you're giving me a hard time. I have to publish." She slapped the table for emphasis. "With three students to mentor, I don't have a minute to myself. I'll do whatever I have to do to get published, and that's it. This has always been the way things are done in academia." Roberta reached down and lifted up her wineglass, gulped down the rest of her wine, and set the glass down. She looked at her watch. "You know, I'd forgotten an appointment I have this afternoon. I'm afraid I have to forego our lunch and our little talk. I guess I'm not hungry." She pushed her chair back under the table. "Thank you for giving me your opinion, Mrs. Trumbull. I hope Jodi hasn't been trying to influence you against me."

"Surely you know Jodi better than that," said Victoria, also standing. "I hope you'll at least think over what I've said. As I'm sure you know, there are laws against plagiarism."

Roberta's face got quite pink. "Thank you for your time, Mrs. Trumbull." With that, she strode out of the cookroom in her lime-green-and-pink kitten socks, through the kitchen, pushed her way through the door, scooped up her boots and jammed her feet into them, threw her foul weather jacket over her shoulders, and ran for her car.

The curtain of rain hid her from Victoria, who watched from the window with a sick feeling that she'd accomplished exactly what Jodi had warned her against.

Two days later, Jodi stormed into Victoria's kitchen. "Mrs. Trumbull, how could you do this to me!"

Victoria got up from her chair in the cookroom and went into the kitchen. "I'm so sorry, Jodi."

"You spoke to Roberta Chadwick after I asked you, begged you, pleaded with you not to talk to her." Jodi pounded her fist on the table. Her face was covered with red blotches and she was weeping. "You've destroyed me. Totally destroyed me. I have no chance now of getting my master's. I'll never be able to sign for court cases. Ever. I told you, Mrs. Trumbull . . ."

"Please, Jodi, sit down. I'll make tea."

"Tea!" shouted Jodi. "You think tea is going to fix the damage you've done? You knew the situation, Mrs. Trumbull. You knew she stole my research. You knew if I ever challenged her she'd win. You knew . . ."

"Stop that, Jodi. Sit down." Victoria handed her a paper towel.

Jodi limped into the cookroom blotting her face and slumped

into a chair. In a few minutes, Victoria joined her with two mugs of hot tea and a plate of graham crackers.

"I know you were trying to help, Mrs. Trumbull," Jodi sobbed. "But you've destroyed me. I'm dropping out of school and . . ."

Victoria slapped her hand on the table. "Stop that! Drink your tea and listen to me."

"There's nothing you can say." Jodi dabbed the paper towel gently around the stud in her nose.

"Has Roberta spoken to you?"

Jodi nodded miserably.

"What did she say?"

"She said . . ." Jodi hiccupped and ran her fingers through her spiky hair. Her purple nail polish was chipped. "She said, it's academic policy, as she had informed me earlier, for an advisor to put her name on an advisee's work, and if I was unwilling to work under that policy, I didn't belong in a university, and every college has that same policy." She plucked at the paper towel. "And in any case, the abstract of the article had already been submitted. And if I thought I would get any sort of recommendation from her"—another hiccup—"ever, I had another think coming." She blew her nose and Victoria winced as an edge of the paper towel caught in the nose stud. Jodi pulled the towel loose and wadded it up.

Victoria handed her another paper towel.

"Thanks," Jodi sobbed. "I tried so hard." Every swipe she made with the towel left a smear of black eyeliner across her cheek, like a nasty bruise.

"I take the blame. It was a good plan that backfired. However"—she held up her hand to stop Jodi, who was about to launch into another diatribe—"however, Roberta Chadwick has shown herself for what she is and she's now on record for threatening you."

"It's her word against mine, Mrs. Trumbull. Who's going to listen to me?"

"She has three student advisees on the Island. One of them came to me because she stole his paper, too."

"Yeah, I know. Christopher something."

"Christopher Wrentham. I remember his name because of the churches."

"What?" said Jodi, looking up.

"Just a way I have of recalling names. She can't intimidate Christopher. He can afford to take this case to court, if necessary, on behalf of all three of you."

"She's stealing from all of us?"

Victoria nodded. "Publish or perish, and she is unwilling to perish."

The second body had taken longer to identify than the first had. Eventually the autopsy and forensic entomologist's reports came back. The body was that of Dr. Journeyman Cash, professor of geology and member of IGCOC, the oversight committee. Professor Cash had been dead for more than two months, which would place his death around mid-July, shortly after the July IGCOC meeting.

Because he was often in the field and out of touch by cell phone, his friends and colleagues had not been concerned about his lack of communication. He had no family.

CHAPTER 10

At the state police barracks, Sergeant John Smalley laid out reports and photos for Casey and Victoria. They were sitting at the conference table, Victoria at the head, Smalley on her left, Casey on her right.

Trooper Tim Eldredge came into the room and set down lined yellow pads and a pen at each place.

Smalley looked up. "Thanks."

"I really don't belong here, John," Casey said to Smalley. "This is way out of my territory."

Smalley allowed himself a tight smile. "It's your deputy I want to talk to, Chief, not you. She's at the college and may have some insight into what's going on there."

Casey folded her arms across her chest. "O-kay."

"Don't be offended, Casey," said Smalley. "Mrs. Trumbull knows a hellava lot more about what's going on around this Island than both of us put together. I haven't even called in the Tisbury cops." He sat back. "Victoria is related to half the Island, and knows where the skeletons are buried—so to speak," he added with a grim smile.

Victoria folded her hands on the top of her yellow pad and waited to hear more. Casey sat back.

"This is what we've got," said Smalley. "Two Cape Cod University professors dead. Both members of that Ivy Green College Oversight Committee. Both strangled. Both found on the campus." He shrugged. "And now we've got a third body."

"A serial killer," said Victoria.

"Looks that way." Smalley pulled his pad toward him and sketched a wavy line. "We'll know more after forensics has examined this third victim." He added two more lines.

Smalley's last doodle had started with a few wiggly tendrils and developed into a full-blown drawing of a grapevine entwined on an elaborate arbor. Victoria was curious to see what would emerge this time.

Smalley continued. "Same modus. Three victims. Dr. Bliss killed roughly six weeks ago, Dr. Cash roughly two and a half months ago." He drew two more wavy horizontal lines. "Condition of the third victim indicates he was likely killed six months ago or more."

"Serial killers have a pattern like that, don't they?" Victoria asked. "A specific time lapse between killings before they're compelled to kill again."

Smalley nodded and tossed his pen down. "Killdeer, the forensics guy, seems to think it's worthwhile to have Walter's dog sniff around the campus."

"Couldn't hurt," said Casey.

Victoria tilted her head to see Smalley's yellow pad better.

Smalley said, "Dogs have a far, far better sense of smell than we humans. Some dogs are uncanny in their ability to sniff out specific odors. Usually, they have to be trained. Could be Brownie is a natural."

"I understand dogs are being trained to sniff out bedbugs," said Casey.

"Yeah." Smalley grunted. "Drugs, bugs, corpses."

Victoria picked up her own pen. "The two professors who were killed supported Ivy Green College."

"Thackery's had a tough time getting both financial and academic support," said Smalley. "Aside from the fact that three corpses have been found on his campus, losing the support of those two is going to hurt."

"He's certainly got the support of Islanders," said Victoria.

78

"Thackery may be a pompous ass, but you can't fault him for trying to educate us." He picked up his pen and flicked the button that retracted the point. "Stubborn guy. He's been working on founding that college as long as I can recall."

"At least ten years." Victoria sat back in her chair. "Apparently some members of the oversight committee think Thackery's college is too small to be considered."

Smalley looked up. "Too small? Hell, I went to a one-room school not that long ago and I'll bet you did, too, Mrs. Trumbull. Good education, lots of personal attention."

"I agree. But there seems to be some kind of personal agenda within the committee. I don't know the committee members and so I can't pinpoint the problem."

"I'll give you a list of the committee members," said Smalley. "To the department they're all 'persons of interest.'" He leaned back in his chair and called to Tim. "Would you make a copy of the IGCOC member list for Mrs. Trumbull?"

"From what I know, the committee was given considerable power," said Victoria.

"Enough to kill the program?" said Casey.

Victoria nodded.

"Sounds as though they're killing one another," said Smalley. He clicked the button on his pen again and drew a series of Vs above the wavy lines. "This personal agenda on the committee. Is it directed toward Thackery? He can be abrasive."

"I don't believe so," said Victoria. "I'll invite myself to an oversight committee meeting and see what I can find out."

Tim laid a paper with the IGCOC names and contact addresses, phones, and e-mails in front of Victoria.

She looked up. "Thank you, Tim."

"Be careful, Victoria," said Casey. "Someone's playing for keeps. You don't want to get in the middle of whatever."

Smalley nodded. He added a triangle above the wavy lines and a storm cloud above the triangle, and Victoria saw the sea, gulls, and a sailboat on Smalley's yellow pad.

On Tuesday, the day after the second body had been identified, the oversight committee announced its intention to return to the Island.

The committee now consisted of Phillip Bigelow, professor of American military history, and chair of the committee, and the other four of the seven original members—Hammermill Jones, business administration; Cosimo Perrini, romance languages; Noah Sutterfield, African-American studies; and Dedie Wieler, engineering. The Reverend Bob White, professor of theology, the sixth member, was newly appointed after the death of Professor Harlan Bliss.

The committee's job now was to appoint yet another new member to fill out the slot left by the death of Professor Journeyman Cash.

Although the odor in Catbriar Hall had faded so it was almost imperceptible, Professor Bigelow, chair of the committee, had decreed that they meet in the administration building, now called, at least by students in the know, Poison Ivy Hall.

The group had not yet arrived.

Walter set six chairs around the card table and was kneeling down, steadying the table's wobbly leg with duct tape.

Thackery bustled around giving directions. "Can't you find chairs that match?"

"No."

Thackery ran his hand over the top of the table. "You haven't dusted this."

Walter got to his feet and threw the roll of duct tape onto the table. It bounced off and rolled under a bookcase. "How about you letting me do my job?" Walter stood by the card table, hands on his hips, feet apart.

Thackery waved an arm. "The committee will be here any minute."

"Soon as you get out of my way, I'll get to work." Walter stood firm.

"For God's sake!" Thackery paused briefly, then, defeated, turned and left the building.

Outside, he almost ran into Victoria. "Now, what?" he snapped.

"I see you've had another confrontation with Walter," said Victoria, unruffled.

"That man is a mule. I don't know why I didn't fire him long ago. What can I do for you?"

"I'd like to sit in on the oversight committee meeting today," said Victoria.

"Bigelow won't let me sit in."

"He'll let me," said Victoria.

"Have it your own way," said Thackery, and stalked off.

IGCOC members waited to seat themselves around the card table until a seat was found for Victoria. Dedie returned from the kitchen, carrying a chrome-legged chair with pink vinyl upholstery and then they sat.

"We're delighted to welcome you, Professor Trumbull," said Professor Bigelow. "We're honored to have such a well-respected poet as an adjunct professor." He introduced the others. "Professor Bob White is our newest member, a Baptist minister. His field is theology."

Victoria nodded to each and made brief notes to herself so she could remember their names.

The Reverend Bob White was a short, plump man with a small beaky nose. He looked so much like the quail whose name he bore, that Victoria wondered if he was aware of his image. He had bushy white eyebrows and white chin whiskers worn in a modified Van

Dyke that looked like bird feathers. He wore a speckled brown-and-rust tweed suit with vest buttoned tightly over his round belly.

"For Mrs. Trumbull's information, we're meeting to appoint yet another new member"—Bigelow nodded at Bob White—"to replace our late colleague Professor Journeyman Cash."

"Bless him," said Cosimo Perrini.

"Thank you," said Bigelow.

Cosimo was wearing the same blue-and-white seersucker suit he'd worn before, again with a white T-shirt underneath. Victoria tried to put an image to his name. Cosmos? A flower on a tall stalk, sometimes pink, sometimes white. That seemed to fit.

Hammermill Jones, the former football player, shifted his weight and the rickety chair groaned. "Two IGCOC members dead. Killed. We'll have a problem finding a willing volunteer."

"Not volunteer," said Bob White. "Appointee. I had no choice in the matter. The provost appointed me after you people nominated me."

Dedie Wieler raised a hand. "I nominate Professor Petrinia Paulinia Kralich, mathematics. We discussed her at our last meeting."

"Trying to get her killed off, eh?" said Hammermill. "We didn't nominate her, if you'll recall, my dear."

"I second the nomination," said Noah Sutterfield, African-American studies. "Professor Kralich and Professor Chatterjee, my nominee, were tied for the position. This time, I'm backing Professor Kralich."

Dedie glanced at him and mouthed her thanks.

Bigelow's tongue flicked out. He looked around the group. "Since we've been through this nomination procedure only a short time ago, shall we agree on Dr. Kralich as our seventh member?"

"Gentlemen and lady. And you, Professor Trumbull," said Reverend Bob White.

Victoria smiled.

"As your new member," Reverend White continued, "I wasn't

82

privileged to go through the selection process. May I make a suggestion?"

Bigelow scowled. "I hardly think that would be appropriate, Bob, since you're new to the group and haven't attended any prior meetings."

"Let's hear what he has to say," said Hammermill.

"If I may say a word?" said Cosimo.

Victoria, making notes, had listed the Reverend Bob White, Dr. Dedie Wieler, and Hammermill Jones. She added Cosimo's name to her list. She studied him. He was a pallid man, someone who could easily be forgotten. She determined not to forget him. Cosimo, pale pink cosmos flowers.

The group turned to their usually silent member.

"Certainly," said Bigelow. "Let's hear what you have to say."

"We have a qualified nominee in Professor Kralich. We discussed her fully at our last meeting. In the interests of time, I think we should nominate her."

Dedie started to say something, looked over at Victoria, then at Noah, who shook his head ever so slightly, and she stopped.

Bigelow turned to her. "Did you have something to say, Dedie?"

"No. That's okay."

"All agreed?" He looked around. "I'll take the vote, then. Dedie?"

"Yes."

"Hammermill?"

"No."

"Cosimo?"

"Yes."

"Noah?"

"Yes."

"Bob?"

"I'll have to abstain, since I'm apparently not permitted to speak."

"I vote no," said Bigelow, ignoring the Reverend White's comment. "Three yes votes, two no votes, and an abstention. Professor

Kralich will be our new member replacing the late Professor Journeyman Cash. Dedie, would you please ask Dr. Wilson to step in?"

"Me?" said Dedie, crossing her hands over her chest.

Victoria stood up. "I believe he's just outside. I'll get him."

After Thackery presented his college progress report, he mentioned that Dr. Wellborn Price had agreed to enroll in Principles and Practices of Education, 101.

"Didn't he win the Nobel Prize in Economics a couple of years back?" asked Reverend Bob White.

Silence. Dedie smiled.

Reverend White looked around the group, most of whom avoided his eyes. "Why a freshman course in education?"

"He's required to be fully qualified to teach," said Bigelow, staring him down.

"Wellborn Price?" asked Bob White. "You expect him to take an introductory course in order to be qualified to teach? Surely you're joking."

Bigelow stood and looked at his watch. "I believe we can catch the three-forty-five boat if we hurry."

"You know, Bigelow, you're asking for a lawsuit." Bob White leaned back and folded his hands over his stomach.

"Hardly," said Bigelow. "No grounds whatsoever." He turned back to the others. "The next IGCOC meeting will be back on schedule, second Tuesday in October."

"I could come up with a half-dozen grounds," said Bob White, "starting with defamation of character."

"I guess you know about lawsuits," said Dedie. "Aren't you suing the university over that statue?"

"Inappropriate. Offensive piece of so-called art."

Bigelow ignored them.

Thackery said, "One other matter."

"What is it?" Bigelow glanced at his watch again.

"I'm sure you've heard by now that a skeleton was unearthed on campus this past week."

"It was in the news." Bigelow sat down again. "Do you have any further information? One hopes the skeleton is, perhaps, an Indian artifact?"

"It's a relatively recent burial," said Thackery. "Within the past year."

The eyes of all the committee members were on Thackery.

"That wasn't mentioned in the news," said Bigelow. "Has the body been identified?"

"There isn't enough left to identify readily. The state forensics team is working on his ID as we speak."

"His?" snapped Bigelow.

"A belt buckle, size twelve shoes."

"At least it's not another member of BIG . . ." Dedie stopped. "Of IGCOC," she finished.

The four regulars gathered on Alley's porch after work that same afternoon. Donald Schwartz, the boat builder, was sitting next to Sarah on the bench.

"Who's the seedy character working for Mrs. Trumbull?" asked Donald.

"No idea," said Joe. "Didn't think she hired anyone to help her." As usual, Joe was leaning against the post near the step where he could spit his tobacco juice off into a tuft of dried grass.

"You're killing that grass," said Sarah.

"Shouldn't be growing there," said Joe.

Lincoln stood in the doorway, scratching his back on the door frame. "If it's who I think it is, he delivers the morning papers. Picks them up from the paper boat."

"Okay, I know who he is," said Donald. "Name's Robert. Has a drinking problem."

"I hear they found another corpse up to the college." Joe cut off a fresh chunk of Red Man and stuffed it into his mouth. "Number three."

"That's old news," said Sarah. "Almost a week ago."

"Mrs. Trumbull find the body?" asked Lincoln.

"Caretaker's mutt dug it up," said Joe. "Must've thought it was a bone he buried."

Donald laughed.

"It's not funny, you guys," said Sarah. "Three dead people?"

"You heard of corpse-sniffing dogs?" said Lincoln. "Like drug-sniffing dogs at airports, only different."

"I heard they use gerbils to sniff drugs these days," said Donald. "Less threatening."

"Stop it!" said Sarah, putting her hands over her ears. "This is awful. Do they know who it is?"

"Was," said Joe. "Nothing but bones."

"They ID'd the second corpse yet?" asked Lincoln.

"Yup. Another college professor. Somebody hates college professors," said Joe.

"Killer's probably a college professor himself who didn't get tenure," said Donald.

"What do you know about tenure?" said Joe.

"Never did get tenure," said Donald.

"Figures," said Joe.

CHAPTER 11

"I'm sure it's not personal, Thackery," said Victoria.

The IGCOC group had walked to the ferry without a word of thanks to him. He was obviously still smarting from Victoria's having attended the first part of the meeting from which he'd been excluded.

"They didn't even have the decency to say good bye." Thackery was standing by the cracked window, his back to Victoria, hands clasped behind him.

"I suspect each of them was thinking about his own self interest," said Victoria. "I don't know why they bothered to come over to the Island. They could have nominated a new member on the mainland."

Thackery still said nothing.

Victoria said, "They may have felt that Reverend Bob White, the new member, needed to see the campus."

"They might have asked me to show him around," said Thackery without turning. "Only common courtesy. It is my campus, after all. I put the whole thing together with no help from anyone."

"What you've achieved is remarkable, Thackery. No one else could have done what you have." Victoria was seated in the chair next to Thackery's desk, still speaking to his back. "The committee members seem to be letting some form of personal animosity get in the way of helping the college."

Thackery said, "After the last meeting, that female member,

Dr. Wieler, took me aside and shed some light on the personal animosities." Thackery returned to his seat.

"What did she have to say?"

"She explained why Bigelow is making it so difficult for us to appoint Dr. Wellborn Price."

"Cape Cod University ought to be delighted to have Dr. Price listed among adjunct professors who teach at Ivy Green." Victoria smoothed her hair. "They didn't seem to have a problem approving me."

"Of course not," said Thackery.

"Even I, who know nothing about economics, am familiar with the name Wellborn Price. Wasn't he a consultant to the White House economics policy group?"

"He was on Bigelow's tenure committee," said Thackery.

"Oh?"

"He was responsible for denying Bigelow tenure."

"Was there justification?" asked Victoria.

"The only justification was personal vindictiveness," said Thackery. "Years before, Bigelow's father had served on Wellborn's tenure committee and blackballed Wellborn."

"Why?"

Thackery shrugged. "For personal reasons."

"And that's the reason Wellborn blackballed his son, our Professor Bigelow? That's as archaic as the Hatfield and McCoy feud," said Victoria. "Did our Professor Bigelow, appeal?"

"He did. But lost the appeal."

"And ended up teaching at Cape Cod University instead of at Stanford."

"Exactly. Tenure denial is a kiss of death for an academician with aspirations for teaching at a major university."

"It must be discouraging to put in five or more years at the beginning of one's career only to be fired. That's what it amounts to, doesn't it?"

Joel Killdeer, the forensics boss, was standing near the lush poison ivy vine that hid the shingles of Woodbine Hall when Walter let Brownie off his clothesline leash.

Brownie turned around in a circle, squatted down, scratched his ear with a hind leg, and yawned.

Killdeer nodded at the vine. "Stuff's pretty."

"Go on, Brownie," said Walter, nudging his dog with his toe. "Sic'um!"

Brownie turned his head to look at his master with sad eyes, and lay all the way down. He dropped his head on his front paws.

Killdeer was chewing gum. His sunglasses covered his eyes, his arms were folded over his chest. He leaned back against the side of the building. "Pretty lively mutt, you got there, Walter."

Walter bent down and lifted Brownie to his feet. "Go on, sic'um!"

At that point, Thackery and Victoria emerged from the building.

"That's poison ivy, Dr. Killdeer," said Victoria. "I hope you're not sensitive to it."

"Oh, shit!" Killdeer straightened up and stared at the vine. "Last case I got damned near killed me."

"Woodbine Hall has an upstairs shower," said Thackery.

"Cool water," said Victoria. "Be careful not to touch your clothes where they've come in contact with the vine."

Killdeer left to clean up. Brownie staggered to his feet and looked reproachfully at Walter. He then put his nose to the ground and started circling, making wider and wider circles, moving away from the administration building. He stopped suddenly and began to dig, almost tripping up Walter, who'd been following closely behind his dog. Thackery and Victoria gathered around.

"Smart dog," said Walter, preening himself.

Thackery scowled.

"I hope he hasn't found yet another body," said Victoria.

Brownie dug furiously with his front paws. Dirt shot out between his hind legs. After a few minutes he stopped, looked up at Walter, and yelped.

Walter bent down to look into the foot-deep hole. "Can't see nothin'."

Thackery turned his head away.

Brownie yelped again. Walter reattached the clothesline leash and held him back.

Victoria leaned over the dark hole. "Something is moving down there." She could just make out a wad of some cottony stuff with seven or eight, or maybe nine, wriggling pink creatures the size of the last joint on her little finger.

"Mice?" asked Walter.

"I don't believe mice would nest underground. These are probably voles." Victoria stood up and patted Brownie. "Good boy," she said. "That was clever of you."

"I hope you don't plan to charge Dr. Killdeer for Brownie's latest discovery," said Thackery, turning back to the scene of the dig.

"At least they're not *dead mice*," said Walter, "if you know what I mean."

"Voles are harmless," said Victoria

Killdeer peered into the hole. "Look like mice to me."

Walter was holding Brownie back with the clothesline. "They're mice."

"They're called meadow mice," admitted Victoria.

"Drown'em," said Killdeer.

Victoria leaned over the hole in the ground. "We'll cover their nest and leave them alone."

Brownie whined, and tugged at his leash.

"Better encourage that dog to look elsewhere," said Killdeer.

Victoria gathered up a handful of fallen leaves and placed them over the tiny pink creatures, then gently mounded dirt back over them.

Brownie looked up at her and wagged his tail.

Thackery, who'd been silently glaring at the goings-on, grunted. "I have business to attend to." He strode back to Woodbine Hall.

Walter led Brownie away from the voles and removed the clothesline from the dog's neck. "C'mon. Get to work!"

Brownie sat down and scratched his ear.

"Good job, Brownie." Victoria leaned down to pat him.

"He's got fleas," warned Walter.

Brownie stood and yawned, then began circling again.

Victoria moved the lawn chair she used for class away from the former magic circle, set it back up in the late afternoon shade of the oaks, and sat down.

Brownie circled. He stopped. He sat and scratched himself again. He looked over at Victoria.

"Go on," said Walter. "What've you got?"

Brownie dug for several minutes, kicking dirt behind him until he'd excavated a shallow ditch.

The katydids stopped singing for a second, then started up again.

"What the hell was that?" asked Killdeer.

"Katydids," said Victoria. "That's their mating song."

"Mating song." Killdeer rubbed the back of his neck. "Wonder if my babygirl would mate if I chirped like that."

"They start calling right around now, late afternoon. They're nocturnal." Victoria glanced up. "They live in trees and look like large grasshoppers."

"Thanks," said Killdeer.

A breeze blew through the tall oaks, and a few leaves drifted down. On the side of Woodbine Hall, the poison ivy vine blazed with color as the low rays of the afternoon sun struck the house. A V of Canada geese flew overhead, and their continuous honking faded into the distance.

Brownie stopped digging, yawned, and lay down in his ditch. He lowered his head onto his paws. His tail thumped.

"For cryin' out loud. Get up!" Walter demanded.

Brownie opened his eyes and looked up.

Walter grunted, turned his back, and shuffled toward the road in front of Woodbine Hall.

Victoria stood up and leaned over, hands on her knees. "That was hard work, wasn't it, Brownie?"

The tail thumped.

"You haven't finished, have you?"

Brownie staggered to his feet, stretched, his rear end up, his front paws out straight, yawned with a sort of groan, moved a foot or so to the right, and recommenced his digging. After a few minutes, as though he'd simply been warming up, he began to dig furiously. Dirt flew behind him. He panted. He yelped. He dug. Dirt flew. Saliva dripped from his grizzled jaws.

Killdeer returned, his sunglasses perched on top of his dark, smooth head. "Your pup earned his salary today," he said with admiration. Walter had returned from his place across the road, and was zipping up his pants. Killdeer dropped his sunglasses into place. "You can retire, Walter, my man, and let that pup support you the rest of his life. Corpse-sniffing dogs ain't cheap."

Victoria was leaning on her stick peering down into Brownie's excavation. Thackery had summoned the police, and the troopers finished the disinterment.

"Number four, I gather," said Killdeer.

"Something like that," Smalley replied. "No question about it. Serial killer."

"Who's been at it for some time." Killdeer turned to Thackery. "Likely have to dig up your whole place, man."

Thackery grunted. "Can you tell how long ago this victim was buried, Dr. Killdeer?"

Killdeer shoved his glasses up on his shiny head again and leaned over. "More recent than the last one. Still has bits of dried flesh. Lab can tell us more."

CHAPTER 12

The next morning, Thursday, a crowd materialized. The Island grapevine had been at work. Five or six people gathered behind Woodbine Hall and another eight or so had walked from Main Street through the oak grove toward Brownie's hole in the ground.

"Sorry folks," said Smalley, as he ordered his troopers to string crime scene tape around the entire perimeter of the campus. "Not much to see. We'll give the *Island Enquirer* and WMVY all the information we can."

"Was this the third body you've found?" asked a gray-haired woman holding a bulging Black Dog shopping bag.

"Afraid we have no comment, ma'am."

"It's number four," said a man standing next to her.

A young woman wheeling a baby stroller asked, "What're you doing to catch the killer?"

"Folks, I'm afraid I really have to ask you to step back," said Smalley.

"They're dealing with a serial killer," said the same man who'd spoken. "Won't catch him until he kills again."

"Do you want me to mind the office while you're gone, Thackery?" asked Victoria. Sergeant Smalley had requested Thackery to accompany him to the state police barracks. Thackery hesitated. He was rubbing his hand over the back of his neck in a way Victoria suspected meant stress.

"I'd appreciate that, Mrs. Trumbull." He turned to Smalley. "How long will this take?"

"An hour or so" Smalley replied.

"Perhaps we'll have some word on the identity of the third victim," said Victoria.

"Let's hope so," said Smalley.

Victoria watched at the cracked window as the two men headed for the police car in the faculty parking lot. The two were about the same height, but Thackery Wilson was almost as gaunt as the skeletons Brownie had unearthed, while John Smalley, a good ten years younger, had the broad chest and tight bottom of a discus thrower. Thackery loped along with an awkward stork gait, Smalley strode along as though he was about to accept his gold medal. Victoria watched until they got into the police car and drove off.

The phone rang. She took Thackery's seat at his desk and answered.

"Was that another body they found?" the caller asked.

"I'm afraid we have no comment," said Victoria.

"That means yes, then." The caller disconnected.

Victoria searched in her cloth bag for something to write on, found a pen and a fuel oil bill in an envelope with a clean reverse side and began to draft her column for the *Island Enquirer* in her loopy backhand.

The phone rang again.

"Understand a dog dug up another corpse?"

"I'm sorry, we have no comment." Victoria hung up.

She would have to be careful not to divulge too much information in writing her column. She had been privy, she knew, to more than the police would care to release to readers of the weekly newspaper.

Another call, another no comment.

Victoria was sorting through her notes when the front door opened and a tall heavyset man entered. She first noticed his hair, a tousled white mane, then his eyes, a clear cerulean blue. He was

94

probably in his sixties, about the same age as her daughter Amelia. He wore jeans belted below his stomach. The top buttons of his plaid shirt were undone showing a clean white T-shirt.

"Wilson around?" He had a deep mellow voice.

"Dr. Wilson should be back shortly," Victoria said. "Is there something I can help you with?"

"Where'd he go, if I may ask?"

The phone rang. "No comment." Victoria hung up.

"I suppose you've been getting that all afternoon."

Victoria nodded. "Thackery went to the police barracks. Won't you have a seat?"

"Thanks." The man sat in Victoria's usual chair and leaned back. "Hear you found a fourth victim."

"I'm afraid we have no comment." Victoria smiled.

He laughed and crossed an ankle over his knee. He was wearing well-worn boat shoes with no socks. He studied her with unsettling eyes. "Victoria Trumbull. I like your work."

"Thank you." She felt quite girlish under the scrutiny of this attractive man. "I'm sorry, I don't know your name."

"No reason to. Name's Wellborn Price." He uncrossed his legs, leaned forward, and held out his hand.

They shook.

"I'm delighted to meet you, Dr. Price. You'll be one of our professors, won't you?" Victoria felt quite at ease talking to one of her fellow professors.

"Adjunct professor." Wellborn grinned, showing slightly crooked front teeth. "That is, if I pass the introductory education course Professor Bigelow insists I take."

Victoria flushed. "That's degrading."

"That's Bigelow." His grin broadened. "But understandable, given the personality involved."

"Even I know something of your reputation as an economist and educator."

Another call. Another no comment.

Wellborn sat back again, crossed his legs, and grasped his ankle. "I certainly don't need the job, Mrs. Trumbull. But I would enjoy tweaking that pointed nose of our little Professor Bigelow." He pinched his own rather grand nose. "Bigelow's convinced I'll refuse to go along with his game." He smiled again. "Might be fun sitting through that course with those eighteen-year-old freshmen women."

"Can't you appeal to the university?"

"I won't lower myself. I could tell Wilson to hell with it. Or I could keep in mind that Thackery Wilson, despite his shortcomings, is doing his best to bring higher education to the Island." He slapped his ankle. "Yes, I plan to take that course."

The door opened and Thackery stalked in along with the raucous sound of the katydids.

Wellborn Price stood and they shook hands.

"God, Price, I'm sorry." Thackery tossed papers he'd been holding onto his desk.

"Don't be. Not your battle. Bigelow and I go way back."

Thackery stepped over to Linda's desk, wheeled her chair over, and sat. "The female member of the oversight committee, Dr. Wieler . . ."

"Dedie. Yes. A remarkable woman. Brilliant engineer. Know her well."

"She informed the freshman ed teacher of the situation." Thackery leaned forward, hands on his knees. "According to the teacher, if you're amenable to delivering an hour-long lecture to the class on the latest methods for teaching economics to non-economists, that would more than qualify you for an A-plus in the course."

Wellborn laughed and got to his feet. "That's all I needed to know, Thackery. Thanks." He bowed to Victoria. "You see, Mrs. Trumbull? I'm not alone in my feelings about our Professor Bigelow."

After the door closed behind Wellborn Price, Victoria yielded Thackery's seat to him and took her usual chair.

Thackery straightened his desk calendar. "Were there any calls while I was gone?"

"Several wanting to know about the body we found."

"Ghouls," said Thackery.

"Have they identified the third victim? I hope it wasn't another member of the oversight committee."

"That mongrel of Walter's is an embarrassment."

"Brownie has some endearing qualities. What about the third victim?"

"A sociology professor at Florida State named Geoffrey Merriman. He was vacationing on the Island."

"Didn't his family report him missing?"

"He and his wife were separated," said Thackery, fiddling with papers on his desk. "This yours?" He held up the Packer's Fuel Oil envelope.

"That's this week's column for the *Enquirer*."

He passed the envelope to her.

"Another college professor," she mused. "Didn't his university miss him?"

"He was on sabbatical."

Victoria tapped the envelope on the arm of her chair. "So sad. No one missed Professor Bliss. No one missed Professor Cash. No one missed this third victim."

Thackery nodded. "Professor Merriman."

"Where was he staying?"

"Smalley's trying to locate the place, but it's a cold trail."

Victoria shook her head. "Three college professors. Two different universities. What's the connection, I wonder."

"They were probably on someone's tenure committee," said Thackery, with a fleeting smile.

CHAPTER 13

Classes at Ivy Green started up again despite the ongoing disruption of police work. Now that their magic circle under the oaks had become a crime scene, Victoria's poetry class moved into Catbriar Hall. It had been five weeks since the body of the unfortunate Professor Bliss was found. Only an occasional reminder drifted into the room when the wind eddied from the northeast.

On Tuesday, Jodi stopped to pick up Victoria, who was waiting at the top of her steps. Jodi had cut last Thursday's poetry class.

October brought the blush of Island autumn, a pastel canvas, unlike the daring scarlets and yellows of the mainland.

"Such a glorious day," said Victoria, climbing into the front seat of the Jeep.

"Yeah." Jodi shifted into gear and headed down the drive. She was wearing a green T-shirt that read ISLAND GROWN and jeans so worn that in places only the warp threads held the cloth together.

"I'm glad you haven't dropped out of the graduate degree program," said Victoria. "Are there any new developments in your plans for publication?"

Jodi glanced at Victoria but said nothing. A car passed by on the road heading from Edgartown.

"Has Roberta submitted your paper to the journal?"

Jodi looked both ways and turned left onto the road. "She submitted the abstract of my paper under her name."

"And?"

"The journal agreed to publish *her* paper, contingent on its meeting the deadline and all publication requirements."

Victoria was silent.

They turned onto Old County Road and passed the Granary Gallery. While she waited for Jodi to say more, Victoria gazed out at the dead oak trees on either side, killed by a two-year plague of hungry caterpillars.

"Is there any possibility publication can be held up?"

"Not that I know of."

"Again, I'm sorry, Jodi. You were right. I should never have spoken to Roberta Chadwick."

"I thought I was so lucky to have her for a thesis advisor." Jodi sighed. "She's nothing but a scheming, conniving bitch." They were both quiet as they slowed for the school zone. "She pretended to be so interested in my work. All the time she was setting me up."

They passed the school before either spoke.

"Did you tape your deaf-mute interviews?" asked Victoria.

"I taped some. Mostly took notes."

"You have the notes, don't you?"

Jodi nodded.

"It seems to me you have legal recourse."

"In a normal world, I guess," said Jodi. "The academic world is not a normal world."

"Stand up and fight."

"Look at me, Mrs. T." Jodi took a hand off the wheel and gestured at her snake tattoos, nose stud, eyebrow rings. "People see me and they think troublemaker. If I challenge my professor, who're they going to believe—her? Or me? I'm gonna need, like, recommendations and her support and her networking, you know?"

"I know a lawyer who would represent you pro bono."

"You don't get it, Mrs. T. Let's say I win. You think she'll help me after that? Look at what happened after you tried to talk to her. She submitted the abstract to the journal under her name. Please, Mrs. T, I asked you before and you didn't listen. *Please, please, please,*" Jodi underlined each word by pounding on the steering wheel. "I don't want your help."

Dedie Wieler strode into the office of Dr. Harold Harriman, dean of the engineering school at Cape Cod University that same morning and stood in front of his desk.

"I don't want Hammermill Jones on my tenure committee. He's a misogynist."

Dean Harriman sat back in his leather chair and steepled his fingers. "You're overreacting, Dedie."

"He's in business administration. He knows nothing about engineering. He can't possibly evaluate my work." Dedie leaned over, her hands flat on his desk.

He moved his chair back and ran a hand over his short hair, cut the way he'd worn it in the Corps of Engineers. "The university looks for balance in our tenure committees. Professor Jones gives the committee that balance."

"Oh, baloney!" said Dedie, standing up straight.

Dean Harriman removed his steel-framed spectacles. "Hysteria doesn't suit you, Dedie."

"I'm not being hysterical!"

"Calm yourself." Dean Harriman studied the lenses of his glasses. He opened his desk drawer and took out a tissue. He breathed on the lenses and methodically polished them with the tissue, then dropped it into his wastepaper basket.

Dedie took a couple of deep breaths, her hands tightly fisted, while the cleaning of the glasses was going on. "Do you call male faculty members hysterical?"

"Please," said Dean Harriman, holding up a hand to stop her. "We don't need a diatribe on feminism."

"This has nothing to do with feminism. And it's not a diatribe. It's okay, isn't it, for my male colleagues to come in here and rage and say *shit* and *fuck* . . ."

"Dedie," said Dean Harriman. "Watch your language."

"It's not *my* language. I'm just down the hall. I hear them say *goddamn, hell, fuck,* and *shit*. As do you, *Harry*."

He cleared his throat. "I prefer to be called by my title, Dedie. *Dean* Harriman."

"The guys call you Harry and you call them Frank and Joe and Bill."

"That's quite enough, Dedie."

"When you call me *Doctor* Wieler, I'll call you *Dean* Harriman."

He crossed his arms over his chest and studied her. "I don't make deals with junior faculty." Dean Harriman stood.

"Don't dismiss me, *Harry*," said Dedie. She was a good five inches taller than he was. "I want you to get Hammermill Jones off my tenure committee."

"Are you sure you're ready for tenure, Dedie?"

"Ready!" sputtered Dedie. "Seven years in this department. I've brought in more grant money over those seven years than all the members of the engineering department combined." She folded her arms and looked down on him. "Not one member of the department has more publications than I do. I've been cited by the community for my engineering advice for the new high school. My students have given me the highest scores an engineering faculty member ever received at Cape Cod University. And you question whether I'm ready for tenure?" She pointed a stiff finger at him. "And *you* let that ignorant bigot sit on my tenure committee to judge *me*?"

"I suggest you leave now, Dedie, before you lose control completely." Dean Harriman walked around his desk and opened his office door. "When you've had a chance to calm down, I'll be happy to discuss matters with you."

Dedie stared down at him. After a moment, she brushed past

him, stalked down the hall to her office, her head up. She shut the door behind her, careful not to slam it.

Catbriar Hall's transformation from garage into classroom had given the building windows on both sides with a view of the parking lot on one side, trees on the other.

After class, Jodi, Victoria's chauffeur, had gone to Cronig's to buy her week's groceries. With four boys, a week's worth of groceries would take time to assemble. Victoria was using the time to plan her next class session.

She glanced out the windows toward the trees and saw a young man with snowy-white hair approaching. When he came through the door, she was stowing papers in a manila folder.

He was tall, about Elizabeth's age, she guessed, maybe older, in his early forties. He had far-seeing blue eyes and a deep tan that contrasted nicely with his sun-bleached hair. He looked vaguely familiar.

"Can I help you?" she asked.

"Is Jodi Paloni around?" A deep voice.

"She's doing errands and should be back soon. Is there anything I can do for you?"

"You're Victoria Trumbull, the poet, aren't you?"

Victoria smiled. "Yes."

"I've wanted to meet you since I was a kid." He held out his hand and she shook it. "My name is Price Henderson. Jodi Paloni and I are two of Professor Roberta Chadwick's Island advisees and I was hoping to talk with her about a problem we both seem to be having."

"I believe I understand. Won't you have a seat until Jodi gets back?" Victoria picked up her folder.

Price Henderson swiveled a chair around so he faced her and sat down, his arms resting on the chair back.

After a few moments of silence Victoria asked, "What are you studying?"

"Sociology. I'd been planning on a career in counseling and thought I needed an advanced degree."

"'Had been'?" Victoria held the folder upright. "Has Professor Chadwick done something to change your mind?"

"I guess you've spoken to Jodi."

"Well, yes. We've spoken."

"No point in repeating what she's told you."

"I assume you've done some research and are, or were, about to publish it?"

He nodded. "A paper on the sociological consequences of an adoptee's search for birth parents."

Victoria said, "I've talked with another of her students, as well."

"Christopher Wrentham?"

She nodded.

"Professor Chadwick is out of control," said Price, shaking his head. "Someone's got to stop her."

"I'm afraid I tried and made things worse for Jodi." Victoria tucked a paper back into her folder.

"I heard about that." He gazed out the window at the yellow crime scene tape strung around the dug up site of Brownie's discovery. "They've really made a mess out there, digging up the whole campus like that."

Victoria nodded. "Most unfortunate."

He looked back at her. "I'm like Jodi. I can't afford to antagonize our faculty advisor either."

"Do you know the third student?"

"Christopher Wrentham. Never met him. No idea what he's like."

"He's willing to take this to court. He claims he has nothing to lose."

Price shook his head. "Won't do any good. I tried going to the grievance committee, or whatever it's called. They met with her. She put up a good defense. They cleared her and now she's got it in for me. Jodi, too."

CHAPTER 14

Ever since Price Henderson walked through the door of Catbriar Hall, Victoria had pondered why he looked familiar. Now it came to her. Wellborn Price, of course, the economist.

Victoria looked up again at the young man sitting in front of her. According to Thackery, Wellborn Price had fathered a son by the daughter of his tenure professor. The young man sitting before her resembled Dr. Price, and was the right age. And, furthermore, was named Price.

"Is Price a family name?" Victoria asked.

"My mother told me she named me Price because she paid a high price for me, and I was worth it." He leaned his chin on his arms, folded now on the back of the chair. "I have to live up to that. I was the result of a serious fling she had with someone my grandfather didn't approve of."

This was not the time to pry. Victoria was quite sure she knew something about this young man's background that he, himself, didn't know. "Jodi should be along any minute."

He glanced at his watch. "I don't mind waiting."

"Are you taking courses with Jodi?" Victoria asked.

"I've never met her. Our only connection is our advisor, Roberta Chadwick."

"Your thesis subject is interesting." Victoria looked up and saw that he was watching her closely. "It wasn't long ago that adoption authorities believed they were doing the right thing by making it impossible for children to reconnect with their birth parents."

"I'm glad that's changed."

"I gather your research is firsthand?"

He nodded. "I know my birth mother. It's my birth father I don't know. I've been searching for information about him." After a moment, he went on. "My adoptive father, John Henderson, married my mother when I was five. He's the only father I've ever known. A real loser."

"What about your mother's family?"

"My grandmother died when my mother was a young girl. When my grandfather learned she was pregnant with me, he whisked her off to Turkey, where he'd accepted a teaching position."

"Didn't your mother have any brothers or sisters? Your aunts and uncles?"

"She has an older brother. She's been estranged from him since he learned she was pregnant."

"What have you learned about your birth father?"

"I was told he was killed in an automobile accident. That's what I'm trying to track down."

Victoria looked down at her folder. She'd torn off a corner without thinking.

Price said, "When I was four or five, my mother and I returned to the States and that's when she met and married John Henderson. They've been divorced for years now."

"I'm sorry," said Victoria. "Did she and your grandfather ever reconcile?"

"She refused to have anything to do with him. He stayed in Turkey and died there. I don't remember much about him."

How sad to be estranged from family, Victoria thought. She had lost her own father when she was three, and her mother took the only job she could find, a governess job off Island. But Victoria had lived with her doting grandparents and aunt, and her mother had written her weekly letters full of funny drawings. She glanced out the window and saw Jodi's Jeep pull into the parking lot. The car door slammed and she realized she had to ask a quick question before Jodi appeared. "Have you ever heard of a Dr. Wellborn Price?"

"Sure. I guess everybody's heard of him. He retired to the Vineyard, and is teaching an economics course here at Ivy Green."

"I hope so," said Victoria.

"I came to the Island hoping to meet him. I want to take his course. Price Henderson taught by Professor Price. I like that."

Jodi breezed through the door. "Sorry it took so long. Oh, I didn't realize you had someone with you."

Price Henderson unwound his legs from the chair and stood up. "Jodi Paloni?"

"Yeah?"

He held out a hand. "I'm one of Professor Chadwick's Island advisees."

"Omigod!" Jodi seized his hand. "You're not Price Henderson, are you?"

He nodded.

Victoria gathered up her papers and stood. "I suspect you two will want to talk." She looked from one to the other eager face. "Don't do anything rash." She headed for the door. "I'll wait in your car, Jodi. Don't hurry. I have plenty to think about."

The day after Dedie Wieler's confrontation with the dean of the engineering department, she was in her office at Cape Cod University, pulling out her desk drawers and dumping them, one at a time, into a large cardboard box she'd picked up at the liquor store in the Falmouth mall.

Dr. Harold Harriman rapped on the side of her door and she looked up. He stood there, stiffly. "May I ask what you're doing, Dedie?"

"I'm emptying my desk drawers, *Harry*," she replied.

"Dean Harriman, Dedie," he said.

"Right-o, *Harry*," said Dedie.

Dr. Harriman came all the way into her small office, pulled up her lone guest chair, and sat down. "I have to tell you, Dedie, your attitude is a problem for me."

"Is that right?" said Dedie, lifting her files out of the wide bottom drawer.

"I must ask again, what are you doing?"

"I believe I answered you the first time, Harry."

"You understand, don't you, that your tenure committee is meeting next week for a preliminary evaluation of your suitability for tenure?"

"Thanks for reminding me, Harry." Dedie swept a jar of pencils and pens off the top of her desk. It hit the contents of the cardboard box with a rattle. She turned to her bookcase, and began to stack books into an empty Smirnoff box.

Dr. Harriman stood, his face flushed. "You must realize, Dedie, given your attitude, I can scarcely give you a hearty recommendation."

"Thanks, Harry, but I don't need or want a recommendation from you of any kind, hearty or not."

He started for the door, turned before he went through. "I'll ask you once more. What do you think you're doing now you've told me you're emptying your desk?"

"Leaving, Harry. I've accepted a position with Ocean Engineering, Inc. here in Woods Hole."

"You'll regret that decision, Dedie."

"I don't think so, Harry." She finished filling the Smirnoff box, and with her foot shoved an empty Dewar's White Label box under the last shelf of books.

"You're a quitter, Dedie. Can't stand the pressure."

"You're right, Harry. I'm quitting."

"You're giving up the prestige of academia, salary, benefits, tenure. Your future."

Dedie brushed her hair out of her eyes. "I've accepted a salary that's twice what you're making. Four times what I'd make as a newly tenured professor. Benefits? You can't begin to match Ocean Engineering's. Tenure? No tenure, thank God." She laughed. "So long, Harry. Tell the tenure committee to go fuck themselves."

Dr. Harriman turned on his heel and in his most military manner beat a retreat.

Dedie thrust her middle finger in the air at his retreating back.

At the same moment Dedie was giving Dean Harriman the finger, Victoria's phone rang. She answered.

"Mrs. Trumbull? This is Jodi."

"Yes, Jodi. I'm glad we had a chance to meet Price Henderson yesterday." Victoria pulled up a chair next to the cookroom table and sat down, thinking Jodi probably had a good bit to talk about.

"Me, too. I'd been trying to meet him, but he's hard to reach. He lives on a sailboat."

"Something I've always wanted to do," said Victoria. "How can I help you?"

"I'm afraid I'm going to miss a couple of classes."

"You've missed one already," said Victoria. "You're allowed only three cuts, you know."

"Yeah, I know. But I heard about this weeklong sociology conference off Island, sort of short notice . . ." Jodi paused.

"If it's a professional meeting, of course you can be excused," said Victoria. "Are you going with Roberta?"

"I'm not positive I'm going yet. I have to make arrangements and stuff . . ." Her voice trailed off. "Budgets, you know . . ."

"I can give you additional assignments. Then whether you go or not, you'll be covered."

"That would be great, Mrs. T. Thanks! Bye!"

"You haven't answered . . ." said Victoria, but Jodi had disconnected. I hope she decides to go, thought Victoria. She needs to get away. And it will be an opportunity for her to settle things with Roberta.

CHAPTER 15

Late that night Professor Roberta Chadwick was reading through the manuscript of "Culture and Society of the Deaf-Mutes of Chilmark." Based on the abstract, the paper was scheduled for publication in the summer issue of the quarterly, *Massachusetts Journal of Sociology.*

As the evening grew chilly, Roberta slipped on her sweatshirt, the same pink one printed with chickadees she'd worn the day Victoria Trumbull had invited her to lunch. As she smoothed the front of the shirt, she recalled Victoria accusing her of plagiarism. Roberta felt her face flush as she recalled Victoria's look of disgust. Plagiarism. Was it possible that's what she was doing?

At first she'd put her name on Jodi's paper as junior author. The department chair had assured her that a student's work, after all, was the result of a teacher's guidance. Students' papers were never accepted on the basis of the students' credentials. Jodi's work would never be published unless Roberta's name was on it. And, her department head warned her, she needed more publications to her credit. Tenure, he'd said. Always keep tenure in mind.

That led Roberta to put her name on the paper as senior author, rationalizing that if she rewrote and edited the paper, it would really and truly be hers, not Jodi's.

And then Mrs. Trumbull had challenged her.

This was the way things worked in the academic world. Jodi needed to know that. Roberta deleted Jodi's name as junior author and put it in the acknowledgments.

The deadline was coming up. She had only a short time to get all three papers ready for publication.

References had to be checked, a time-consuming chore. Footnotes. She sighed. Really, she did deserve to be senior author. Lone author. After references and footnotes she would have to rewrite to reflect her style. The students had written with entirely different voices. Jodi had submitted hard copy and she would have to retype the entire paper into her word processor. She pushed her keyboard away from her, stood up, and stretched. She would have to pull a couple of all-nighters and she didn't look forward to that.

Fortunately, Professor Chadwick's house was on a semicircular road near Oak Bluffs. Most of the houses along the road were summer homes. Owners had left and the houses were deserted this time of year, so it would be nice and quiet. She'd be able to get a lot done.

She brewed a pot of coffee and took a mug to her desk. She'd seated herself again when her cat jumped up onto her lap and stood staring at her.

"Settle down, Ruffles. Come on, sit." She stroked him absently while she tried to make a list of what had to be done and when. The cat's tail was in her face. He meowed.

"What's the matter with you?"

He dropped off her lap onto the floor, circled the room, and jumped back onto her lap, where he stood again, paws kneading her jeans-clad thighs. He stared at her.

"You hear something?" Roberta stopped writing and listened. "A mouse? Mice?"

Ruffles dropped off her lap and disappeared.

When she heard knocking on the door a moment later, she glanced at her watch. It was almost eleven o'clock, and she'd forgotten all about supper. She'd forgotten to feed Ruffles. That was his problem.

Her legs were stiff from sitting for such a long time and were starting to cramp. She braced herself against her desk for a few seconds until she could work the cramps out.

A second knocking, louder.

"Just a minute!" she said. "Be right there."

Who would call so late at night? Mrs. Hamilton was her only neighbor this time of year. Did she have an emergency?

The timer had shut the porch light off at ten, and her hallway and porch were in deep shadow.

She limped to the door but before she reached it she called out, "Come in! The door's not locked."

Immediately after she said that, she wondered if she should have invited in an unknown caller. But this was the Vineyard and she liked the feeling of security she had, living on the Island. "Who is it?" she asked, belatedly.

She reached the door just as it opened. She couldn't make out the caller in the darkness. Her students never came to her home. Her sister, Linda, would have knocked, opened the door, and called out, "Anybody home?" All this went through her mind before she decided what to do.

She still couldn't make out the person or persons on her porch. "It's late," she said, her eyes blurry from focusing on the papers, and not yet adjusted to the night. "Unless it's an emergency, come back tomorrow."

A chill breeze rustled the dry leaves in the oak in her front yard, and Roberta shuddered.

She began to close the door to block out the dark silhouette against the less black night sky, when the caller pushed a damp, acrid-smelling cloth into her face.

She reached for the light switch, and that was the last thing she knew.

Victoria was preparing for next week's class when the police Bronco drove up and the chief knocked on the door.

"Good morning, Casey. I've made a fresh pot of coffee."

"Thanks, I could use some." Casey wiped her boots on the doormat and stepped up into the kitchen.

Victoria poured coffee into two mugs, and handed one to the chief along with milk and the sugar bowl.

They sat in the cookroom and Casey stirred a spoonful of sugar into her coffee. "Professor Roberta Chadwick is missing," she said abruptly.

"I beg your pardon?"

Casey stirred a second, then a third spoonful of sugar into her coffee. "Your so-called friend, Roberta Chadwick. She's missing."

"What are you talking about?"

"Mrs. Hamilton, her neighbor, noticed her cat clawing at the door this morning. No sign of Chadwick."

"Jodi talked about a meeting off Island. I imagine she's attending that."

"Her car's in her driveway and Mrs. Hamilton said she'd never leave the cat for any length of time without telling her." Casey continued to stir her sweetened coffee.

"I'm sure she'll turn up. Why did Mrs. Hamilton notify you instead of the Oak Bluffs police?"

"Her grandson is in the same grade as Patrick in the West Tisbury school. She didn't want to be an alarmist and call the police. So she called me."

"And . . . ?"

"I knew you'd had an encounter with Professor Chadwick." Casey sipped her coffee. "Figured you might be able shed some light to pacify Mrs. Hamilton, who's a bit of a pain, if you know what I mean."

"I know Mrs. Hamilton." Victoria looked up at the philodendron hanging above the table. There were a couple of dead leaves she should trim off. "I invited Professor Chadwick here for lunch during the nor'easter. Things started out well but she didn't stay for lunch."

"Mrs. Hamilton is in the category of nosy neighbor," said Casey. "You're probably right. Chadwick is at a meeting or doing something ordinary like a friend stopped by and they went for a ride."

"Still, that's curious about her cat."

Casey reached for the sugar bowl.

"That'll make four spoonfuls," said Victoria. "Not that I mind."

"Thanks." Casey pushed the bowl away. "I wasn't paying attention." She stirred her coffee again.

"I don't really know Roberta Chadwick," said Victoria. "Tell Mrs. Hamilton that she'll show up eventually. How long has she been missing?"

"Mrs. Hamilton said the last time she saw her was yesterday."

"Oh for heaven's sake," said Victoria. "Hardly something to be alarmed about."

"I agree." Casey sipped her coffee. "She's an adult, after all. Who knows why she didn't plan for her cat."

"Cats can take care of themselves." Victoria nodded at McCavity, perched on the chair next to her, cleaning himself. "If she'd left without making plans for a dog, that would be different."

"Reminds me, what do you think about Walter's dog?"

"He's remarkable," said Victoria. "He's apparently a natural cadaver dog, a great rarity. Dr. Killdeer has hired Brownie to sniff all over the Ivy Green campus."

Casey grinned. "Thackery Wilson must be delighted."

Later that afternoon, Mrs. Hamilton again called Casey at the West Tisbury Police Station. "Roberta still hasn't come home and it's been almost a full day."

"What about her cat?" asked Casey.

"I'm feeding him. He was at her door and I just can't help it, I feel so sorry for him."

"Her car?" asked Casey.

"It's still in the driveway. I looked through the glass at her box in the post office, and it hasn't been emptied."

"Mrs. Trumbull thinks she might be attending a meeting off Island," said Casey. "I wouldn't worry about her, if I were you. I did call the Oak Bluffs police after you reported her missing and gave them your number."

"Thank you so much, Mrs. O'Neill."

Casey winced. She'd shed that title some time ago. "Let me know if Professor Chadwick shows up."

"I will. I certainly will. I don't feel safe on this street this time of year with no one around. And with Roberta missing, I'm just sure she's met with . . ."

"I understand," said Casey.

Chapter 16

Professor Roberta Chadwick awoke to a fierce headache and a sickening rocking sensation. She was lying on her back on a narrow mattress covered with a stiff, prickly fabric.

It was pitch black. Her head hurt so much she couldn't think straight. She was still wearing her pink sweatshirt, jeans, and Nikes, and she felt as though she'd been wearing them for weeks.

Her world spun, but she didn't feel drunk. The last thing she remembered was working on her papers when someone knocked on her door late at night. It had been after ten because the porch lights that were on a timer were off. When she'd opened her door, someone stepped toward her. That was all she recalled.

She wasn't in her own bed or on her own couch, she knew that much. She was surrounded by a faint musty smell. Water splashed somewhere. Nothing felt or smelled or sounded familiar. Her head hurt. She felt queasy. The darkness was disorienting. She tried to sit up and slammed her aching head on something solid right above her. She tried to hold down the panic that rose. She felt around her. Wood overhead. She wasn't in a coffin, was she? Slanted wood to her right. The overhead, where she'd bumped her head, seemed to continue for a foot or so. Down to her right and left she felt the edges of what must be a narrow mattress. She moved her hands around until she defined her space and realized that if she slid her body out from under the shelf-like protrusion over her head, she could sit up. In the blackness, everything she could feel slanted in crazy directions. Everything was moving. Her head pounded. The sloshing sound reverberated in her brain.

"Is anybody here?" she called out. "Help!" Her voice sounded weak and echoed in her throbbing skull.

No answer.

Her strange world reeled and pitched. Her stomach churned. Wood creaked around her. Metal clanged against metal above her. A chain rattled.

"I'm going to throw up! I'm sick!" she cried. "Help!"

No answer.

She held her hands over her head to gauge the space above her. Every part of her body ached. Her stomach roiled. Water surged and splashed.

A boat. She was on a boat. She'd sailed a few times with friends and knew something of the layout. She was on the V-shaped berth up forward, where two skinny mattresses on either side met at the pointed bow. The rattling chain must mean they were at anchor and the anchor chain was tensing and loosening with the motion of the waves.

How long had she been unconscious? She had no memory between seeing the dark shapes at her door, reaching for the light switch, and this ghastly awakening.

She had to get to a toilet, and fast.

The V-berth was in the front of the boat, that much she knew. The toilet would be somewhere toward the back. Immediately to her right as she felt her way aft was a door. A closet. She had to hurry. She continued toward the back of the boat, unsteady with the boat's motion, past a table on her right, a settee on her left. Beyond the settee, another door. Found a handle. Opened the door. Felt around for the toilet. Lifted the lid, just in time.

She found toilet paper and cleaned herself up as best she could in the dark, not knowing how to flush the marine toilet, not knowing how to get water out of the faucet.

She'd heard enough about seasickness to know she needed fresh air. She felt around. Three wooden steps near the toilet door led up. Lurching with the rocking of the boat, she located a railing by the steps and gripped it tightly with both hands. Another wave of nausea hit. She swallowed hard and felt for a door to the outside.

Dear God, don't let me be locked in, she prayed.

A latch. She clicked it and the low door opened out. Fresh, fresh cold air washed over her and she almost cried with relief. She climbed up the steps into a semi-enclosed space. With her eyes accustomed to darkness, she could make out a roof overhead, windows on three sides, a steering wheel and console to her left. This must be the wheelhouse. Straight ahead was a wide, open deck. Beyond the deck the dark sea merged into the starry sky without a defining boundary. She felt as though she was floating in a gigantic snow globe with stars instead of snow.

A red light flashed above her, startling her.

She lurched toward the back of the boat, almost falling down a wide step onto the open deck. She had never seen so many stars, above her and reflected in the roiling sea that lifted and dropped the boat.

The red flash swept over her head again.

The only boats she'd been on, besides the ferry, were fiberglass sailboats. Here, everything was wood. The back and sides of the open deck were wood, about two feet high, wide enough to sit on. In the middle of the deck she'd almost stumbled into a chair on a pedestal, a strange thing to find on a boat. She looked up for a mast, and saw only a ladder leading to the roof of the wheelhouse. She was not on a sailboat. She knew nothing at all about power boats.

Still nauseated, she moved to one side and sat down on the wide ledge, and leaned over the side, eyes closed, hoping to relieve some of the queasiness. But she had nothing left to heave up.

As the boat swung back and forth on its anchor, she breathed in the chill air. Back here in the stern the motion wasn't as bad as it had been up forward.

The red flash swept overhead.

Until now, she'd been concentrating on her aching head and nausea and keeping her footing.

Now she felt anger. Fury, in fact. Where was she? Who'd brought her here? Why? She slammed a fist on the wooden ledge beside her, and a piercing pain shot through her head.

Another red flash swept over her and she felt dizzy.

I've got to think this out. Where am I?

Since the boat was at anchor, it must be in fairly shallow water, close to land. She looked off the stern and could make out only stars. Stars in the sky. Stars in the water. She was sailing through the night sky.

Stop it! she told herself. You're hallucinating.

The red light flashed again. The flashes seemed to be about four seconds apart. The boat must be anchored near a lighthouse. If they were off the Vineyard, which of the five Island lighthouses flashed red? She had no idea. The Gay Head light, she knew, flashed red and white alternately, and the East Chop light, she thought, flashed green.

She sketched in her mind the location of the five lighthouses, something every visitor to the Vineyard seemed to know. All five were on the northern part of the Island. Gay Head, to the far west, then the West Chop and East Chop lights, which guarded the entrance to the Vineyard Haven harbor. Then came the Edgartown light, which was well inside the harbor, and on the farthermost eastern tip of the Island, the Cape Pogue light.

She had no concept of how much time had passed. She couldn't tell whether it was early or late night. She pressed the button that illuminated her watch dial. After six. At this time of year this could be either night or morning. Probably night, with all those stars. Clearly not the same night when she'd been working on her papers.

Was it the following night? Or had she been unconscious for more than twenty-four hours?

She turned slowly to keep from moving her head unnecessarily and looked behind her. Only a few lights dotted the shore, dark against the sea of stars.

The red beam swept past her again, and she remembered being told about the red sector of the West Chop light. The red sector warned mariners of shallow water and rocks. Where waters were safe, the beam showed white.

What could she do? She could stand up and scream for help, but she was sure no one could hear her. She was too far from shore, and besides, the noise of the wind and waves and the creaking of the boat were louder than she could possibly scream. This time of year, this time of day, no one would pass by in a boat.

She had no idea how to start the engine and get the boat moving. She was a prisoner and her captors must have known she'd be helpless.

She wasn't a strong swimmer. Even if she were, October's cold water would lead to hypothermia in a hurry. Besides, she'd been warned about the strong currents around the Island that could sweep her out of reach of any help.

A signal of some kind. Flares or an air horn. Weren't boats supposed to be equipped with such things?

She would need daylight in order to search the boat.

Breathing in the cold air, she felt marginally better.

She was beginning to shiver. She got up slowly from her seat, felt her way to the pedestal chair, and ran her hands over it. Almost like a dentist's chair with arms and a footrest. A fighting chair on a sport fishing boat, where a fisherman would sit hoping to reel in a giant trophy fish.

She peered into the starlit black water behind the boat. No rowboat trailed behind, nothing but blackness speckled with stars.

Whoever had brought her here must have taken the boat, leaving her with no way to get to shore.

This brought up another question. How had she arrived here? Clearly, she'd been doped or drugged. At least two people must have been involved. It seemed unlikely that such a distinctive boat, a wooden sport fishing boat, had pulled up to a dock and her captors had carried her aboard. The harbors were busy. Ferries came and went into the Vineyard Haven and Oak Bluffs harbors, and the fishing derby was in full swing. Fishermen, on their insane quest to win the derby, wandered about night and day. Carrying an inert body would have been conspicuous.

Think, think. She passed her hand over her hair. Dampness had curled her short hair even more tightly. The boat must have been anchored here already, and she must have been lifted up into it. From another boat. A rowboat or an outboard motorboat. Or another big boat. One person couldn't have done it. Near the West Chop lighthouse, if that's where she was, she was a long way from the Vineyard Haven harbor.

But why would they have kidnapped her?

She was a teacher, wrapped up in her work. She liked her students and she knew they liked her. She wasn't wealthy, in fact she had money worries. She shook her head, and cringed at the pain.

She wrapped her arms tightly around her shivering body, then let go long enough to retrace her steps to the wheelhouse, then down the three steps into the cabin. There she braced against the door to the toilet. In the dark she felt around, found a counter with what seemed like a small stove on it. Felt around some more until she found a box of matches on a shelf above the stove. She struck a light and in the flickering flame saw a kerosene lamp fixed to the bulkhead above the table she'd identified on her way aft. The first match went out and she lit a second, lifted the lamp's glass chimney, and held the flame to the wick. In the warm light that illuminated the cabin, she looked around. The cabin was tidy and seemed more like a place where someone lived than simply a weekend retreat. Behind sliding Plexiglas doors she could see books, classics as well as books on navigation. On the floor, deck, she supposed, was an Oriental rug, a nice old one. The settee behind the table was scattered with several bright cushions.

She was almost accustomed to the swaying and dipping and rocking and began to feel better, even hungry. At least a full day since she'd last eaten. Perhaps she'd lost a pound or two. She'd been intending to take off about ten pounds. A positive thought. In the soft light of the kerosene lamp she opened lockers and found crackers and peanut butter, cardboard boxes of juice. She'd be able to make herself a meal. Surprisingly, the lamp had warmed up the small cabin like a miniature stove, and as she warmed, she tried to make sense of her situation.

But no matter how she tried to analyze what she might have done to deserve this, or why someone would go to such considerable trouble to kidnap her, nothing made sense.

She took stock of the food. There was enough to last her a long time. As much as two weeks, possibly. Even three. An ice chest held fresh vegetables and fruit, cheese and cold cuts. When she realized how much food was on board, she had the horrid feeling that the boat had been stocked on purpose to hold her captive for some time.

Perhaps this was a case of mistaken identity.

In the hanging lockers she found warm jackets. On the side of the V-berth across from where she'd lain, were two rolled-up sleeping bags. She wouldn't suffer from the cold.

A medicine chest. She opened it, took out a couple of aspirins, and swallowed them. After a bit, her headache receded to a dull numbness.

She had to eat something, and peanut butter and crackers didn't appeal to her. Something hot and comforting. That meant lighting that unfamiliar stove. She staggered over to it. The stove swung back and forth with the motion of the boat, and she realized that it, like the lamp, was held in some kind of metal cradle that kept it level even when the boat tilted. In the dim light she could make out printed directions on a plate above the stove that showed her how to operate it.

An alcohol stove. Pump it up with the plunger as shown in the diagram, open a valve to let alcohol run into a cup under the burner, light the alcohol . . .

She figured it out and found satisfaction in watching the flame flare up.

She found bottled water and a saucepan, and in the familiarity of heating water, felt a bit more in control.

The water boiled and she made a cup of tea. Opened a can of beef stew and heated that.

Once she'd eaten, she felt better. She curled up on the L-shaped settee behind the table with a second cup of tea, pulled a down sleeping bag over her, tucked a pillow behind her head, and found a book she'd read years before.

Before she opened the book, she thought of her two nagging concerns. She hoped Mrs. Hamilton fed her cat.

The other, and really a more major concern, was for the papers she was preparing for publication in the journal. She was on a tight deadline. When the caller or callers had come to her door, she'd had only four days to submit the manuscripts, e-mail preferred. What day was this?

She needed every one of those four days to prepare the papers for submission.

The tenure committee would recognize, when the papers were published, a wide range of knowledge, her exacting research, and her understanding of the requirement to publish. That was the one thing her tenure advisor had emphasized. She must have publications to her credit, and her list of publications was much too sparse. She'd already been rejected for tenure last year. This was her last chance. She wouldn't get another.

Publish or perish. Were her captors going to release her in time? If they only knew how important it was for her to mail those papers off.

If she missed that deadline . . . She didn't want to think about it. But she had to. If she missed that deadline, the papers would not be published this academic year.

Three papers that would make the difference between tenure approval and rejection.

She swallowed down the lump she felt in her throat. At the moment, there was nothing she could do. Nothing.

She snuggled the sleeping bag around her, turned up the lamp, opened the book, and sipped her tea. Tomorrow was another day. She would look for the boat's papers and identify the owner. Perhaps she could signal a passing boat in some way.

She opened the book at random and her mind lightened at the familiar words. *"Grace Stepney's mind was like a kind of moral fly-paper, to which the buzzing items of gossip were drawn . . ."*

CHAPTER 17

Joe and Sarah were the first of the porch sitters to arrive at Alley's Store for their Friday afternoon commentary on the goings-on about town. Sarah seated herself on the bench.

"Thank God it's Friday." Sarah stretched her hands over her head. She was wearing a bloodred sweatshirt emblazoned with tomahawks. "This past week felt like a year."

"Don't complain to me," said Joe, leaning against the post. "I get called out at two a.m. on Sunday morning because some asshole hears water dripping. Forgot to turn off the bathroom cold water faucet."

At this point a silver Porsche pulled up to the curb. Sarah nudged Joe with her booted foot. "That's him, isn't it?"

"Who?" demanded Joe, scowling.

"That television guy. You know, *Family Riot*?"

"So?" said Joe, spitting off to one side of the steps.

"You're the one who told me who he was."

The driver stepped up onto the porch, and Sarah whispered his name. "Bruce Steinbicker!"

Joe stood up straight.

The stranger paused at the door. "Nice day."

"Yup," said Joe.

"It's a lovely day," said Sarah. "Just beautiful. Are you visiting the Island?"

The man dropped his hand from the door handle and smiled. "I'm here for the Bass Derby."

"You look a lot like Bruce Steinbicker," Sarah said.

"I'm not surprised." The man grinned. "That's me." He pointed to his chest. "You watch my show?"

Joe turned to face him. "She don't watch TV."

"Joe!" said Sarah.

"Not much worth watching these days," said Steinbicker. "You both from around here?"

"Born and bred," said Joe. "She's a wash-ashore."

"I've only lived here since I was in second grade," said Sarah. "Where are you staying?"

"On my boat. I powered over from Falmouth. That's where I keep it."

Sarah pulled her sweatshirt sleeves over her knuckles. "I heard you lived in California?"

"Most of the time. I'm from the Cape originally, so I'm back here a lot. I wouldn't miss the derby for anything. I take time off in October. You fishermen?"

"Not me," said Joe.

"Well, nice talking to you." With that he disappeared into the store.

Sarah folded her arms over the tomahawks. "How about that!"

Joe shrugged. "You hear about that disappearing lady college professor?"

Sarah nodded. "Are there any new developments?"

"Old Lady Trumbull is on the job." Joe reached into his shirt pocket and drew out a package of Red Man.

"What do you mean?"

"The state cops called her in." Joe carved off a chunk of tobacco with his pocket knife. "Seems one of her students has a bee in her bonnet. Claims the professor stole her research." He stuck the chunk into his mouth.

"How can you steal someone's research?"

Joe shifted the tobacco to his cheek. "Who knows?"

"Who's the student?"

"Jodi something. Lives here in West Tiz." Joe leaned back against the post, stuck his hands in his pockets, and crossed one foot over the other.

"Jodi Paloni?"

"You know her?"

"Sure I know her," said Sarah. "She's dynamite just waiting to blow up. Messing with her is like swimming around a great white shark after you hit your head on a rock and you're bleeding all over the place. You ever seen her?"

"Don't recall ever seeing the lady. A few of them sharks around, these days. Global warming."

"She's not exactly what I'd call a lady." Sarah picked lint off her black jeans. "She wears her hair in a buzz cut, she's tattooed all over, and she's body pierced every place you can see." She finished brushing her jeans. "Who knows what you can't see."

"The cops say she's attending a meeting off Island."

"The professor?"

Joe shrugged. "I guess."

The door opened and Bruce Steinbicker came out, carrying the *Wall Street Journal* and a brown paper bag. He lifted a hand in acknowledgment. "Nice meeting you."

"Heading back to your boat?" asked Joe.

"Not tonight," said Bruce. "A buddy and I traded a couple weeks' stay on my boat for a couple weeks' stay in his guesthouse. With a friend, you know." He winked. "Boat's a little too close for two."

Joe uncrossed his feet. "Sounds like a plan."

When daylight came, Roberta Chadwick examined her prison boat from stem to stern.

First, she went up the steps to the sheltered wheelhouse. The morning was bright, windy, and chilly.

The boat was about forty feet long, she guessed. A wicked current swirled past the bow as if the boat were tearing through high seas, but the taut anchor line angled out, holding fast. In the distance, she could see a white speck. The ferry, too far away to spot a signal, even if she waved a blanket. No other boats were in sight on the horizon, not even a fishing boat.

She held onto whatever support she could reach as the boat rolled and pitched in the rough sea.

She looked toward shore. It seemed a long, long distance away, far greater than she could swim, even without the current. Even on a summer's day.

She'd never been comfortable on boats. She stepped down from the shelter of the wheelhouse onto the open afterdeck, not sure what she was looking for. A signaling device? A flotation device? A way to move the boat?

She eased her way to the side and shaded her eyes against the reflected sunlight dazzling off the turbulent water and looked forward. The expanse of white deck at the front of the boat was broken only by a foot-square of framed Plexiglas, a hatch that could be opened from where she slept. No point in going forward. A streamer on a short mast at the bow fluttered straight out, away from land.

On either side of the afterdeck were lockers. She lifted the lids, one by one, and looked inside. Neat, clean, and empty. No life jackets, no lines, no floats, not even a fire extinguisher. Nothing.

She lowered the lids and plopped down on top, frustrated. The boat had an engine, didn't it? She'd need a key. She stepped back up into the wheelhouse. Behind the wheel was an instrument panel, almost like a car's, but not quite. Two engines? There were slots for keys, but no keys.

The brisk wind chilled her. She went below to the cabin and continued searching, not feeling particularly hopeful.

She searched in vain for the key. Then she turned to the radio. Her hopes rose. She'd never worked a marine radio before, but she was sure she could figure it out. No matter what she did, no lights lit up, no static, no sound, nothing. They'd disabled it. Of course.

She opened doors and drawers and found the first-aid kit again, but no flares, no signaling device, no whistle. She tried the horn. No sound.

Boats had to have life jackets, didn't they? Surely her captors wouldn't remove that necessary safety gear. Perhaps they were here belowdecks. She might chance swimming to shore, despite the chill, offshore wind, and strong current, if she could construct a sort of raft of life jackets.

None.

They had thought of that, too.

She stood in the center of the small cabin, bracing herself against the motion of the boat.

Tears welled up. She was frightened, she finally admitted to herself. Terrified.

What were her captors planning? With two weeks' supply of food on board, was she imprisoned here for two weeks?

With all that food aboard, they must not intend to kill her. Why would they? It must be mistaken identity. She was no threat to anyone, owned nothing of value, had no enemies. What insane reason was behind her captivity?

She couldn't stay here for two weeks. She simply couldn't. She had to get those papers to the journal within the week to meet that deadline. After all the work she'd done. If they didn't get published this year, the tenure committee would never, ever, approve her tenure application. Never.

Damn all tenure committees. Crabby old men. Retaining the status quo. Medieval. Academic freedom? Hardly. But she had to get their approval. She had to. Period.

She wiped away the incipient tears with the back of her hand and lit the two-burner alcohol stove. While the water was heating, she looked through the boat's papers. The owner was a Bruce Stein-bicker, a name that seemed familiar, but she couldn't place it.

The water started to boil, so she put the boat's papers back in their zippered waterproof case and made a cup of tea (there was no coffee). She found a package of oat-bran rusks, slathered a couple with raspberry jam, then eased herself onto the settee behind the table, balancing her breakfast of tea and rusks against the pitching and swaying and rolling of her prison.

Think! Think!

Someone had planned this imprisonment carefully. Anchored offshore with no escape, no way to contact anyone, every object that could help her removed or disabled, and a two-weeks' supply of food.

If only she could contact one of her three Island students. They were loyal. They cared for her. They would get her out of this crazy mess.

CHAPTER 18

Victoria sat patiently in the West Tisbury Police Station waiting for Casey to get off the phone. Sergeant Junior Norton was at his desk sharpening pencils with a mouse-shaped pencil sharpener. He stuck a pencil in the mouse's mouth and twisted, and the mouse squeaked.

Victoria smiled. "You won't have much left of your pencils, Junior."

Junior held up the sharpener and wiggled its ears. "Amazing what they think of these days."

Casey set the phone down. "That was Sergeant Smalley, Victoria. He says Mrs. Hamilton is worrying over nothing. He talked to Jodi's husband, Jonah, who said she's gone off Island for a week-long conference."

"Jodi mentioned it to me," said Victoria. "She asked to be excused from classes."

"She's got her cell phone. Jonah says she checks in with him and the boys regularly." Casey leaned back. "We needn't worry about Professor Chadwick's absence."

Victoria scratched at a rough spot on the back of her hand. "There's something odd about the situation, though. Why would Roberta neglect her cat? Or leave the papers on her table? Why didn't she take her car?"

"Jodi probably drove."

"Jodi and Jonah have only one car. A Jeep. She wouldn't have left Jonah with the four boys and no car."

Casey turned to her sergeant. "Cut it out, will you Junior? You're driving me nuts with that squeaking thing."

"Yes, ma'am." Junior dropped the mouse into his desk drawer and scraped the pile of pencil shavings into the wastebasket.

"Professor Chadwick is undoubtedly at the conference," said Casey. "Probably forgot the cat."

Junior brushed pencil shavings off his hands. "I checked with the Steamship Authority, Chief. No Paloni or Chadwick booked passage over the past three days."

Casey sighed in exasperation. "They probably used one of the other student's cars. We've got murders to worry about, Victoria. A whole bunch of them. We can't get distracted over a problem that doesn't exist."

The phone rang and Junior answered. He said "Yes, sir" several times and hung up.

"What was that about?" asked Casey.

"Smalley wants us to help with crowd control at the college tomorrow and Sunday. Seems Brownie has been hard at work, and the public is gathering around."

"Another body? This takes precedence." Casey stood.

Victoria, too, stood and headed for the door. "I don't like the feel of her disappearance." She turned at the door. "Has anyone checked to see if there *is* such a conference?"

"Come on, Victoria." Casey sighed in exasperation. "Loosen up, will you?"

The Ivy Green College campus was pitted with excavations, seven in all. Led by Brownie, the forensics team had worked steadily. The entire block was cordoned off with crime scene tape, and both Tisbury police and West Tisbury police helped with crowd control.

Even though it was Saturday and a glorious day for fishing or walking on the beach or hiking the Island's trails, half the population seemed to have gathered around the perimeter of the dug-up area. There was a continual buzz of questions, of comments, of concern, of fear.

A serial killer was at work.

Brownie, Walter's dog, seemed to understand his importance. His scruffy coat had become glossy. His eyes shone. His ears had perked up. His tail stood out straight behind him like the wing feather of a great raptor. He held his head up and his pink tongue didn't so much hang out as add to the effect of Dog on the Spot. He wore a new bright red collar that Walter had purchased from Good Dog Goods.

Walter held the matching leash and stood out of the way, mourning the mess of his beautiful lawn yet preening at the success of his masterful corpse-sniffing canine.

Thackery was nowhere to be seen.

Every one of the four corpses identified had been a faculty member at a college or university. Four had yet to be identified. The known victims were all tenured faculty members. The dates of burial went back at least seven years.

"How come nobody reported any of these guys missing?" Joel Killdeer, the head forensics specialist, asked of nobody in particular. He smoothed his glistening, freshly shaved scalp. "Four profs, maybe eight." He chewed, mouth open. "Not one soul cared enough to ask where they were?" He snapped his gum and there was a faint fruity aroma.

The state troopers and Tisbury cops continued to dig up the site of Brownie's latest discovery.

"Sabbaticals?" Tim, the state trooper, paused in his work to wipe his forehead with a red bandana.

"Sabbaticals come once every seven years. They don't last seven years," said Killdeer.

"Fieldwork, then. Leaves of absence? Assignments to another

university?" Tim tucked his grubby bandana back into his pocket. "Professors get buried in their ivory towers all the time and don't appear until they retire. Nobody notices, once they've got tenure."

"C'mon, Tim. Back to work!" barked his co-digger. "We don't have all day."

"Close to full moon tonight," said Killdeer. "You can dig all night by the light of the moon."

Tim bent down over his work again. After a couple of minutes he brought his arm up to block his nose. "Jee-zus Kee-rist! Lemme outta here. Another one."

The Ivy Green College Oversight Committee reconvened on the Ivy Green campus the next day. Professor Bigelow led the march up the hill from the ferry to the muddy shambles that was once splendid green lawn. Hammermill Jones strode along next to him, puffing slightly at the pace set by the older but more athletic Bigelow.

Math professor Petrinia Paulinia Kralich, the newest member of the committee, followed along with Cosimo Perrini, romance languages; Noah Sutterfield, African studies; and Reverend Bob White, religious studies.

"I'm so sorry Dedie's no longer with us," said Professor Perrini. "I'm happy for her, of course, that she was offered that wonderful position, but, still . . ."

"But, still," replied Professor Kralich, "she quadrupled her salary." Professor Kralich's white hair floated halfway to her waist and lifted slightly with each step she took. In her sixties, Kralich was tall and gaunt, her face a wrinkled dried apple. Granny glasses, of course. She had gathered up the hem of her long diaphanous lavender-and-green printed skirt, which apparently had impeded her. Exposed unshaven legs ended in combat boots. She held a briefcase. Although her boots seemed almost too heavy to lift, she was outpacing her two younger colleagues.

"A great loss to the university," said Professor Sutterfield, switching his own briefcase to his left hand. "Certainly to the oversight committee." He brushed his dark forehead with the back of his hand. "Warm for this season."

"Am I walking too fast for you?" asked Professor Kralich, slowing her pace slightly.

"Not at all," said the Reverend White. "Speaking of Dedie Wieler, the university's loss is the business sector's gain." He cleared his throat and added in a reverent tone, "A bright, spiritual woman."

Professor Kralich turned, not slowing her pace. "Spiritual?" She guffawed. "Dedie? She's a dyed in the wool atheist."

The Reverend White flushed.

Cosimo Perrini said, "Bigelow and Hammermill are getting awfully far ahead of us."

"Do we know where we're going?" asked Professor Kralich.

"Left onto Greenleaf, where you see the crowd," said Sutterfield. "That's the Ivy Green campus."

Yellow plastic tape fluttered in the light breeze. The hum they'd heard as they approached became distinct voices. The words "serial killer" echoed through the crowd gathered in the shade of the tall oaks.

Professors Bigelow and Hammermill had crossed the street and were waiting for the other four members.

Bigelow looked at his watch. "We need to step lively. Lot to discuss with Dr. Wilson, and I want to catch the three-forty-five boat back to the mainland." Bigelow's khaki trousers were still sharply creased, his shirt still seemed freshly ironed, his blue blazer pressed.

Hammermill was sweating. He undid the second button of his hibiscus-printed Hawaiian shirt exposing straggly gray chest hairs.

Someone in the crowd pointed to the six IGCOC members, and the noisy hum of voices died.

"What on earth are you staring at?" said Professor Kralich in a loud voice. "Ghouls."

Hammermill wiped the back of his neck with his handkerchief, and put his handkerchief away. "They think we're next. Eight bodies. Eight professors . . ."

"We don't know that they're all professors," said Cosimo Perrini gently. "Only four, so far."

"I'm quitting this committee as of now," sputtered Hammermill. "This place gives me the willies."

Bigelow smoothed his mustache and frowned. "Don't be such an ass, Hammermill."

CHAPTER 19

Victoria and Casey met with Sergeant Smalley and Dr. Joel Kill-deer at the state police barracks on Monday morning. The barracks was a quaint Victorian building painted a soft Colonial blue. A picket fence was out front.

They met again around the conference room table with yellow pads and pencils at each place. Trooper Tim Eldredge carried in a tray of coffee and doughnuts, and plugged the coffeepot into a wall outlet to stay hot.

Smalley introduced Dr. Killdeer, who nodded at Victoria. "Seems to me we met a few bodies back, Mrs. Trumbull."

They shook hands. He was taller and more slender than Victoria had recalled, completely bald, his skin dark and polished. He was wearing a yellow collared knit shirt that showed off broad shoulders and muscular arms.

Victoria said, "I believe Brownie had just unearthed the third victim. And now there are, what, four more?"

"Five more," said Killdeer. "Total of eight so far, and that dog is still sniffing around." He sat to Victoria's right, Smalley to her left, and Casey next to Killdeer.

Casey unfastened her utility belt and hung it on the back of her chair with a heavy thunk. "Eight deaths, and no one reported them missing?"

Smalley poured coffee into mugs. "They were reported missing from their own locales, but nobody tied their absence to the Island. "Coffee, Doc?"

"I'll pass," said Killdeer.

Smalley handed a mug to Victoria and a mug to Casey, who reached for the sugar.

"Brownie is quite remarkable," said Victoria.

"A natural. One in a million. Who'd have thought that flea-bitten cur would be a champ?" Killdeer brought out a package of chewing gum and held it up. "Anyone?"

Head shakes around the table. "No, thanks."

"I told Walter he could retire on what he'd get for that dog," continued Killdeer, stripping the foil wrapper from a stick of gum.

"You mean, sell Brownie?" asked Victoria. "I don't think so."

Killdeer folded the gum into his mouth and Victoria marveled at his splendid white teeth.

Smalley cleared his throat. "We called you in, Mrs. Trumbull, because you are not only part of law enforcement on the Island"—at this, Victoria smiled—"but as a faculty member of Ivy Green, you are in a unique position to help the investigation." He pulled his scratch pad toward himself. "Dr. Killdeer can explain where things stand as of now." He picked up his pencil and nodded at Killdeer, who was chewing steadily.

"I'm ready to help in any way I can," said Victoria, attempting to sound modest. "Have you determined how the victims were killed?" She looked from Smalley to Killdeer, and clasped her hands on top of her own yellow pad.

Killdeer looked across the table at Smalley, who lifted his hand. "It's okay, Doc. Go ahead."

Killdeer leaned back in his chair. "Most were strangled, possibly a cord or wire with handles at each end. Two may have been asphyxiated. Buried alive."

Victoria scribbled a note on her pad.

Killdeer crossed brawny arms over his chest. "Eight corpses. The first was the one you found in that old garage . . ."

Loyal to Thackery Wilson, Victoria said, "That's Catbriar Hall, our auditorium and classroom."

"Yes, ma'am." Killdeer grinned. What teeth! "Brownie's first find was underneath that poisonous vine."

"Poison ivy," said Victoria.

"Whatever." He snapped his gum and eyed her. "Brownie's second find—the third body—was where, I understand, your class usually met."

Victoria nodded.

"Once we turned Brownie loose, he located five more. Diggers having a hard time keeping up with that dog." He grinned again.

Victoria twisted her pencil around in her gnarled fingers. "You've identified four of the eight so far."

"Yes, ma'am." Killdeer looked up as Tim Eldredge came into the conference room and gave him a printed sheet. "'Scuse me a moment." He studied the paper, chewing steadily, then passed it to Smalley. "Fax from Sudbury."

"Autopsy report?" asked Casey.

Killdeer nodded. "Fifth and sixth bodies ID'd. Males. College professors. Range in age from around forty-five to under sixty-five."

"Where were they from?" Casey brushed her doughnut crumbs into a tidy pile beside her scratch pad.

"Two from Cape Cod University. Two from Ohio. One from Florida. One from Ontario, Canada." He studied Victoria. "Thoughts, Mrs. Trumbull?"

"Were they all tenured professors?"

"Let's see that fax again, John," said Killdeer, holding out his hand for the paper. He looked it over again and shook his head. "Doesn't say."

"I don't suppose it would," said Victoria, thinking. "How far back do the killings date?"

"Seven years, best guess." The gum snapped.

Victoria dropped her pencil onto the table. Her thoughts were of Roberta Chadwick and her desperation for tenure. "I can imagine someone who'd been denied tenure at some point. Rage built up and finally, seven or so years ago, that anger pushed him—or her—over the edge."

"Hundreds of Ph.D.'s denied tenure," said Killdeer.

Casey dipped the remains of her doughnut into her coffee. "It won't be the first time someone tried to kill off her tenure committee."

"Do we assume our killer is male?" Victoria asked.

"Most likely," Killdeer answered. "There are female serial killers, but most are males. A female's more likely to use poison."

"It was a female who shot up her tenure committee," said Casey, defending the role of woman as killer.

"Why would the killer choose the Ivy Green campus to bury his victims?" asked Victoria. "Were all the victims killed on campus?"

"No way of knowing." Killdeer leaned back again, arms folded, and watched Victoria. "Keep talking."

She looked down at her coffee, at the swirls of steam rising from the surface. "The victims were most likely visiting the Island and were probably killed here. It would be cumbersome to transport bodies on the ferry." She sipped her coffee, closing her eyes against the steam.

Casey said, "The Steamship Authority requires a passenger ticket for a corpse."

Killdeer laughed. "He kills and buries them on the Island to save ferry fare."

"How would the killer know they were faculty members?" Victoria continued. "The victims were probably not frequent visitors, or someone would have missed them."

Killdeer nodded. "Umm hunh."

"The killer must know the Island well. He either lives here or spends a great deal of time here."

Killdeer chewed steadily.

Victoria said, "He had to know when the Ivy Green campus would be deserted so he could bury his bodies. Each burial must have taken some time."

"Want to guess his age?" asked Killdeer.

Victoria lifted up her coffee mug and held it in both hands then set it down without drinking. "Do they teach strangling in the military?"

"Depends on the branch of service, but yeah. The military would teach him how to use a rope or a wire."

"Age," murmured Victoria, looking down at her scratch pad. "He'd have to have completed his graduate work at the doctoral level in order to be on a tenure track."

"Figures," said Killdeer.

Victoria sighed and then sipped her coffee. "Let's say he graduated from high school at eighteen and went into the military to pay for college. Three years or more in the service, four years of college, two years to get a master's degree, four years for a Ph.D." She paused. "Was that the route you took, Dr. Killdeer? Military service?"

"You got it. So by then he was thirty-one, -two. Somewhere around there."

"He may have accepted a teaching job right away, on a tenure track. I think that ranges from five to seven years." She deferred to Killdeer. "You would know more about tenure track time than I."

"No, ma'am," said Killdeer. "Never wanted that academic shit.'Scuse me. Puts him at around forty."

Victoria nodded. "Assuming he was denied tenure, he may have tried to get another academic position."

"Being denied tenure is not necessarily a career killer," said Smalley.

"Not if he'd taught at an Ivy League college," said Killdeer.

"But if he taught at a less-than-top-ranked institution and was denied tenure, he'd have had a difficult time finding another position," said Victoria.

Smalley was sketching what looked like a brick pattern on his pad.

Killdeer leaned over, examined the sketch, and snapped his gum. "You want ivy on that brick wall, man. Some of that poison stuff."

Smalley tossed down his pencil.

"I'm really just guessing here," said Victoria. "Would it take three years, four before he started killing?"

"You're doing just fine, Mrs. Trumbull. So we're looking for a guy early forties."

Victoria said, "I don't mean to tell you what to look for."

Killdeer leaned back in his chair again, arms behind his head. "You got a great future as a profiler, know that? Eight or nine years, you'll be tops in the field." He grinned. "So this guy has a Ph.D., taught at some Podunk college, lives on the Island or at least knows it well, and hates professors."

"Not just professors." Victoria's face had an attractive pink flush. "I'm guessing tenured professors." She looked down again and smiled at the growing acceptance of her as fellow investigator. "Perhaps he's jealous of tenured professors."

Smalley stood and refilled Casey's coffee. "Warm yours up, Mrs. Trumbull?"

Victoria pushed her mug toward him. "Thank you."

"The killing hasn't stopped," said Casey. "The body we found in Catbriar Hall was only a couple of weeks old."

"Yes, ma'am," said Killdeer. "Following a pattern. He needs more and more stimulation to satisfy that urge he's got. Killings get closer and closer together."

"Looks like he's not following the pattern, though," said Smalley. "Seven of the bodies were buried. The most recent one's been different, found inside a building."

"Yup." Killdeer set his chair back down and put his elbows on

144

the table. "Latest body was easy to find. The body before that was only lightly buried. He wants us to find the bodies. Probably wants us to find him."

"He had to have access to a key to Catbriar Hall," said Casey.

"Pick the lock on that garage door with a toothpick," said Killdeer with a snort.

Smalley stood. "We've got work ahead of us. A forty-something-year-old, well-educated male, attended a lesser-known college, military background, knows the Island."

Victoria said, "He's likely to be well-known and respected on the Island. He may attend gatherings and lectures where he'll meet his future victims."

"The guy's killed eight men in cold blood," said Casey. "You'd think he'd stand out as being different."

"Take a look at convicted serial killers," said Killdeer. "Neighbors thought almost every one of them looked like a normal human being." He adopted a falsetto. "'I never dreamed that nice man next door . . . He's so polite.'" His voice dropped back. "Yes, ma'am. That smell isn't the homemade beer he's brewing in the cellar. He's got twenty-three dead young boys buried there."

CHAPTER 20

Since Jodi wasn't available to chauffeur her after class, Victoria had an hour or so to wait for her granddaughter to pick her up after work.

She walked to the administration building still known as Woodbine Hall to turn in her attendance records. The afternoon was golden. In the distance she heard the whistle of the ferry leaving for Woods Hole. The air was full of the whisper of falling leaves. The fragrance of autumn almost hid the faint aroma of death. It was difficult to think of the campus to her right as a crime scene, the once-velvet lawn now pitted and muddy.

She heard voices of policemen she'd known as children. Shovels chinked on stones in the sandy soil. Flung dirt thudded rhythmically onto a growing pile beside a new excavation.

Victoria looked up at the oak trees, where the katydids were tuning up for their evening serenade. Beyond the treetops, Canada geese flew in formation, honking a nostalgic song of far-off places.

After the body of Dr. Journeyman Cash was found under the accumulation of leaves sloughed off by the lush vine that clung to the outer walls of Woodbine Hall, students had renamed the building Poison Ivy Hall. Victoria, too, now thought of it by that name, although she was careful not to say it aloud in the presence of Thackery Wilson.

She trudged up the creaky front steps with a firm hold on the railing. The wooden steps could use a few solid boards and a coat of paint—soon, before winter set in.

Afternoon sunlight reflected off the stained-glass panels in the front door. As she opened it, purple and green images of glass grapes and leaves shifted on the worn floorboards of the front hall.

At first, Victoria didn't notice that Thackery was meeting with someone. She was listening to her own thoughts about poetry. Reflections would be a good theme for a sestina. She would need six words for the framework of the poem, a tricky form, with its repetition of those six words at the end of each stanza. Musing on this she walked into Thackery's office.

"Oh," she blurted out. "I'm so sorry, Thackery. I didn't realize you had someone with you."

Thackery stood as did his guest. When he turned to greet her, she recognized, with a start, the older version of Price Henderson, who'd come to her about Roberta Chadwick. No question about the relationship. Dr. Wellborn Price, the man standing before her, had to be his father. Images. Echoes. Reflections. Three words. This flashed through her mind before she could speak.

Apparently mistaking Victoria's hesitation as trying to place who he was, the man held out his hand. "Professor Trumbull, I'm Wellborn Price."

"Of course," said Victoria, taking his large hand in hers. "We met when I was here in the office, trying to handle phone calls."

"Succeeding, I would say, not trying. I believe that was the day Brownie discovered his fourth body."

"Won't you join us, Mrs. Trumbull," said Thackery, wheeling over the chair from Linda's desk. "Linda's gone home for the day."

"She's not sick again?" asked Victoria.

"She's upset about her younger sister, who seems to have disappeared."

"Sister?" Victoria leaned forward and the chair tilted with a squeal.

"That needs WD-40, Thackery, old man," said Wellborn.

Thackery opened his lower desk drawer. "Paint, new windows, squeaking chairs, new steps, new roof." He produced a spray can and shut the drawer again. "Duct tape holds this place together and WD-40 makes things work."

"Linda's sister?" repeated Victoria.

"Roberta Chadwick," said Thackery. "You know her, don't you?"

"Yes, of course. Jodi Paloni's advisor."

Thackery stood and approached Victoria's chair with the spray can. "Here, let me get at that."

Victoria moved aside. "I had no idea Roberta had an older sister."

Thackery nodded. "Ten years older. Linda, the consummate hypochondriac, is sick with worry. You'd think Roberta was her child." He returned to his desk and put the WD-40 away. "I told her Professor Chadwick is attending a meeting off Island. Try rocking that chair again."

"That seems to have done it," said Victoria. "The police agree with you about an off Island conference."

"What do the police have to do with it?" asked Thackery.

"Roberta's neighbor was concerned about her cat and reported her missing."

"I know Mrs. Hamilton," muttered Thackery.

Wellborn had watched the chair repair with interest, and swiveled his own, as though testing its noise level. "Roberta Chadwick. I've come across that name somewhere."

"She teaches sociology at Cape Cod University," said Thackery. "Up for tenure this year and she's under a good bit of stress."

Wellborn smiled. "That demon word *tenure* again. My guess is she's taking a break."

"I must admit, I'm a bit uneasy," said Victoria. "She's single-minded about tenure. She was working on papers she planned to submit to a journal . . ." She stopped and thought about the three students whose research papers Professor Chadwick had appropriated.

Undoubtedly those were the papers found on her dining room table. "I don't believe she would have abandoned those papers to attend a conference."

Wellborn asked, "What about the papers? You hesitated when you mentioned them."

"Roberta Chadwick was working on a publications deadline. I can't believe she would have left before she submitted those papers." If Roberta was not attending a meeting, where could she be? Until she knew, Victoria didn't want to say anything that would implicate the three students.

"Much ado over nothing," said Thackery.

Victoria swiveled to face Wellborn Price. "An interesting young man came to Catbriar Hall the other day after my class let out. His name is Price Henderson."

"Oh?" said Wellborn.

"He's spent several years traveling around the world, and is here on the Vineyard, living on his sailboat."

"How old is this young man of yours?"

"I would guess he's in his early forties. He's working on a master's degree at Cape Cod University. I gathered he already has an advanced degree."

Thackery was listening, his head tilted to one side, his elbows resting on his chair arms.

"He reminded me of you, Dr. Price. Even his name."

"Price. Hardly a common first name."

"He was adopted as a child by his stepfather. His mother is still alive, divorced now."

Wellborn got to his feet and went to the window. "I don't suppose he mentioned his mother's name?"

"No."

Thackery said, "Right age for Bigelow's nephew."

"Impossible," Wellborn said under his breath. He stared out of the cracked and dusty window.

"When did you last see your son?" Victoria asked.

"I never did." Wellborn turned away from the window. "We planned to get married, but her father was opposed."

"Why? Even at that age it must have been clear that you had a promising future."

Wellborn interrupted with a short laugh. "It involved academic politics. Her father rushed her off to Istanbul, I learned later, where he'd accepted a teaching position at Robert College." He returned to his seat. "We had plans, she and I. Her father and brother, our Professor Bigelow, squelched that." He rocked his chair. "We were in love." He paused. "I still am. Never married."

Victoria said nothing.

The song of the katydids seeped into the room.

Thackery shifted papers around on his desk, opened the shallow drawer, straightened pencils, and shut it again."

"I traced them to Turkey," Wellborn said, "then lost the trail. I finally gave up hope of finding him."

"What about her?" asked Victoria.

"I assume she married and established a life of her own. I had no right to disrupt that. A face out of her past. But my son . . ."

Thackery turned to Victoria. "How did the boy end up on the Vineyard?"

"He'd heard that Dr. Price would be teaching an economics course here, and came to the Vineyard to see about taking the course."

"Hardly a coincidence." Thackery steepled his fingers.

"Price was told his birth father had been killed in an automobile accident. He's been searching for years for information about his father's death." Victoria glanced at Wellborn. "Has he contacted you?"

He shook his head.

They sat without talking, listening to the repetitious song of the katydids. After a bit Wellborn said, "He's enrolled in a master's degree program?"

"Sociology. He's one of Roberta Chadwick's students."

Wellborn said, "You've got an expressive face, Professor Trumbull. What about Roberta Chadwick?"

Victoria nodded. "The papers Roberta was editing when she disappeared were the work of three of her students."

"CCU students?" asked Wellborn.

"Two from Cape Cod University, one from Ivy Green."

"Jodi Paloni, I assume," said Thackery.

"I assume one of the CCU students is Price Henderson," said Wellborn.

Victoria nodded. "His paper was on the sociological implications of the search for birth parents by adoptees."

Wellborn groaned.

"The students gave Roberta their papers understanding she would submit them to a journal under their names."

"I suppose Professor Chadwick intended to add her name as co-author? That's quite usual," said Wellborn.

"She was submitting them under her name alone. When I spoke to her about this, she said it was imperative for her to publish."

"The tenure issue has been cause for murder at times in the past," said Wellborn, smiling. "I don't suppose . . ."

"The three students are upset by what they perceive as injustice. Plagiarism," said Victoria, sitting forward. "Two of the students went to the university authorities and were brushed off."

"Soooo," said Wellborn, drawing the single word out. "You think they've taken matters into their own hands."

"I'm afraid so," said Victoria.

Elizabeth walked into Thackery's office just as Victoria stood. She looked from her grandmother to Thackery, whom she knew, then to Wellborn Price, who'd stood when Victoria did.

"I hope I'm not interrupting," said Elizabeth. "I'm parked outside and can wait."

"Not at all," said Thackery. "I don't believe you've met Dr. Wellborn Price. Elizabeth Trumbull, Victoria's granddaughter."

"Trumbull?" Wellborn raised his eyebrows.

Elizabeth laughed. "My mother kept her maiden name, and I kept hers. I don't know why our name can't carry through the female line."

Wellborn stuck out his hand and they shook.

"I'm ready to leave," said Victoria. "We'd been discussing Roberta Chadwick's disappearance."

"Among other things," said Wellborn.

The two women left, descended the worn steps, and climbed into Elizabeth's waiting Volkswagen. The convertible top was down to take advantage of the warm day. Duct tape on the folded-down canvas top fluttered in the light breeze.

Victoria smiled at the thought of the ubiquitous duct tape and WD-40.

They detoured past Tisbury School without speaking and went around by the Waterworks.

"What happened in there?" asked Elizabeth.

Victoria told her about Wellborn Price and his lost son. "And Roberta Chadwick has disappeared, as you know. I'm concerned about her students, who are understandably upset. Let's get home and sit down with a drink."

They drove past the Tashmoo overlook, a scene that always lightened Victoria's mood. The tawny grass of the sloping meadow waved gently in the light breeze, rippling like the waters beyond.

"We can stop for mail, first," said Elizabeth, "if you're not in a hurry for that drink."

"I am, but it can wait a few minutes."

Three of the regulars were on Alley's porch, Joe, Sarah, and Lincoln. Elizabeth parked in front of the store.

"Mrs. T, how're you doin'?" asked Joe the plumber, leaning, as usual, against one of the posts that held up the roof as well as

Joe. He pushed his faded red baseball cap back and scratched his head.

"Nice to see you, Joe," said Victoria, stepping up onto the porch. She nodded to Lincoln, who was standing next to the sign above the rusted red Coca-Cola ice chest that read CANNED PEAS. Elizabeth had already gone into the store for the mail. Sarah moved to one side to make room.

"Nice day, Mrs. Trumbull," said Lincoln. "Won't have too many more like this. You teach today?" He was a tall, gangly man, a landscaper.

"I've just come from the college."

"Found any more bodies lately?" asked Joe.

"Stop it, Joe." Sarah patted the bench. "Have a seat, Mrs. Trumbull."

"Thank you," said Victoria. "Elizabeth is picking up a few groceries. Do you have any news for my column?"

"Tell her about that TV star," said Lincoln.

"This really buff guy came into the store." Sarah smoothed her bright orange T-shirt. "I didn't recognize him but Joe did."

Joe spit and wiped his mouth on his sleeve.

"That's disgusting, Joe." Sarah turned back to Victoria. "It turned out he was Bruce Steinbicker, the TV actor." She looked expectantly at Victoria, who took a small notebook out of the cloth bag she was carrying.

"I don't have television," Victoria said.

"He's in a show called *Family Riot,* and he lives in California."

"What is he doing here?" Victoria scribbled notes.

"The Bass Derby," said Joe. "Comes here every October." He jammed his hands into his pockets and leaned back against the post.

"He keeps a boat in Falmouth and lives on it when he's here," said Sarah.

"Did he tell you the name of his boat?" asked Victoria.

"*Star Lite,*" said Joe. "You know, star, actor. Lite as in lite beer."

154

"Yeah, Joe, we know," said Sarah.

"Does he keep his boat in the Oak Bluffs Harbor?" asked Victoria. "That's where Elizabeth works."

"Vineyard Haven," Sarah answered. "He loaned his boat to a friend in exchange for staying at the friend's house for a couple of weeks."

"Got a girlfriend. His boat's too small, he says."

"I won't intrude on his privacy," said Victoria. "It will make a nice mention in the column that he's on the Island."

Sarah looked up. "Hey, Elizabeth."

"How are you, Sarah?" Elizabeth stepped down onto the porch from the store with a jug of cranberry juice and an armload of catalogs.

"What a waste of paper." Elizabeth held up a lingerie catalog and an inch-thick book of office supplies.

"Let's see that." Joe held out his hand. "Not that one," he said of the office supply catalog.

Lincoln, who'd been silent up to this point, guffawed. "Get your jollies any way you can, Joe. Ladies' undies."

Chapter 21

The evening was mild, not really cool enough to warrant a fire, but Elizabeth lighted one in the parlor fireplace anyway. They settled down with their drinks, Victoria in her wing chair, Elizabeth on the horsehair sofa.

Victoria held up her cranberry juice and rum to let firelight flicker through the ruby-colored drink. "Just what I needed. Thank you." She sipped her drink, then set it down on the coffee table. "Roberta is so anxious about tenure, I doubt if she would go off Island voluntarily."

McCavity strode into the parlor with something in his mouth and headed toward Victoria. A large mouse, clearly beyond rescue.

"Good kitty," Victoria said.

McCavity stalked out of the room with his trophy, and a moment later, there was a crunching noise in the kitchen that didn't sound like his normal cat chow.

Elizabeth got up and put another log on the fire. Sparks rose and the fire flared up. "I saw you took notes at Alley's. Did Sarah give you some news?"

"A nice item about a television star coming to the Island for the Bass Derby."

"Who was it?"

"Bruce Steinbicker. Have you heard of him?"

"Sure. He stars in that Christian TV series, *Family Riot*. All about family values and morals. Where is he staying?"

"He usually stays on his boat, but he's at a friend's guesthouse in Vineyard Haven."

"Where's he keeping his boat?"

"Apparently anchored off Vineyard Haven."

"I'd love to take a look at it next time I'm out on the water. Vineyard Haven's not my territory, but, hey. Bruce Steinbicker is a big name. Since he's not staying on board, I won't be intruding, at least not on a big TV star. If it's nice tomorrow, I might take the harbor launch on my lunch hour." Elizabeth looked up at her grandmother. "Want to come?"

"I'll pack a lunch," said Victoria.

"Should be a nice day. The NOAA weather station is calling for another cold front day after tomorrow."

McCavity returned and settled in front of the fire. He licked a paw and rubbed it behind his ear again and again. When he finished, he stretched out with his soft belly fur to the fire and dozed off.

The following day was as fine as Elizabeth had predicted, bright with a low row of summery clouds on the mainland horizon and a gentle mild breeze. Casey dropped Victoria off at the Oak Bluffs harbor and Victoria walked down the dock to the harbormaster's shack, swinging her lilac wood stick. She was greeted by Domingo, the harbormaster.

"Sweetheart! Haven't seen you for a while." His dark face lighted up with a broad smile. He took a last puff on his cigarette and flicked it into the water. "Understand you're taking a cruise to Vineyard Haven."

"With a picnic lunch." Victoria indicated the bulging paper bag she was carrying.

"Better keep a weather eye out. Storm's predicted for tomorrow, but since this is New England, who knows." He pulled his faded NYPD hat down on his forehead. "You know the weather better than I do. Got your sunscreen?"

"I have my hat," she said, holding up the wide-brimmed straw hat she'd bought in Mexico years before.

The short, stubby harbormaster and his tall, ancient companion strolled to the end of the pier. Elizabeth had just pulled up in the launch after checking moorings out in the harbor. She tossed a line to Domingo, who wrapped it around a cleat, then climbed onto the dock, brushing her sun-bleached hair away from her face. She bent down and held the boat close for her grandmother to climb in.

Victoria had spent most of her life around boats and was determined not to appear infirm. Balancing herself carefully, one hand on Elizabeth's back, she stepped gracefully into the launch and seated herself in the bow facing the stern.

Elizabeth sat in the stern, Domingo tossed the bow line into the boat, and Victoria coiled it neatly. Her granddaughter put the motor into gear and they went slowly out of the harbor, past a lobster boat in need of paint, past the *Island Queen,* and past the dock of the paper boat. Long before sunrise, summer and winter, no matter what the weather, the *Patriot,* more familiarly known as the paper boat, made a daily run from Falmouth to the Vineyard to transport the *New York Times* and other mainland newspapers to the Island while most readers were still asleep.

Once out of the channel, they sped up and soon neared East Chop, one of two chops or headlands that marked the entrance to Vineyard Haven harbor. Despite the warm sun and light breeze, it was cool, and Victoria, knowing the water as she did, tugged on one of the sweaters she'd brought, pulled on her windbreaker, and tied a scarf over her floppy straw hat to hold it in place.

She held onto the gunwale, delighting in the sounds of the motor, the slap of the bow hitting each wave, the splash of wake that trailed behind them in a V. She lifted her great nose to breathe in the scent of salt water and seaweed, fish and plankton. A gull flew down over the water and rose with a fish in its beak, and Victoria clapped her hands in approval. The breeze was at her back and she turned her head to face into it.

High on Telegraph Hill she could see the East Chop light, one of the five lighthouses on the Island.

"The lighthouse was painted brown in my childhood," she called out to Elizabeth above the sound of the motor. "We called it the Chocolate Light."

Elizabeth laughed and looked up at the dazzling white column high on the bluff as they passed beneath it. "Why'd they call it Telegraph Hill?"

"In whaling days, a semaphore system signaled that a vessel was approaching and what sort of cargo it carried."

"A visual signal?"

Victoria nodded. "From East Chop to Chappaquiddick to Nantucket. They could signal the mainland and the signals were carried up the coast as far away as Boston."

They rounded the chop. Elizabeth asked, "Where did Sarah say he'd anchored his boat?"

"All she said was outside the Vineyard Haven harbor."

"I'll skirt around past the harbor then. I don't suppose she knew what make of boat it is?"

Victoria shook her head. "A power boat. I didn't ask the make, and I doubt if she knew."

They ran along the stretch of East Chop Drive where a line of cottages faced the harbor, only a foot or two above the water, only a few feet from the shore. The frail buildings looked extremely vulnerable to the elements. The cottages had been there for years, since Victoria was a young woman. Above the small houses, the huge new hospital was a bright landmark. Cars sped along the barrier bar that separated Lagoon Pond from the harbor, close enough so they could make out drivers and passengers.

"Not many boats on the water this time of year," said Elizabeth.

It was easier to talk now they were going more slowly. "At the Eastville beach I'll cut directly across to Owen Little Way, north of the jetty, and head along the shore. That will save us some time."

"Once we round Husselton Head, we should be able to see all the way to the West Chop light," said Victoria.

"If we get to West Chop and don't see his boat we can head back and check the harbor on the way."

"Where would you like to eat lunch?" asked Victoria.

Elizabeth checked her watch. "Not yet noon. Let's stop off West Chop and drift. If tide's running, we can anchor."

During the week she'd been a prisoner-at-sea, Roberta Chadwick examined every nook and cranny on her boat prison looking for some means of escape. She opened every hatch she could find. Some were screwed down and she used a table knife for a screwdriver, since there was no tool chest aboard. She didn't like heights and left the deck over the wheelhouse until last. When she worked up nerve enough to scale the ladder, she found another place to run the boat, with identical controls, a wheel, and a seat. But no key.

Every day she watched the ferry ply the waters between Woods Hole and Vineyard Haven, so close and yet so far. She knew its schedule. Each time a ferry passed she went out on deck and waved on the off chance that someone on board might scan the horizon with binoculars and see her.

She had now become more concerned about herself and what would happen to her when the food ran out than she was about those three papers. Her hopes of submitting them to the journal on time to meet the deadline were fading.

There was too much work to be done on them. She'd run out of time.

She ran her fingers through her hair. She had no comb and the only way she could control her wild curls was to finger comb them.

Fortunately, there were enough good books aboard so she had her choice of reading material. She lost herself in them. Her captors had left paper and pencils, and she started a journal.

She'd used up the salad makings, but still had plenty of food. She spent a long time each day planning what she would eat and anticipating mealtimes. She'd lost several pounds.

She'd seen nothing of her captors.

No boats had come within hailing distance during the entire week. During the first day or two, she'd thought of starting a fire. Maybe signal with a torch. After all, she'd been left with matches and alcohol for the stove.

She'd dismissed the idea. By the time someone spotted the fire, it would be too late. She'd be drowned or cooked.

Occasionally, she would think about Jodi, her Ivy Green College advisee. The girl didn't understand how things worked in academia. When she, Roberta, had been a student, her first few papers had been published under her professors' names.

Damn the tenure committee! She'd always had positive comments on her teaching. She had a creditable record of community work. Publications and the inflexibility of the tenure committee were all that stood in her way.

When Mrs. Trumbull had invited her to lunch and accused her of plagiarism, Mrs. Trumbull, a mere adjunct professor, hadn't understood the academic world. Mrs. Trumbull had been so self-righteous. Roberta burned at the thought.

During the first few nights, it had taken her a long time to get to sleep, but eventually the rocking, the swish of water, the coziness of the down comforter lulled her, and she slept well.

When she awoke on Wednesday, it was almost ten o'clock, far longer than she'd intended to sleep. The night before she'd rinsed out a few things and dressed again in her pink sweatshirt and jeans, the clothes she'd been wearing since she'd been abducted.

She was fixing her breakfast—lunch, actually—when she heard the distant sound of a boat engine. She immediately turned off the stove and rushed up on deck.

Chapter 22

———

Before they reached the jetty that protected Vineyard Haven harbor, the summery clouds Victoria had been admiring had risen over the mainland and spread, giving the air an eerie greenish tinge. The sea surface was a flat mirror, reflecting the ominous sky.

Victoria nodded toward the distant Cape, now hidden by a gray mist. "The weather is moving in fast."

"The radio predicted a cold front," said Elizabeth. "It wasn't supposed to hit until tomorrow. I was hoping we could beat it."

"I suppose we should start back?"

Elizabeth glanced at the sky. "I think you're right. The sea's too calm. I don't like the looks of it."

"We can always take shelter in Vineyard Haven," said Victoria. "Rounding East Chop in this," she nodded at the sky, "might not be a good idea."

They'd been heading north of the jetty along the shore. On their left the large, elegant summer homes, most far older than Victoria, lined the shore. The eerie light touched windows that overlooked the Sound, reflecting back the threatening sky. A heavy curtain of rain now obscured the mainland and was moving rapidly toward them.

Victoria, who faced the stern, turned to see where they were heading and shaded her eyes with a hand. "I don't see a sign of a boat. If Bruce Steinbicker anchored much farther away, he has a long way to row or motor to Vineyard Haven."

"Seems odd to anchor that far out," agreed Elizabeth. "When

you're famous, I guess you need privacy." She pushed the outboard motor's handle away from her and the launch turned, trailing a curving wake in the flat sea.

Victoria now faced West Chop. "Wait! I see a boat."

"We'd better get back quickly." Elizabeth glanced up at the cloud cover and down at the strangely calm sea. "It's not that important to see his boat. I'll head into the Vineyard Haven harbor."

A puff of wind sprang up and Victoria tightened the scarf around her hat. "We've had a nice outing," she said.

When Roberta went out on deck, the sea surface was a slick dead calm. Clouds covered much of the sky and the light was a foreboding bilious green. Lightning flashed in the distance. She scanned the water and at first could see nothing. Her vision was slightly fuzzy from sleep.

Had wishful thinking made her hear a motor?

She could see bits of seaweed drifting near the surface of the glassy water. She searched from the waters beyond the West Chop light, where the tidal current rippled over the shallows, to the far shore of the mainland, around East Chop, to the indentation of the Vineyard Haven harbor.

There! A small boat with two people in it was traveling away from her. Where the boat had circled back, a wake spread outward on the mirrorlike water, marking the boat's retreat.

They'd turned back! Too far away for a shout to be heard. They must see her. They had to. She stood on the lower rung of the ladder and waved frantically.

Victoria wrapped her second sweater around her. "We can eat our lunch in the Steamship Authority terminal. I'm sure they won't mind." She looked up at the lowering sky, then at the boat in the distance. She shaded her eyes with her hand. "It looks as though someone's on deck waving."

A few drops of rain splattered on the floorboards.

Elizabeth turned to look. "Oh my gosh, that's the last thing I wanted to do—invade his privacy." She glanced up at the sky. "I'm speeding up. We have to run for cover."

"I think that's wise," said Victoria, still watching the boat near the Chop as it grew smaller and smaller.

Roberta tore off her pink sweatshirt and waved it.

"You've got to see me! Don't leave!"

The boat continued to move away from her.

She plopped down on the cold seat and burst into tears.

"Whoever is on the boat is waving something pink," said Victoria. "Perhaps they're in trouble. Should we turn back?"

By now, the once calm surface was wrinkled with small waves. A jagged flash of lightning split the clouds over the mainland. Several seconds later, thunder boomed.

"That's our answer," said Elizabeth, gunning the motor. "I'll tell Richard Williams, the Vineyard Haven harbormaster, about the person waving. His boat is larger and handles better than this in a storm."

The wind picked up. The sea surface peaked into sharp whitecaps that began to break over the stern. Lightning flashed and thunder followed. Elizabeth pressed for more speed, and the bow of the launch lifted. Victoria held on to her seat with both hands. Approaching the jetty they had to follow along it to the end. That meant turning broadside to the wind and waves. With the impact of the waves, the launch heeled, tilting dangerously to one side. Waves dashed over the high side that faced the wind. A thin sheet of water poured in over the low side. Victoria leaned into the wind for balance. Another flash of lightning, another roll of thunder. The floorboards were awash and Victoria reached for the coffee can bailer that had floated near enough for her to reach without changing the balance.

Elizabeth's expression was stony, her jaws clenched, her lips were pressed in a tight line.

Water poured in faster than Victoria could bail. Just as she thought they would surely swamp, and just as she was reaching behind her for the life jackets, they approached the end of the jetty. The boat turned sluggishly away from the wind and righted itself. Water no longer poured in. Victoria kept bailing.

Suddenly, they were in the lee of the jetty, protected from the wind. The waves were no longer the fury they'd been seconds earlier. Victoria bailed out most of the water and the coffee can scraped against sand in the boat's bottom.

They were soaked. Victoria's outer sweater hung on her like wet seaweed. Her windbreaker had kept her inner sweater dry, but her corduroy trousers clung to her legs. The brim of her straw hat was limp. The scarf dangled under her chin. She felt half drowned, and Elizabeth looked worse.

Elizabeth ran the launch onto the beach near the ferry dock, jumped out into the shallow water without removing her shoes, and pulled the boat high onto the shore.

Victoria sat where she was, in the bow, high but hardly dry, catching her breath. Rainwater streamed down both sides of her hat.

"Well!" she said, wiping salt water from her face with her hand. "That was an adventure."

From the ferry terminal in Vineyard Haven, Elizabeth called Domingo, the Oak Bluffs harbormaster, to let him know they were safe and that someone had been signaling to them from a boat that might belong to Bruce Steinbicker.

Bridget, the ticket taker, took one look at Victoria and came out from behind the counter. "You're half-drowned, Mrs. Trumbull. Follow me. Let's get you dried off. I've got towels and dry clothing upstairs." They headed up to the crews' quarters. "I've read all your books," she said as they reached the top of the stairs. "I love your poetry."

She opened a cupboard and brought out a towel and a large dry sweatshirt that read STEAMSHIP AUTHORITY: LIFELINE OF THE IS-LANDS.

The storm held up the exhumation of bodies on the Ivy Green campus. Brownie, however, continued to search. He trotted around and around in an ever widening circle, nose to the ground, wearing the yellow oilskin slicker that Joel Killdeer, the forensic scientist, had special ordered from Good Dog Goods. The slicker had POLICE DOG in bold black letters on it. Killdeer followed the dog. He wore a matching yellow slicker with a simple POLICE on the back. Every time Brownie stopped, pawed the ground, and looked up at Killdeer with large eyes, the under lids rimmed with red, Killdeer pounded a wooden stake painted orange into the ground to mark the spot for the diggers.

Including three sites he'd found today in the rain, Brownie had identified fifteen altogether. Three were homes of field mice and one was a buried ham bone.

The rain had just started when trooper Tim was on digging duty. He thrust his shovel into the ground, stopped suddenly, bent down, and pulled something out of the dirt.

"What in hell's this?" he'd called out, holding up a muddy black lace thing with underwires and dangling garters. He shook off the soil. "Only a couple inches below the surface. What do you want done with it, Doc?"

Brownie sat down on his haunches and scratched behind an ear.

Killdeer pushed his hat back, smoothed his already smooth scalp, and snapped his gum. "Bag it," he said, taking an evidence bag out of an inside pocket. He sheltered it from the rain with his jacket.

"Think we'll find whoever was wearing it, like . . . ?" Tim asked, dropping the garment into the bag.

Killdeer tucked the bag inside his foul-weather jacket. "You never know."

Brownie yawned and lay down.

The black lace find was as much of a mystery as the eight corpses they'd so far unearthed.

Killdeer ordered the diggers to rebury the field mice the way he'd seen Victoria Trumbull do, with a protective cover of leaves before they shoveled the dirt back on top. The ham bone he gave to Brownie, who ignored it.

If two of the three sites Brownie had found today turned out to contain bodies, that would make ten in all. That is, so far, Killdeer corrected himself.

The wind picked up. Branches swayed wildly, snapped, and fell to the ground. Rain slashed sideways.

"Enough, Brownie," Killdeer said. "C'mon, boy."

Brownie glanced up, then looked back down again.

"Time to stop. You've done a good job, dog."

Brownie sighed, shook himself, and trotted after Killdeer, who went into the house everyone now called Poison Ivy Hall, at least when the director wasn't around. The state police had set up a sort of rough laboratory in the kitchen and had taken over Linda's office. Linda was still out sick, worried half to death, she claimed, because sister Roberta was still missing.

Thackery was moving his work from Woodbine (Poison Ivy) into Honeysuckle, the classroom building.

"Have you any word on the missing female, Professor Chadwick?" Killdeer asked Sergeant Smalley, who was filling out paperwork at what had been Thackery's desk.

"She's the least of our worries," said Smalley, clicking his pen. "All indications are she's been attending a conference off Island. She won't be getting back tonight with the ferries not running."

The Vineyard Haven harbormaster's office was a short walk in the downpour from the ferry terminal. Elizabeth was so wet, she didn't care. She couldn't get wetter. She pushed the door open and entered, rain lashing her back.

"It's Steinbicker's boat and I know he's not aboard," said Richard Williams, the harbormaster, after she'd explained about the person waving. "Wonder who is?"

Williams was about Elizabeth's age, early thirties, and deeply tanned. He wore khaki uniform slacks and a short-sleeved shirt with a U.S. flag patch on the sleeve.

He nodded toward the window, where rain beat against the panes. "No point in going out in this." He got up from his desk and returned from the washroom with a less than clean towel. "Afraid it's been used."

"Looks good to me. Thanks." Elizabeth toweled her hair.

"I don't know who'd be on his boat. He had no need to inform me, of course. They're safer staying put on board than trying to make it to shore."

"Did the person on the boat radio you?" asked Elizabeth, running the towel over her wet shirt.

"I tried to raise the boat on the radio, but no answer. Was there any indication of a problem?"

"We were too far away. He was waving something pink," said Elizabeth. "I decided we'd better head for shelter before the storm hit."

"Lucky you did," said Richard. "Dirty out there."

From the harbormaster's shack they could see the harbor and Vineyard Sound beyond through rain-drenched windows. The northeast wind had whipped up breakers in the normally sheltered harbor.

Elizabeth finished blotting her shirt and slacks, and handed him back the towel. "Thanks. That helped."

"Where's Mrs. Trumbull?" he asked.

"Bridget took her under her wing."

"She's a great fan of your grandmother's," said Richard. "If there's a break in the weather, I'll check out Steinbicker's boat. The wind and sea will probably die down later this afternoon. Rain's no problem. Want to come?"

Elizabeth checked her watch. "I'd better call Domingo."

Roberta stayed out on deck until the boat was out of sight. Fat drops of rain splattered on the teak woodwork and the once calm water was now confused. Her prison pitched and rolled, swinging in an arc on its anchor line. Feeling demoralized and abandoned and sick, she went down below into the cabin. Rescue had been so close.

CHAPTER 23

Price Henderson, Jodi Paloni, and Christopher Wrentham had spent the past week on Price's sailboat, a twenty-eight-foot O'Day anchored off Lambert's Cove. The three coconspirators were about five miles by water from where Roberta's prison boat was anchored.

"Gorgeous morning." Price brushed his white-blond hair out of his eyes. "Too gorgeous." He slid his sunglasses into place. "NOAA is calling for a severe storm tomorrow. I'd better row ashore while I can and pick up bread, milk, and eggs. How are we doing for other things, Jodi?"

Jodi opened the ice chest and peered down into it. "We're out of salad stuff." During the past week the sun had bleached the tips of her cropped dark hair giving it a silvery frosted look. She was wearing the cutoff jeans and purple tank top she'd alternated with a sweatshirt and long cotton skirt during the week. She was barefoot, as were the others. "Tomatoes and lettuce. Otherwise, we've still got plenty of canned and dried food, carrots, potatoes, onions."

"What about fuel for the stove?" Christopher looked up from the crossword puzzle he was working. He'd stayed out of the sun as much as possible, but even with sunblock he'd acquired a painful burn.

Jodi opened the cabinet under the stove. "Looks like three half-gallon jugs of alcohol."

"That's more than enough," said Price. "While I'm gone, one of you run the engine for a couple hours to recharge the batteries."

"I'll do that," said Jodi. "Chris has got to stay out of the sun." She shut the cabinet door. "Bring back whatever news you can."

"Goes without saying." Price unhooked a backpack from inside a storage locker, slung it over his shoulder, and picked up his boat shoes. "If that's it, I'll probably be back around two. Once I get to shore, I've got that long hike to the road. I'll hitch a ride to North Tisbury." He checked his watch. "It's around nine now. Even if I don't get a ride, it's only a couple of miles to the store."

"Looks like a good day for whatever," said Christopher, stretching his arms over his head, pencil in one hand. "I might even go for a swim."

"Be careful," said Price. "The water's colder than you think." He went to the stern of the sailboat and tugged on a line. The dinghy wobbled to the boat like a recalcitrant puppy on a leash. "Take care, you guys. Even if I have to walk both ways, it shouldn't take more than four hours."

"Got your life jacket?" asked Jodi.

"Always." Price held the dinghy close and stepped in carefully. "Pass me the oars, Jodi."

Jodi turned on the blowers to evacuate fumes from the bilge. Christopher finished his puzzle and returned the puzzle book to the bookshelf behind him.

"Need a hand, Jodi?"

"No, thanks."

"Stupid of me getting this badly sunburned."

"Your wife's going to wonder where you've been."

"She'll think golf course. She's so excited about Bruce Steinbicker staying in our guesthouse, she doesn't give a damn about me." He yawned and stretched. "I believe I'll take my morning constitutional before the sun gets any higher." He slid out from behind the table, climbed up the short ladder to the cockpit, and walked the few feet to the bow, testing the tension on the wire shrouds as he swung around them. He stopped and shaded his eyes with a hand to watch Price pull the dinghy high onto the shore almost a half-mile from the boat. He waved and Price waved back.

When the engine started up its vibration added to the sway and roll as the boat swung at anchor. Once she'd started the engine, Jodi, too, made her way to the foredeck.

"Hard to believe it's October," she said. "It's more like summer. Look at those puffy clouds over the mainland."

"I'm going in the water." Christopher released his hold on the stay. "I could sure as hell use a bath." He tugged off his jeans and T-shirt, dropped them onto the deck, and wearing only his briefs made a smooth dive into the clear green water. He came up spluttering, shook his head. "Whoosh! Cold, all right." He ducked under a couple of times, then swam around to the boarding platform on the stern and hoisted himself up.

Jodi passed him a towel. "Wouldn't catch me diving into something I didn't feel the temperature of first."

"At least I'm clean. First bath in a week."

Jodi ran her hands over her exposed arms with the snake-and-vine tattoos and sat next to him in the cockpit. "You know, Chris, I can't help worrying about her."

"Nothing to worry about. When she woke up she probably had one helluva headache. Price and I were careful not to hurt her." Christopher toweled his bright hair, and got up, leaving a wet spot on the seat. He made his way to the bow and retrieved his shirt and pants, then sat down again. "She's got everything she needs on that yacht—food, clothing, blankets, books."

"But still . . ." Jodi's words trailed off.

"Look, Jodi, we went over the plan ad nauseam. We three agreed. Plain and simple. We didn't want her *dead*, we wanted her to miss that *dead*line." He smiled at his small joke. "We didn't want to harm her, we didn't want to get ourselves in trouble, and we didn't want to worry our families. Your husband and kids or my wife and kids. Everything's working out just fine."

Jodi gazed at the deck. "When is Bruce Steinbicker returning to his boat?"

"He said two weeks. Another week to go."

"The journal's deadline is Friday, two days from now. We're, like, cutting it kinda close, having her on the boat for a week. The journal might extend the deadline."

Christopher shook his head. "She has several days' work to do on our papers—references, footnotes." He blotted his sore face and arms gently with the towel. "She has to edit our writing for her style."

"Her style," repeated Jodi, scowling. "Bitch."

Christopher pulled his jeans over his legs, stood up, and zipped up the fly. His wet briefs soaked through the seat of his jeans. He sat down again and pulled on his T-shirt. His drying hair curled around his temples, a bright red-orange.

He tossed the damp towel over the steering wheel. "The journal editors are strict. They can't cut her much slack. They've got their own printing deadlines to meet."

"Suppose someone in a passing boat spots her?"

"Come on, Jodi. Unlikely. We went over all that. Every possible contingency." He reached over and patted her leg. "Don't be such a worrywart."

"I can't stay out here any longer, Chris. Jonah thinks I'm at that conference for a week. A week with the kids, he can handle." She stood up, moved the towel aside to reach the throttle, and pushed the lever forward. The engine vibrated at a higher pitch and an even rhythm. "Price sure takes good care of this boat."

"It's his home." Chris stood up again. "I'd better get inside before I get more sun." He turned. "If you recall, we never intended for you to stay away longer than a week. You'll be home tomorrow or the day after."

"Yeah. I guess. I'm homesick, I want my kids. What about your wife and kids?"

"They think the conference was a week. I told them I might stay another day or two to schmooze with colleagues." He watched the clouds rising over the mainland. "I also said I might go up to Boston, spend a few days doing research at the library."

"I hate lying to Jonah." She tugged her cutoffs down so they were more comfortable.

"I know how you feel. You're not really lying, you're dissembling."

"Lying," said Jodi.

"It's kind of late to be having second thoughts, Jodi. We discussed your situation, all of us. You were in on it. Price is single, doesn't matter what he does. Anyway, this boat is home for him. You can leave tomorrow. We'd put the word out, hinted, that you and Roberta were going to the same conference I was going to."

Jodi curled her hands, palms up, and looked at her fingernails. "When we planned this, I didn't expect to look so cruddy. How do I explain this?" She straightened out her fingers so he could see the dirt under her nails.

"Fieldwork," said Christopher. "Take a swim. It's a great way to get clean. Invigorating."

Jodi shuddered. "No, thanks. What do I say about Roberta?"

"You seem to have forgotten everything." Christopher's voice was exasperated. His blue eyes looked through her and beyond. "Jonah thinks you're at a conference, right?"

Jodi squirmed. The cutoffs were really too tight for comfort. "I told him there was a conference. I didn't say I was going. I said I was thinking about going."

"What did we tell you to say to him when you get home?"

"I'm exhausted, which is almost true, I need to take a long, hot bath, and that is true, and that I've missed him a whole lot, and . . ." She looked up and smiled.

"He'll have missed you, too. You'll be so wrapped up in your reunion, nothing else will matter, right?"

"Sort of. Yeah."

"He'll ask you about the conference. What do you say?"

"'You can't imagine how many people were there,' and then I'll say, 'Did the boys behave?'"

"Um, hmm," said Chris. "He'll ask you about Roberta."

"She and I didn't see much of each other at the conference."

"Good girl," said Chris. He looked at the horizon. "Those clouds are building up fast."

"Pretty." She looked back at Chris. "Are you sure Roberta won't connect us with her kidnapping?"

"Not kidnapping," said Chris, moving into the shade of the furled sail. "Detention."

"Whatever." Jodi stood and tugged down what remained of the legs of the cutoffs. "You never told us how you got to know Bruce Steinbicker."

"We went to prep school together. Mount Herman."

"La, de dah!" said Jodi.

"We've been friends for years. Long before he became a star. Like I told you, he asked to borrow our guesthouse for a week or so, I said sure. Make it two weeks."

"A girlfriend?"

"I didn't ask. I said I'd keep an eye on his boat."

"So that's where the kidnapping idea came from."

"Foolproof. Hasn't the engine been running long enough?"

"What's the matter with you? It hasn't even been an hour."

"Cabin fever," said Christopher. "I really got to get below out of the sun."

"Tell me again. Bruce returns to his boat, and Surprise! A woman's aboard, all upset."

"You got it," said Christopher, who was now down in the cabin. "How about a game of Scrabble?"

"And the woman will be so thrilled that Bruce Steinbicker, the famous actor, has discovered her, that she won't press charges."

"You got it," said Christopher again.

"Steinbicker will know full well who was involved."

"Another prep school prank," said Christopher. "Come on, get out the Scrabble board."

"People go to jail for stuff like this."

"You think the authorities will touch Bruce Steinbicker? Not a chance. They'll ask for his autograph. You think he'll give me away?"

"Yes," said Jodi. "As a matter of fact. I do."

"Hah! Not after he's spent two weeks in my guesthouse with a friend who's not his wife."

Price Henderson, owner of the sailboat, rowed to shore, pulled the dinghy high up on the Lambert's Cove beach, hiked the quarter-mile to the road, and stuck out his thumb to the first vehicle that came along. The vehicle, a blue dump truck, stopped.

"Where're you heading?" asked the driver, turning down the volume on the stereo, which was blaring out a mournful country-and-western tune.

"Up Island Cronig's," said Price. "You going that far?"

"Where I'm heading. Get in."

Price climbed up into the high passenger seat and the truck took off. The driver extended his hand. "Name's O'Malley. Bill O'Malley."

"Price Henderson," said Price, grasping the hand.

"About to have some weather," said O'Malley, nodding at the threatening sky.

"Looks like it," said Price.

"Been on the beach?"

Avoiding a direct answer, Price said, "Great place to walk. Pick up stones."

"Almost warm enough for a swim."

"Almost," said Price.

From that point until they reached the intersection with State Road neither spoke. O'Malley pulled into the parking lot, Price got out.

"Thanks," he said.

"No problem," said O'Malley. "If you're done shopping for boat supplies, I'll be coming by soon as I drop off these stumps."

"How . . ." Price started to ask.

"Saw you anchored in the cove this past week and figured it was about time for you to get a few supplies. See you." With that, O'Malley grinned, put the truck in gear, and drove off, leaving Price with the sick feeling of having been discovered, and by the wrong person.

CHAPTER 24

Price Henderson bought enough supplies for the boat to fill his backpack at Up Island Cronig's, and peered out of the grocery store window to see if O'Malley and the dump truck were waiting for him. He did not want a ride back with that guy. Where had O'Malley been that he could have seen the boat? And who was he, anyway?

Price didn't see the blue truck, but he did see leaves and papers blowing across the parking lot. The trees on either side were swaying in the wind. The sky had turned a greenish black. A jagged streak of lightning flashed nearby followed by a crash of thunder.

A woman with a cartload of groceries stood next to him watching the storm. "We timed our shopping pretty well, didn't we?" She looked like someone's grandmother, with a long white braid trailing down her back, and bright blue eyes set in round rosy cheeks.

"Yes, ma'am," said Price.

"I love thunderstorms," the woman said.

"Umm," Price responded, thinking about the two innocents on his boat, hoping they wouldn't do anything foolish.

"You feel sorry for the poor fishermen caught out in this," said the woman.

"Yes, you do," said Price.

The blue dump truck pulled up close to the door and O'Malley dashed out, yellow slicker pulled over his head. The store's automatic door swung open to admit him.

"There you are." O'Malley pushed back the hood of his slicker. "How're the chickens, Katherine? Still laying?"

She wobbled her hand, palm down. "Maybe one or two eggs a day."

"I'll take as many as you've got." He turned to Price. "I don't suppose you want to row back to your boat in this."

"Boat," said Katherine. "I wouldn't think so. I was just remarking that I feel sorry for anyone out at sea right now. It's out of season for a hurricane."

"You never know," said O'Malley.

Price, distracted, was worried. He couldn't row back to his boat in this weather. Staying put in the store was probably the wisest thing to do.

"Be glad to give you a ride back to the cove. Your shipmates don't seem to know which end is up," O'Malley said.

"I gotta ask," said Price, "how come you know so much about my boat?"

"That's my home opposite Paul's Point. Saw you anchor there a week ago." O'Malley grinned. "You've had some fun trying to shape up that crew of yours."

The crew was not comfortable. When the storm hit, the northeast wind swept down Vineyard Sound pushing ahead of it horizontal sheets of rain and a ferocious chop. The sailboat pitched and rolled. The Scrabble board slipped off the table, spilling tiles on the deck.

"I don't like this," said Jodi. "This is not fun." She retrieved a sweatshirt from her suitcase.

"Best place to be in a storm at sea is in a sailboat," said Christopher.

"What about those charts showing all the wrecks around Martha's Vineyard?" Jodi kept from falling over by bracing her hand on the overhead. "They don't even note dinky little sailboats like this."

"Stop fussing, will you?" snapped Christopher. "You're tiresome." He bent down to pick up the Scrabble tiles.

"It wasn't supposed to rain until tomorrow," said Jodi.

"Well, it's raining now." He dropped the tiles he'd recovered into the plum-colored velvet Crown Royal bag.

"We ought to check the anchor."

"Check it if you want, Jodi. I'm staying put where it's warm and dry." He sifted through the tiles in the bag. "I think we lost the *Q*."

"It's by your foot." She lurched suddenly. "What was *that*?"

"The wind. I hope Price isn't rowing back now."

She spread her bare feet for better balance. "You know, it feels like the boat's moving." She grabbed a handrail near the settee. "Something's crazy wrong. I'm starting up the engine again." She staggered up the ladder, crawled out on deck, and lifted herself upright, holding onto the wheel stanchion. Rain and blowing spume slashed at her face.

She wiped the spray out of her eyes and glanced toward the stern. The wind shifted briefly and she suddenly saw Paul's Point, the western point of the cove, much closer. The stern was backing directly toward it.

"Christopher!" Jodi hollered and started the engine. "Get the anchor up!" She shifted into gear and spun the wheel. The boat turned away from the wind and toward the open Sound, the stern swiveled away from the rocky point of land. Christopher clambered up on deck. They were almost clear of the Point. On his knees, hanging onto the railing as the boat tossed, he edged up toward the bow. The anchor line, instead of stretching out ahead of the boat at a low angle, was now riding under the boat.

"Hey!" he shouted. "Cut the engine! You're running over the anchor line!"

Jodi hadn't heard. She pushed the throttle to full power. Just as it looked as though they would clear Paul's Point, the engine shuddered and cut out.

"Shit!" Jodi cried. "The anchor line! Caught in the prop. Oh, shit!"

———

Back in Vineyard Haven, the harbormaster peered out the rain-streaked window. "The wind's let up a bit," he remarked to Elizabeth. "Want to try for it?"

"I'm ready," said Elizabeth. Her clothes were still damp, but her hair had dried and was curled around her head like a crown. "We've got to pick up my grandmother."

"I don't think . . ." Richard shuffled papers on his desk.

"She knows more about boats than both of us put together."

"Suppose something happens . . ."

"What?" said Elizabeth. "You're the boss, aren't you?"

Richard looked up from his papers and grinned. "Okay. You win. Get your ninety-two-year-old grandmother to the dock and I'll bring the boat around and help her aboard."

"She doesn't need help," said Elizabeth, and started toward the door and the still pelting rain.

"Here, catch!" Richard tossed her one of the yellow oilskins that hung by the door, and she grabbed it and left before the harbormaster could change his mind.

When she reached the Steamship Authority waiting room she saw a throng of day trippers gathered around Victoria, who was autographing books. The visitors had been marooned when the ferries stopped running because of the wind. Bridget had hustled up to the Bunch of Grapes Bookstore a block away and returned with a shopping bag full of Victoria's poetry books.

"You can't go out in this," protested a large woman in a lavender sweatshirt. "You'll catch your death!"

"If you're still here when I return," said Victoria with a smile, "I'll be happy to autograph the rest of the books. Good-bye!" She waved airily.

"Here's a slicker," said Bridget, helping Victoria into a hooded yellow oilskin. "Belongs to one of the guys."

"Thank you," said Victoria, heading out into the storm. Elizabeth followed. They crossed the staging area to where Richard had

184

pulled his boat next to the floating dock. Elizabeth went down the ladder first and Victoria climbed carefully after. She set both feet firmly on the floating dock, then took the hand Richard offered in a gentlemanly fashion, and stepped aboard.

She sat on the bench near Richard, and they pulled away from the dock. The whaler, the harbormaster's boat, was larger than the one Elizabeth had piloted from Oak Bluffs, and had a cabin that sheltered them from the wind and rain.

As they rounded the jetty, the seas were still heavy, and the boat pounded and shuddered as it hit each wave.

They passed Husselton Point and had just made out the boat anchored south of the lighthouse when the engine quit.

"Damn!" said Richard.

"Water in the fuel line?" asked Victoria.

"Hand me the mike, Elizabeth." He radioed the shipyard, and the Travelift guy said someone would be there in ten minutes to give them a tow back, and what the hell did you idiots think you were doing out in this?

"Ten-four," said Richard and hung up the mike. "Gotta put the anchor out." He went forward and once the boat was no longer drifting, he checked the engine. He ducked back into the cabin. "You're right, Mrs. Trumbull. Water in the fuel line."

CHAPTER 25

Professor Bigelow, wearing the ubiquitous yellow foul-weather gear, jacket and trousers, held his hood in place against the wind and rain. He struggled into the Woods Hole Steamship Authority terminal.

"When's the next boat?" he asked the ticket taker, looking at his watch. He'd received an urgent message from the university's provost to get over to the Ivy Green campus immediately and begin damage control.

The ticket taker was a pale man with thinning gray hair and steel-rimmed glasses. He'd been sorting a stack of printed schedules when Professor Bigelow interrupted him. "All sailings cancelled. Rest of the day." He went back to his sorting without looking up.

"I've got to get to the Island," said Bigelow, rapping his hand on the counter.

"So do a lot of other people." The ticket taker peered over the top of his glasses and waved at the staging area full of cars, shapes barely visible through the rain.

"I have an important meeting." Bigelow paced away from the ticket window, then back. "Is there another boat?"

"Try the paper boat out of Falmouth."

"Paper boat?" demanded Bigelow.

The ticket taker shook his head. "Crazy fools will go out in anything." He stuck the schedules in a box and set the box where passengers could reach them. "Falmouth harbor. They deliver newspapers to the Island."

"Thanks for your help," said Bigelow, turning away.

"Don't need to get sarcastic with me," said the ticket taker. "I don't make the weather."

Bigelow tugged the hood of his jacket back over his head and strode out through the automatic door into a blast of windblown rain and salt spray. He braced against his car as he opened the door into the wind.

On the Falmouth road, his was the only car. Fallen branches littered the asphalt. Trees on both sides swayed in the wind, as though about to crash down on him.

Given the weather, it took him a half hour to get to the Falmouth harbor, although it was less than five miles from Woods Hole. But even the *Patriot* wasn't running.

Bigelow had to force the door open against the wind to enter the shack that seemed to house the boat's operations.

A huge, black-bearded guy looked up from his mug of coffee. Thick black eyebrows almost met under the peak of a scruffy captain's hat.

"Where's the captain?" asked Bigelow.

"You're looking at him," said the man.

"I've got to get over to Martha's Vineyard."

"Yeah?" The captain leaned back in his chair and scratched the back of his neck. "What's the emergency?"

Bigelow's eyes twitched. "I have business to attend to in Vineyard Haven." His tongue flicked out and in again.

The captain shoved his hat back with a hairy knuckle. "That right?"

Bigelow smoothed his thin white mustache with his forefinger. "I'm the head of the Ivy Green College Oversight Committee, and I must get there immediately. The police have uncovered several bodies there."

"Heard about that." The captain covered a yawn with his hairy fist. "Sounds to me like you're a bit late."

Bigelow flushed. "I'm Professor Bigelow, and I . . ."

The large man set his chair down on all four legs and stuck out a big paw. "Howdy, Mister Bigelow. I'm Captain Littlefield. Big meets Little, right?" He grinned.

Bigelow ignored the extended hand. "I want some cooperation."

"Why sure," said Capt. Littlefield. He pushed his chair back and stood up. He towered above Professor Bigelow. He straightened his shoulders and tugged his trousers up by the belt. "Got a nice rowboat out there I can rent you. Even a set of oars to go with it."

Bigelow turned on his heels, yanked the door open, and the wind slammed it behind him, shutting out the loud guffaw.

When he reached his car, his yellow slicker streaming rainwater, he punched the Ivy Green College number on his cell phone, trying to reach Thackery Wilson. A robotic voice told him there was no service.

He slammed the cell phone down on the passenger seat and drove back to the university, only to learn that the wires were down over much of the Island, which meant most phones weren't working.

He pushed away from his desk, swiveled his chair, and thought. Three members remained on his oversight committee. That pompous ass, Hammermill Jones; that superannuated hippie math professor, Petrinia Paulinia Kralich; and that arrogant black man—African-American, he corrected himself—Noah Sutterfield. That self-satisfied young woman, Dedie Wieler, had accepted a job paying double what he, a full tenured professor of military history, was making.

Rain lashed against his window. His stomach growled. He glanced at his wall clock. After two, but he wasn't hungry.

The minister who looked like a pigeon had resigned because of moral issues. What moral issues? Coward, that was all. And that effeminate wimp, the romance languages man Cosimo Perrini. Probably gay. Couldn't stomach the murders.

He, Professor Bigelow, had a right to be informed about what was going on over at that college. He needed to know how many bodies had been recovered, how many had been identified, and most especially, what persons of interest the police had named.

Worst of all, Wellborn Price had pulled another fast one. When Wellborn had cheerfully agreed to take that introductory course, he, Professor Bigelow, should have been suspicious. Instead of putting Wellborn in his place, the instructor had invited him to deliver a lecture, just one. Gave him a five hundred dollar honorarium when he did—which he contributed to the university's scholarship fund. She also presented him with a document certifying that he'd completed the course with an A-plus. Just thinking about the way that insufferable man had turned things around made Bigelow's stomach boil with acid.

Wellborn Price. Bigelow still felt outrage when he thought of the associate professor who'd fathered his sister's bastard son. He'd gotten even, to some extent. He'd convinced Laurel that Wellborn had been killed in an automobile accident. As far as he was concerned, Wellborn *was* dead.

Bigelow intended to do everything in his power to make sure Wellborn Price stayed dead.

He must get over to the Island before the police found any more bodies.

"Throw the anchor out!" shouted Jodi. "We're heading for the rocks!"

"The anchor's already over, idiot!" Christopher shouted back. He was wearing a red wool shirt that clashed with his orange hair. The shirttail flapped like a danger signal.

The anchor dragged along the sandy bottom and slowed the boat somewhat. But the engine wouldn't start. The wheel wouldn't turn. With the anchor line caught in the propeller, they were now stern first to the wind, and pointed directly at Paul's Point.

"The jib! Raise the jib!" shouted Jodi.

The small sail at the front of the boat lay on the deck in a sail bag. Christopher tugged off the bag with one hand and the bag flew overboard. He held onto the mast with his free arm. His shirt fluttered around him.

"Hurry!" shouted Jodi.

"I'm going as fast as I can, dammit!" He shouted back. As Christopher hauled up the jib, the wind shook the canvas, and it rattled and snapped like gunshots.

Suddenly, the dragging anchor caught on the shoaling bottom. The boat juddered to a stop and Christopher lost his footing on the slick wet deck.

He lifted up his arms and flew overboard. "Help!" he yelled. The boat swung back and forth. Jodi snatched the ring buoy out of its wire holder and threw it out. The wind caught the buoy and carried it beyond the swimmer.

Christopher swam frantically. She saw his orange hair, his red shirt. He caught the ring. The wind and sea swept him toward shore. He disappeared under a breaking wave and Jodi screamed. She was soaked through. Her cropped hair was plastered to her scalp. Water dripped off the gold rings in her eyebrows and off the stud in her nose. She covered her eyes with her hands and peered out through her fingers, dreading what she might see. A flash of red just this side of the breakers that dashed on the point. She could hear the roar above the wind and the slapping sail. She could barely see him through the rain, still clutching the ring buoy.

His head rose above a wave and disappeared again. He was in the breakers now, tumbling and twisting, still hanging onto the buoy. A towering wave flung him onto the beach and she saw him stagger to his feet, take a few steps, and fall.

The jib, the forward sail, snapped, caught on a stay, and ripped with a shriek. Lines running from the foot of the sail whipped and twisted around the stay.

Jodi was too frightened to think of crawling forward to fix the mess. She wouldn't have known what to do anyway. She mustn't fall overboard. She wasn't a strong swimmer. She knew how cold the water was and she'd seen Chris get beaten up and pounded by the surf.

She shivered. She thought of her four boys. Would she ever see them again? Her muscles cramped.

What could she do? Was Chris alive or dead? Would the anchor hold? There was no way she could unwrap the anchor line from the prop. Even if she could, the boat would be tossed onto the rocks.

All this raced through her mind and with it the ever-present thought of her four boys. Her cell phone was dead. How would she get home? What would she tell Jonah?

Too many questions. She dropped into the cockpit, where she was sheltered from the wind, and cried.

At Cronig's big storefront window, Price Henderson and Bill O'Malley watched the deluge for some minutes without speaking. Katherine, the egg woman, had left them and slogged through the rain to her car. She'd taken off with a rooster tail of water trailing behind her.

Price thought about his boat. The boat was safe enough, but he wasn't confident about the two he'd left in charge.

O'Malley set his foot on the low sill and leaned an elbow on his thigh. "I'm leaving as soon as there's a break in the rain. I'd be happy to drop you off at the path to the cove, but this isn't going to let up for a long time." He pointed a thumb at the bag of groceries that filled Price's backpack. "I don't suppose you'd care to wait for the rain to let up at my place, would you? I can offer you a nonalcoholic beer. I don't drink."

Price looked at his watch. Going on three.

"You'll be able to see your boat from my living room window."

Price lifted the heavy backpack from his shoulders and set it on the floor. "I don't want to trouble you . . ."

O'Malley laughed.

"Well . . ." said Price.

O'Malley set his foot back on the floor and stood up straight. "Whatever you three are doing out there is pret-ty strange." He arched his back and sighed. "However, I figure it's none of my business. I have my own affairs I don't choose to share."

Price paused while he thought of his options. Wait at the store and hitch a ride when the rain let up, or take up O'Malley's offer.

"Thanks," he said. "Appreciate it."

There was a slight lightening of the sky and O'Malley said, "Looks as though we can make a dash for it."

Price hefted his backpack and the two raced out to the dump truck and slammed the doors, just as the downpour resumed.

"It's not what you'd call great rowing weather," O'Malley said, starting up the truck with a roar. "As soon as it clears, you can walk from my house to your dinghy. It's shorter than the path."

The heavy truck passed the Lambert's Cove turnoff and wound its way up a long dirt road, slick with mud and newly washed out in places. They stopped next to a sprawling old house that must have been there for generations. The house was on top of a cliff and faced the Sound. Off to one side was a barn. In clear weather, the view must be spectacular, Price thought. Right now, the rain was a curtain that closed off everything beyond the cliff edge.

Price set his backpack on the entry floor and realized he was filthy. He stepped into the kitchen and hesitated before going any farther. He could take his shoes off, but he knew his feet were filthy, too, and probably stained from the wet leather of his boat shoes.

While he stood there, O'Malley lit the fire. Price could see the living room through the kitchen. Beige and cream overstuffed chairs, an antique rug.

"Go ahead, take them off," said O'Malley, returning to the kitchen and nodding at the shoes. "There's a towel by the door to dry your feet. Don't worry about the furniture. It's seen worse."

The fire and the beer, nonalcoholic though it was, soothed Price, and he relaxed.

"Is this a family house?" he asked.

"Built by my great-grandfather," said O'Malley.

After they talked about O'Malley's house, they had nothing more to say. Price had no intention of discussing his academic work—that would lead to awkward questions. Nor did he want to talk about his search for a dead father. He certainly didn't want to talk about the reason he'd anchored his boat for the past week within sight of O'Malley.

He stood and went to the window that overlooked the Sound. Sheets of rain slashed against the small panes.

"See your boat?" asked O'Malley.

"I can't even see the cove," said Price.

"You'll catch a glimpse when the rain lets up."

A few minutes later, while he stood at the window, wishing the view would open up, it did, briefly. Then the curtain closed again.

"You see it okay?" asked O'Malley.

"No. I must not be looking in the right direction."

O'Malley got up from his chair, his bottle of O'Doul's in hand, and stood next to Price. "Next time it clears, look right there."

"I did," said Price. "But I didn't see my boat."

Chapter 26

The disabled whaler, with Victoria, Elizabeth, and the Vineyard Haven harbormaster aboard, was towed back in the pouring rain to the harbormaster's dock by the *Annie B,* the shipyard's boat. Victoria was right—water in the fuel line.

"Thanks, Butch," said Richard Williams.

"No problem." Butch, a black-bearded, curly-haired Newfoundlander, was the pilot of the *Annie B.* He let go the tow lines and jerked his thumb at the harbormaster. "If you and Mrs. T apply for a job at the shipyard, she gets it." With that, he spit out a stream of sunflower-seed shells, shifted into gear, and took off.

Elizabeth laughed.

"Pain in the rear end," muttered Richard, turning to work on the fuel line.

Victoria, still in the seat next to the console, crossed one long leg over the other and, with a faint smile, examined her fingernails.

Christopher Wrentham pushed himself to his knees and tried to get to his feet. No strength left. He was soaked and chilled. Rain beat down on him and wind whipped his wet jeans around his legs. His red wool shirt clung to him. He had crawled out of the reach of the angry surf. He was shivering and knew he had to get warm somehow. He suspected he'd been hurt, but was so numb he could only think of getting warm. The beach had a narrow sand strip bounded by cobbles the size of baseballs at the surf line, and by a low cliff at his back. Surf broke over partly submerged car-size rocks, sending sprays of icy water high into the air. It was a wonder he hadn't been smashed against them. He had to get warm. He had to get out of the wind and rain.

The low cliff faced the wind and provided no shelter. He didn't have much strength left. Inch by inch he crawled around the point until he reached a slightly hollowed-out place that was out of the wind. He understood hypothermia. But he didn't care anymore. He curled up, knees bent, arms tucked close to his chest, and wrapped his wet wool jacket around him as best he could.

Bruce Steinbicker's woman friend, Daphne, had intended to stay for the entire two weeks, but decided to leave early. She planned to take the three-forty-five ferry. Bruce, who had looked forward to this rendezvous, was relieved. After a week, Daphne had lost much of her allure.

Starting at noon, all ferry runs were cancelled.

He wanted to check on his anchored boat after Daphne left. With the wind and rain lashing the Island like this, there was absolutely no way he would go out on the water.

So Bruce and Daphne decided to make the best of it. They lit a fire in the main room of Chris Wrentham's guesthouse and snuggled down for a cozy time. Wind howled, rain beat against the windows. Branches lashed the shingles and the electricity flickered on and off, giving them just enough time to find the candles and matches all Islanders keep for such occasions.

"This is so romantic, darling," said Daphne, snuggling close to Bruce. "A lovely way to end a special time. I really ought to call my husband. He'll be so worried about me in this storm."

"Ummm," said Bruce, nuzzling her neck.

"I just hope he doesn't decide to call Marylou."

Bruce's voice, so familiar to television viewers, was muffled. "Marylou?"

"Oooooh!" said Daphne. "I told my husband I was staying with Marylou. Stop that, darling! I really should call."

"Phones are out," said Bruce, unbuttoning the top button of her blouse.

"It's been a glorious week," she murmured. "What a . . . oooooh! special time."

Bruce didn't answer.

"Ummmmmm!" said Daphne.

Price Henderson turned away from the window. "I don't see my boat."

Bill O'Malley set his bottle of O'Doul's on the coffee table, got up from the couch, and went over to where Price stood staring out into the storm.

"Can't see a thing," said O'Malley, wiping condensation from the glass.

There was a brief view of the cove through the heavy rain. "There!" said Price.

"I still don't see anything," said O'Malley.

"That's it. That's where my boat was anchored."

"Maybe you got your bearings wrong."

Price turned to him. "You saw my boat, O'Malley. You've been watching us for a week." He pointed at the storm raging outside. "Right there. That's where she should be. I know my boat. She's not there."

"Probably slipped anchor." O'Malley took a long swig of his O'Doul's. "Not much you can do about it now. When she drifts into shoal water, the anchor will grab hold."

"If she drags her anchor, she could fetch up on the rocks on the lee shore. Those two people aboard know zilch about boats." Price left the window and headed for the entry where he'd left his jacket and shoes. "I've got to get out there. Would you give me a ride back to the cove?"

"What do you plan to do there, row your dinghy out in this?" O'Malley gestured at the raging storm.

"I have to locate my sailboat."

"It'll be dark in a couple of hours."

"Listen, O'Malley, I've got to do something. I can't just stand by the window wondering if my boat is smashing up on the rocks with those two hanging onto the rigging."

"Okay." O'Malley set his bottle on the floor and got up. "I'll go with you." He went to the hall closet and brought out yellow foul-weather jackets, life jackets, a coil of rope, and a Maglite. "We can take my boat. It's at the foot of the bluff. Closer than driving."

They headed to the cliff path with the wind flattening their oil-skins against their backs, sailing them along. Once they reached the path and had gone a few feet down they were somewhat sheltered. The steady downpour worked its way through openings in Price's jacket, sending trickles of cold water down his back.

A small boathouse stood at the foot of the bluff, the front half built out over the water on pilings. Its wide front door faced the water. O'Malley opened a side door and Price saw a powerboat, about eighteen feet long, hanging in slings above the water.

From here, with his back to the wind, the cove was protected and the water seemed almost placid. Price knew this was misleading. The storm had built up hazardous waves only a few hundred feet from shore. He had a sick feeling about his boat. If the anchor didn't catch, one of two things could happen. His boat could wreck on the rocks of Paul's Point, or she might clear the point and be swept out into Vine-yard Sound. And from there . . . Who knew where it would end up?

Visibility was only a few feet with an occasional break where they could see several hundred feet. Not enough to see the opposite shore of the cove, a mile away. In those brief glimpses, Price could see the backsides of heaving waves, almost like a pod of whales breaching.

Inside the boathouse, O'Malley handed Price a winch handle,

and they lowered the boat in its slings into the water. O'Malley started the engine blower to clear out any fumes, checked the instruments, and they headed out. They'd gone only a short distance from the shelter of the bluff when the full force of the wind hit them.

"This is really stupid!" shouted O'Malley, turning to Price, who was standing behind him. The hood of his jacket blew back. Rain plastered his hair to his forehead. Wind blasted them from behind and they surfed over the backs of breaking waves. Price looked back at the boathouse, but it had already disappeared in the rain and spray. A mountainous wave broke over the stern, filling the cockpit with icy water.

"That's it. I'm turning back," shouted O'Malley. "This is insane! Next breaker is going to flood the motor."

He turned the wheel sharply. During the seconds it took the boat to respond, they were broadside to the waves. A torrent of water poured over the side into the cockpit.

"Bail!" shouted O'Malley, and Price scrambled for the cutoff Clorox bottle that floated in the bilge. He scooped water overboard as rapidly as he could, feeling helpless as he tried to keep up with the chilly water that poured in over the side. Once around, they faced into fearsome breakers, quite different from the smooth backs they'd sped over in the other direction. The following wind had swept them along a quarter mile or more. Now they had to beat back against the wind. With rain and sea spray in his face, Price could see nothing.

Suddenly, when Price had lost hope of ever getting back to their starting point, they reached the shelter of the bluff. The water was unnervingly calm.

O'Malley let out a deep breath, turned the boat to face out, and backed into the boathouse.

Price continued to bail until what remained he could sop up with a wrung-out rag. Without saying a word, they winched the boat out of the water and made their way up the slippery muddy path back to O'Malley's house.

They shed their wet gear and relit the fire. Inside, the rattle of rain on the windows and the howl of the wind made their journey out into the storm seem remote.

Price stood near the fire, wet clothes steaming.

"I'm sticking to O'Doul's," said O'Malley. "Go ahead and pour yourself a stiff Scotch."

"Thanks," said Price. "I will."

CHAPTER 27

Professor Phillip Bigelow spent most of a sleepless night listening to the howling wind and beating rain, worried about things over which he had no control. He finally fell asleep and woke in time to drive over to the paper boat dock in Falmouth. The sun wasn't up yet.

"Mornin'," said Capt. Littlefield cheerfully.

"Yes," said Bigelow, frowning.

"Not too bad this morning," Capt. Littlefield said, taking Bigelow's money and stashing it in an ancient cash register drawer under a heavy metal shackle. "Sea's down, but there's a few rollers out there. Got your sea legs?"

Bigelow, who hadn't had time for coffee, grunted.

Capt. Littlefield heaved a bundle of newspapers onto the deck of the boat docked beside the shack and climbed aboard. Bigelow followed. The entire afterdeck was stacked with bundles of newspapers. *Boston Globe. New York Times. Washington Post. Wall Street Journal.*

The engines were running and the boat shook with the rhythm. Diesel fumes made Bigelow a touch queasy.

"We land in Oak Bluffs, you know," the captain said, over the sound of the engine. "If you're going to Vineyard Haven, you'll have trouble getting a ride at this hour. You can always walk. Only about four miles."

Bigelow looked at his watch. "How long will it take us to get to the Island from here?"

"Little over a half-hour. We're faster than the Steamship Authority boats." Littlefield uncleated lines and tossed them onto the dock, then went back to the wheel and pulled away, looking over his shoulder.

Bigelow said nothing as he seated himself on a bench beside dozens of stacks of newspapers. Once settled, he folded his arms over his chest. The fumes were getting to him. "Order a taxi for me, if you would, please, Captain."

The captain pushed his hat back and guffawed. "You're a pretty comical feller, I'd say."

Bigelow stared at him, but the captain was intent on the boat's instruments and didn't seem to notice Bigelow's disdain. He'd pulled out a microphone from above his head and was muttering into it something Bigelow couldn't hear above the engine noise. Clearly, he was not calling a cab.

They eased out of the harbor and in a short time were on the open Sound. Heavy swells lifted the boat and then dropped it again with a sickening motion. Capt. Littlefield pushed the throttle forward and the boat sped up, trailing a curling wake astern.

For the entire trip across this vast, heaving sea, with its oily swell and its sensation of imminent death, Capt. Littlefield didn't say another word to Bigelow, who was just as glad not to be obliged to hold a conversation with this man. He couldn't have heard him, anyway.

The boat pulled up to the dock in Oak Bluffs just as Bigelow was feeling the growing pressure of seasickness. A half-shaven man with grizzly gray hair was leaning against the hood of a battered white station wagon that was parked near the dock. He wore a torn army jacket and was smoking a cigarette. He dropped the cigarette, crushed it out with the sole of his shoe, ambled over to the paper boat, and flung a line to Littlefield.

"Mornin', Robert." The captain heaved a bundle of newspapers up onto the dock.

"Mornin', Skip," said Robert. "Rough ride?" He lifted the bundle and stacked it in the back of his car.

The captain heaved a second bundle. "Not too bad."

Bigelow waited uncertainly to get off this craft.

Another stack got shifted into the station wagon.

Capt. Littlefield turned to Bigelow. "Thought you wanted to get off here, son."

Bigelow looked up at the dock, then down at his feet.

"Ladder," said Littlefield, pointing to a set of three rusty iron bars bolted onto the side of the dock.

Bigelow started the uneasy climb up.

"Robert, you heading for Vineyard Haven first?" called up Capt. Littlefield.

"I guess."

"This gentleman"—the captain grinned, showing large yellow teeth, and indicating Bigelow, who was halfway up the ladder—"needs to get to Vineyard Haven."

Bigelow reached the top and stood, still feeling a bit rocky. He faced Robert, who was rolling a cigarette one-handed. "I'd appreciate a ride."

"No problem," said Robert, licking the cigarette paper. "Can drop you at Cumbys."

"Cumbys?" asked Bigelow.

"You know. Cumbys. Convenience store."

Bigelow nodded. "Cumberland Farms. That would be fine."

The station wagon reeked of stale cigarette smoke and the floor was littered with Milky Way candy wrappers and empty cans of Diet Pepsi.

"You deliver papers every day?" asked Bigelow.

Robert held his hands high on the steering wheel as though it was his only support. "Every day." He spoke with what seemed to be a final breath.

"On a day like yesterday . . ." Bigelow began.

Robert coughed. "Customers didn't get their paper."

Bigelow decided to give up on the chat and concentrated on mentally urging the ancient vehicle onward.

Robert pulled into the Cumberland Farms parking lot and the car shuddered to a stop.

"How much do I owe you?" asked Bigelow.

Robert shrugged. "Whatever," he said.

Bigelow handed him a twenty. "That enough?"

"That'll do," said Robert, eyeing the bill with great weariness.

"Thank you." Bigelow got out of the car.

"Yeah," said Robert, opening up the back and lifting a stack of newspapers. "See you."

Bigelow made his way in the growing dawn from Five Corners up the hill to Main Street and turned right. The college campus was only five or six blocks from here. He was feeling better by the time he reached the street that bounded the campus. The air was fresh, everything was rain-washed and sweet smelling. The sun, still below the horizon, had lit up the clouds in a spectacular display of gold and rose.

For the hundredth time, Bigelow wondered why the provost had ordered him to the college in such a hurry. Made it sound like life or death. As chair of the oversight committee, of course, he, Professor Bigelow, was responsible for damage control, getting to the Island before they found any more bodies. Check out the open graves. Get a line on that corpse-sniffing mongrel.

Well, he'd tried. There was no reason why this morning shouldn't be early enough.

Bigelow was so intent on his thoughts, he scarcely noticed the stillness of the morning.

The brisk walk cleared away the remains of his nausea. He crossed Upper Main Street and reached the corner of the Ivy Green campus. He heard a bird call, a mourning dove. A vehicle stopped somewhere nearby. He left the sidewalk and decided to cut diagonally across the wooded area that bordered the property. Check out the locations of the bodies. A strip of yellow tape blocked his way. Dawn hadn't reached inside the night-black thicket that grew under

204

the tall oaks bordering the street. He lifted up the yellow tape and took a step into the darkness, then paused to let his eyesight adjust. He probably should walk the long way around, but that would mean an extra block. This was shorter.

He shoved a foot into the undergrowth. He'd better watch for ticks, check his legs first thing when he reached the administration building everyone now called Poison Ivy Hall. He smiled and took another small step.

Thackery Wilson, that pompous ass. Founded a college, did he? Thought he could run one. Thought he could teach. In a very short time, he, Phillip Bigelow, would bring this charade to a halt. His sister's seducer, too. He knew exactly how to deal with that fool, Wellborn Price. He laughed out loud.

From the thick darkness under the oaks he could see out to where the shadows ended and an area of lightness began. He recognized that as what used to be the grassy campus. The place was dug up and pitted like a bombed-out war zone. Once he could see where he was setting his feet, he'd be able to move faster. He took another step and heard a cough.

"Who's there?" he called out.

No answer.

"Is someone there?" He took another step. "Speak up!" His feet hit a mound of dirt surrounding one of the half-dozen or more graves and he stumbled.

He heard another cough. Closer.

He recovered his balance. "Who's there?" He turned to see if he could probe the deep blackness and as he turned, he tripped over the dirt mound and tumbled into the grave beyond. He was too startled to cry out. He landed on his back with a thud that knocked the wind out of him. He peered up. The grave was at least six feet deep. He could see the dawn's grayness far above him. He tried to get to his knees but there wasn't room enough for him to turn around easily. Dirt tricked down onto him from the side of the grave. The dirt smelled foul. Before he had time to recover himself, a figure loomed over him, blocking the little light there was.

"Who are you?" Bigelow croaked, struggling to get to his feet. "Who are you?"

Victoria was an early riser. She loved the awakening day. On the morning after the storm before the sun came up, the phone rang. Dawn was still only a promise, a faint line between dark gray land and light gray sky. She recognized the mellow voice of Richard Williams, the Vineyard Haven harbormaster.

"Mrs. Trumbull," he said. "Thought you might be willing to go with me again to check out Bruce Steinbicker's boat. I could use an extra hand."

"Of course. I'd be delighted." Victoria immediately began to plan a lunch she could pack quickly.

"Tried again to reach Steinbicker on the radio," said Richard. "No luck. He's not answering his cell phone either."

"That seems strange," said Victoria.

"Yeah, it is. Figured I needed to take along someone who can troubleshoot engine problems." He laughed.

"Thank you," said Victoria, primly. "I'll be there shortly."

"Need a ride?" asked Richard.

"I hitchhike," she replied.

"I'll be there in fifteen minutes," he said. "I know where you live."

"Hitchhiking is faster," said Victoria. "Also greener. The first car that passes will pick me up." she added.

"You wait for me," insisted Richard.

Victoria packed her cloth bag with cheese and crackers, a couple of hard-boiled eggs, carrots, and a hardened end of salami, filled an empty cranberry juice jug with good well water, and topped the bag with her police deputy hat. She gathered up sweaters and a scarf and was waiting in the drive when Richard pulled up in the harbormaster's van.

He helped her up into the high seat. "Not likely to have trouble on the water today. Heavy swell running, but it's calmed down since yesterday." He was wearing his khaki uniform with a blue wind-breaker and looked quite handsome with his tanned face and dark wavy hair trimmed neatly around his ears. As they pulled out of her drive, Victoria studied this nice young man. He was about Elizabeth's age. No wedding ring. He and Elizabeth would make an attractive couple.

He turned onto Old County Road.

Victoria said, "I'm really quite sure I saw someone on the boat waving as though they were in trouble."

"Doesn't hurt to check," Richard said, glancing at her with a smile. "I called Domingo at the Oak Bluffs harbor to see if your grand-daughter was available, but she's out in the harbor in the launch."

"How did the launch get back to Oak Bluffs?" Victoria asked, thinking of Elizabeth pulling the heavy boat up onto the sand near the ferry dock.

"Calmed down a bit last night and I ran it down there. A friend brought me back."

"Ah," said Victoria, wondering who the friend was.

Richard pulled into an empty place at the foot of the Owen Park road and went into the harbormaster's shack to take care of last-minute business. Victoria sat on a bench overlooking the harbor.

He came out of the shack after a bit.

"Got a message from Bruce Steinbicker on my answering machine. Wants a ride out to his boat. He should be here in twenty minutes or so. Mind waiting?"

"Not at all," said Victoria. "I'd like to meet him."

"I'll be ready to take off soon as he arrives." Richard strode down the dock and Victoria followed. He stepped onto the whaler, took her bag from her, and offered her a hand, which she accepted. She settled herself on the bench in the wheelhouse and kept out of his way while he checked the engine and jotted notes in his log.

It was less than twenty minutes when Steinbicker showed up and stepped aboard. His hair, light brown, was artistically tousled. His tan accented his bright blue eyes. Above his strong jaw his mouth was slightly crooked, keeping his otherwise perfect face from looking too perfect.

"Thanks for giving me a ride, Richard," he said.

Victoria smoothed her hair. Even though she didn't have television, she recognized that mellow voice.

"No problem. Meet my mate, Victoria Trumbull. Mrs. T, meet the famous TV star."

"How do you do," said Victoria, holding out her hand, which Bruce took gently in his.

"Delighted to meet you. I own two of your poetry books and would love to have you autograph them for me. I'm afraid they're pretty well worn."

"The best kind." Victoria smiled. "That means they're well read."

"And well loved," he said. He then explained to Richard, "I don't have my dinghy. A buddy of mine has it. He's looking after my boat."

The harbormaster started the engine, Bruce let go the lines, and they were underway.

It was hard for Victoria to believe that only yesterday she'd thought her granddaughter's launch was going to founder. Just yesterday breakers had been smashing against the jetty sending up geysers of foaming water. How quickly the angry sea could calm. This morning the harbor's surface reflected the sunrise and hulls and masts of a dozen anchored boats, all facing the incoming tide.

"Beautiful morning," Bruce Steinbicker commented.

"It couldn't be nicer. We were worried about your boat and wanted to check on it," said Victoria. "But yesterday wasn't the best day."

"Certainly wasn't," said Bruce, rubbing his chin, still a bit tender from the week with Daphne. "But my boat has weathered worse storms than yesterday's."

The whaler's wake broke the calm surface of the harbor. Shards of pink, orange, blue, white, and silver mingled the reflections of sky, boat hulls, and masts. A seagull swept overhead, mewling.

"Someone on your boat waved to us," said Victoria, "but the weather was so foul we had to turn back."

"A person on my boat?" asked Bruce. "Are you sure?"

"Quite sure," said Victoria, feeling less sure than she had been. "The person was waving something pink."

Bruce rubbed his chin again.

"I did ask my buddy to check the boat. I suppose that's who it was. Wonder why he was waving?"

They rounded the jetty and Richard pushed the throttle forward. Outside the harbor a heavy swell was running. The bow lifted and Victoria felt the thrill she always felt on the water. Salt water in her veins, she thought. She would have been a grand sea captain.

They'd know the explanation for the mysterious person on this nice man's yacht. In the meantime, she intended to enjoy the morning. Even though the wheelhouse was sheltered, it was chilly. She put on the two sweaters she'd brought along.

They rounded Husselton Head and passed the gray-shingled summer houses on West Chop. Before the sun was high enough to warm them, they sighted the lighthouse.

Victoria shaded her eyes with her hand. "I'm sure this is about where we were when we saw the boat."

"We'll spot it in a couple minutes," said Bruce. "I anchored below the light."

The whaler surged ahead up the long, gentle swells that lifted them, then lowered them until land was hidden.

Victoria strained her eyes. "There!" she said. "There it is. I see it. Someone is out on deck, waving."

"Well, I'll be damned," said Bruce.

CHAPTER 28

Jodi awoke before dawn. Surf crashed on the beach, tumbling the band of cobbles along the shore with a continuous rumble. Heavy swell lifted the sailboat, then dropped it with a sickening lurch. She crawled out onto the deck and peered through the growing light. Through an occasional gap in the breakers she could glimpse the place she last saw Chris.

He wasn't there. Yesterday, she'd watched him get to his feet and stagger a short distance, then collapse. He'd been battered by surf and rocks. He must be dead, his body washed out to sea. She tried to imagine how she'd feel if his corpse drifted past. What would she do?

Her stomach hurt. Her head ached. Her fingers were wrinkled from salt water, her nails were broken.

Her phone was useless. She tried the radio, but got nothing but static. She certainly couldn't swim to shore.

The boat rose, swiveled, dropped.

How would Price react? His boat gone, Chris dead. Omigod! She couldn't even think the word *dead*. He'd have returned from the grocery store during the storm. Perhaps he'd sheltered under an overturned boat with the bag of groceries, probably all soggy.

Surely, he would find them. Rescue them soon. Today.

Rescue her, she corrected herself. She shuddered when she thought of Price's reaction. Oh, Chris! His death was her fault. His daughter, playing softball with her son.

That made her think of her four boys. Her husband. She'd misled

Jonah. When the storm hit and the boats weren't running, he'd probably assumed she'd stayed safely in a hotel on the mainland. How would she explain this whole horrible, ghastly situation to him?

She held onto the wheel as a swell passed beneath the boat, lifting it. A seagull cried. She shivered.

The torn jib flapped idly in the morning's breeze. She glanced again toward the rocky point where Chris had landed. *If only I'd thought before I started the engine. I should have figured the anchor would dig in again as the water got shallower. It was my fault the rope wrapped around the propeller. Chris would never have fallen overboard. He's dead, and it's my fault.*

She was not a churchgoer, but she prayed. *Please, dear Lord, let me see my boys and Jonah again. I'll confess the whole awful story.*

She thought of Roberta Chadwick on the yacht and a hot flush of shame washed over her. *Roberta probably didn't believe she was doing anything wrong by stealing our papers. She probably didn't see it as plagiarism.*

We kidnapped her.

We should never have kidnapped her.

That's what we did, kidnapped her. A criminal offense.

Jodi's last meal was yesterday's breakfast. But she wasn't hungry. She couldn't think of eating. Chris would never eat again. She sat numbly on the cockpit seat, her mind closed. She pulled her feet up onto the seat and wrapped her arms around her legs, rested her head on her knees.

Howland Atherton, who lived near Paul's Point, was walking his dogs along the rocky beach, bracing himself against the wind, when he saw what looked like a mound of red cloth washed up by yesterday's storm. Bowser, his mostly black Lab, raced ahead to investigate. Howland held onto the collar of Rover, his mostly German shepherd, who was whining to join the investigation.

"Bowser! Here, boy, come here!" but the dog paid no attention. He'd taken some of the red stuff in his jaws and was trying to tug it free.

Howland went over to pry the dog loose. What seemed like detritus from a distance, turned out to be a red jacket covering a man, probably in his thirties. At first, Howland thought he was looking at a dead man washed off a fishing boat by the storm. He steeled himself for the sight of death, the sad and broken remains of a person who had lived and loved just a few hours ago.

But as he got closer, the body took a shallow breath.

Howland pulled out his phone, sheltered it from the wind with his hand, and punched in 911, hoping to get a signal. When the communications center answered, he explained about the half-dead man.

"Paul's Point? You gotta be kidding," the dispatcher said. "It's going to take one hell of a long time to get the EMTs there."

"The man's alive," said Howland. "Hypothermia. I'll do what I can to warm him."

"Stay with him," said the dispatcher. "We'll get there soon as we can."

Howland ordered the two dogs to stay, which they did, and stripped off his down jacket to cover the man. A redhead. Under a sloughing-off layer of sunburned skin that made him look like something long dead, he was deathly pale. His skin had a bluish tinge. His eyes were closed. His lips, chapped and raw looking, were parted, and he breathed through his mouth in shallow gasps. His jaw had a light stubble of beard. Howland felt for his pulse. Weak.

A fire. He had to get a fire going. He always carried a disposable lighter and a pocket knife, a holdover from his boyhood scouting days. Plenty of wood had washed up, but it was soaking wet. Searching along the shore for dry wood he found dead branches on the beach plum bushes that clung to the cliff, and broke off as many as he could. The bark was wet but the inside was dry.

He collected a good-sized stack of wood and piled it in a semi-circle around the man to shelter him from the wind. Once the fire was going, the wet stuff would dry out enough to burn.

Before taking the dogs for their walk, he'd stopped at the post office and still had bills and catalogs in his pocket. For once, he was grateful for junk mail. He crumpled up the pages, arranged the beach plum twigs on top, and piled the smaller pieces of wet wood where they would dry and burn. He held the lighter under his electric bill and was satisfied at seeing it burst into flame. The twigs flared up, the small pieces of wood started to glow.

The man groaned.

Howland bent over him. "You'll be okay, buddy."

Before dawn, when the black of the sea was still merged into the black of the sky, Bill O'Malley grabbed a flashlight and he and Price Henderson followed the same route they'd traversed the evening before—down the cliff to the boathouse. The cliff path was slippery from yesterday's rain and Price fell twice, the second time skidding a dozen feet and fetching up against a lush vine that he couldn't make out in the dark.

"That was close," he gasped, getting to his feet unsteadily. "I was headed for the edge of the cliff."

"Vine stopped you?" asked O'Malley.

"Thank God it did."

"Poison ivy," said O'Malley, shining the flashlight on the glistening leaves. "All over the place. Great erosion control."

"Hell!" Price stumbled and fell again. "I'm sensitive to the damn stuff." He scrambled up, trying to avoid the tough vine that had entangled his feet. His shoe came off and he retrieved it gingerly. It was still too dark to make out details.

"When we get down to the cove, soak yourself with seawater. It helps some," said O'Malley, sounding amused.

"Not funny," muttered Price.

When they reached the foot of the cliff, waves were lapping gently along the edges of the cove.

"I'll take care of the boat," said O'Malley, "You better wash yourself. Get the oil off."

O'Malley checked out the motor and turned on the blower. Price waded into the chill water, clothes and all, until the water was above his waist. He ducked under, spluttering as he emerged, and scrubbed his hands and feet with sand.

"Climb aboard," O'Malley called out from the boathouse. "There's a towel in the cabin. Let's go."

They headed out into the lightening dawn. Price shivered in his wet clothes.

O'Malley shucked off his sweatshirt and tossed it to Price. "Here, put this on."

"Thanks," said Price.

The line between sea and sky emerged, the sky pale pink, the sea a steel gray. As they reached the middle of the cove, the clouds flared with gold and rose. The water had calmed somewhat since the night before, but was still rough.

They were well out into the middle of the cove before Price spotted his boat close to the far shore and to their left. "There she is!"

"She's stern into the wind. That's odd," said O'Malley, changing direction to steer toward the disabled sailboat.

"Hey, there's Jodi!" Price stood up and waved his arms over his head. Wind slapped and fluttered his wet trousers against his legs. "Something's wrong. She's all hunched over. I can't see her face. Where's Chris?"

Chris was on a stretcher. The EMTs summoned by Howland Atherton had carried him the long distance from his resting place on Paul's Point to the closest dirt road. He was now in the Tri-Town

Ambulance heading for the Martha's Vineyard Hospital. He was conscious, could talk, but had no idea where he was or who he was.

"Temporary amnesia," Erica, the lead EMT, had told Howland before they'd taken off. "He seems to be in good shape otherwise. Probably fell off a fishing boat in the storm. It's lucky you found him. He's really, really lucky to be alive."

Roberta Chadwick had been violently seasick during the storm. Her prison boat lifted and dropped, swung back and forth, rocked in crazy unpredictable directions. She wanted to die. She'd looped an arm around the ladder on the port side and heaved up everything in her stomach, then tried to heave up her stomach as well. She'd finally gone below, flopped onto her bunk, and fell into a fitful doze. When she awoke the next morning, the storm had passed and heavy swells shifted the boat in a slow rhythm that made her almost as sick as the stormy confusion of the day before.

She hadn't eaten. She felt weak and helpless and depressed. It seemed as though she'd been held captive for months, not days.

Her new life had developed a routine that was like nothing she'd ever followed before. Wake up when the sun comes up. Heat water. Breakfast. An apple or an orange. Cereal. Bathe. Walk around the deck. Watch for rescue boats. Read. Write. Lunch. Check supplies. Walk. Write. Read. Watch. Supper. Read. Write. Rinse out underwear. Bed.

Except for her seasickness during the storm, when she wished to die, she'd begun to appreciate her peaceful, contemplative life. There was a certain freedom to it. Her only responsibility was survival, and that was simple.

She continued to wonder who had kidnapped her and why. She'd given up thinking about when they would come for her. In the past few days she'd begun to talk to herself.

The deadline for submitting her papers had passed. The importance of tenure faded. She thought of her students, Jodi, Christopher, and Price. They would be so disappointed that the papers they'd helped her with would not be published.

She was taking her morning walk, hoping to feel a bit better and perhaps eat something for breakfast. She adjusted her stride to the motion of the boat. Every morning she walked to the bow along the port side and back on the starboard. Posh, she amused herself by thinking. The word dated from the days of the British Empire, when the most desirable cabins aboard ships bound for India were Port Outbound, Starboard Homebound. Evenings she varied her route. Starboard to the bow, port return.

The glorious sunrise began to lift her spirits. Pink clouds above bright orange clouds, set in the bluest sky she'd ever seen. She stood in the stern facing the rising sun and took a deep breath. She had no right to be depressed. She raised her arms to greet the day, and it was then that she saw a boat approaching. It rose to the top of a swell, then disappeared behind it. She waved. The boat was heading directly toward her. It was true! She was about to be rescued. She was saved!

Professor Bigelow closed his eyes. He was lying in several inches of water. Dirt tumbled from the sides of the open grave onto him. The earth around him stank of mold and decay. He'd lost his glasses. Was he lying on them? Could he find them, and were they broken, and did it matter? His ankle hurt. He must have twisted it when he fell.

How would it feel to be buried alive? He thought of dirt filling his nostrils and lungs. Would his life flash before his eyes? He sensed he was about to find out.

He would learn the identity of his killer, but no one would ever know. Such an untimely and ignominious end. He tried to pull out his handkerchief, but the grave was too narrow for him to get a hand into his pocket.

He opened his eyes and looked up at the figure still looming over him, crouching, hands on knees, a black silhouette against the pale blush of dawn. His last view of the sky. The figure coughed. More dirt trickled from the side of the grave onto his chest.

Bigelow groaned.

"Hey, down there. You okay?"

"I . . . I . . . I . . ." stammered Bigelow, closing his eyes again.

"Need a hand?"

"I . . . I . . ." said Bigelow. "I . . . beg your pardon?"

"You hurt?"

"I . . . I . . . my ankle." The weak high voice that emerged sounded far, far away. Couldn't have been his.

"Can you stand up?"

Bigelow, feeling more than nine-tenths of the way to his eternity, didn't know whether he could stand up or not.

"Got some newspaper twine in the wagon. Wait here, and I'll get it."

Wait here? Wait here? thought Bigelow. Newspaper twine?

Dimly he heard, or rather, felt, footsteps retreating. He dropped his head back into the water, now slightly warmed by his body heat. Water trickled into his ears, giving all sounds an ethereal quality. He thought of his glasses, and tried to lift himself to feel beneath him, but it was too much trouble. The footsteps returned.

"Twine's pretty strong," the voice said. "I'll double it up. Should hold you."

Hold me? Bigelow, drifted. I wonder if I can go to the meeting wearing these clothes.

"Hey!" said the voice. "Wake up! Don't weak out on me."

A hairy, thin rope descended into the grave.

"Grab ahold!"

Bigelow lifted a hand. His arm followed. He allowed the twine-rope to wrap around his hand. Then his arm dropped back again.

"Come on, now. You gotta help," said the voice.

Bigelow was beyond caring.

"Wasn't that bad of a fall," said the voice. "Grab ahold."

While Bigelow drifted, drifted, he heard the voice mumble something about damn cell phones and lousy reception and heart attacks and the next thing he heard were sirens.

The Sirens were coming for him. Ah, yes. He understood now. The Sirens' song. Greek mythology. That's what he was hearing. The end of that song was death. The Sirens would carry him away.

CHAPTER 29

Bruce Steinbicker shaded his eyes against the glare coming off the water. "What's a woman doing on my boat?"

"Guess we'll find out in a couple minutes," said Richard, easing back on the throttle to slow the launch. "Bruce, put out a fender. We don't want to scratch your paint job."

The woman waved frantically and did a sort of happy shuffle. She cupped her hands around her mouth, apparently shouting something they were still too far away to hear.

Richard circled the yacht and drew up alongside.

"Thank God!" the woman cried. "Who are you?"

"Harbormaster," said Richard.

Bruce flung a line around a deck cleat and stared up at the woman. "Who are *you*?" he demanded.

Victoria had been sitting on the bench inside the cabin. Now that the launch was coupled with the yacht, she moved carefully into the cockpit, watching her footing and matching her steps to the roll of the boat.

She looked up.

"Roberta?" she asked, astonished. "Roberta Chadwick?"

"Mrs. Trumbull! Thank God you've come!"

Bruce was holding the bitter end of the line he'd just cleated. "What's going on?" He tossed the line onto the deck of the yacht, a good two feet above him.

"I have no idea what's going on," said Roberta. "Who are you?"

"We're coming aboard," said Richard. "Let me take your hand, Mrs. Trumbull. High step up."

Victoria grasped the firm hand that lifted her up and over the railing. "Thank you," she said, slightly out of breath.

"This is my boat," said Bruce to Roberta. "What are you doing on her?"

"Your boat! I'm being held prisoner on your boat, that's what!"

"What in hell are you talking about, lady?"

Victoria stepped over to Roberta who seized her in an enthusiastic hug. "I'm so glad to see you, Mrs. Trumbull!"

"We've been worried about you," said Victoria, extricating herself. Roberta looked quite attractive. She'd lost weight. She had a nice healthy tan and her hair had sun-bleached streaks that any hairdresser would aspire to copy.

"How did you ever find me, Mrs. Trumbull?" She grasped Victoria's hands. "Thank you, thank you!"

"We're so glad you're safe." Victoria pulled her hands away.

Bruce cleared his throat.

Roberta glanced at him, then asked Victoria, "Who is this man?"

Before Victoria could answer, he said, "I'm Bruce Steinbicker."

"The television star," said Victoria, with pride.

Roberta turned on him. "You're the TV star? Is this some fantastic plot in your miserable television series? You think this is funny, holding a woman captive on your yacht? I suppose you've got hidden cameras all around?" Roberta's face was flushed an attractive pink that contrasted nicely with her tan.

"Wait one damn minute," said Bruce. "You're trespassing on my boat."

Richard was checking out the yacht, moving forward slowly toward the bow, ignoring the drama behind him.

"Trespassing!" shrieked Roberta. "You think I swam out here for fun?" She swept her arm at the roiling water that separated her from the Island.

"Just a moment," said Victoria. "I need to sit down."

"Yes, of course," said Bruce, brushing off the bench seat and holding out his arm for Victoria to take.

She sat down and smoothed out her gray corduroy trousers.

"You know this woman, Mrs. Trumbull?" He gestured at Roberta. "Roberta, you've been reported missing, but the police believe . . ."

"Police!" said Roberta.

". . . the police believe you're attending a conference off Island," Victoria continued. "They're so involved in searching for the serial killer, they haven't taken your disappearance seriously."

"Serial killer?" asked Roberta, paling. "What serial killer?" She glanced quickly at Bruce.

"Don't look at me," said Bruce. "I want to know how you got onto my boat."

"So do I," said Roberta, flushing again. "I woke up on your miserable hulk a week ago, and have been trying to get off ever since."

"Ever think of using the radio?" asked Bruce.

"I tried it, of course. It doesn't work."

"You have a cell phone?"

"My kidnappers weren't considerate enough to leave mine."

"I'd like you to meet Professor Roberta Chadwick. She's with Cape Cod University," Victoria said to Bruce. "Did I understand you lived on your boat?"

"I've been staying in a buddy's guesthouse for a week or so." Bruce turned away.

"And the buddy?" asked Victoria.

"He was supposed to check on my boat occasionally."

"Did anyone come to check on the boat during the time you've been here, Roberta?"

"Certainly not. If they had, I'd have jolly well gotten off this stinking barge."

"It's not a barge and it doesn't stink," said Bruce. "It's an antique Egg Harbor, and was in pristine condition, at least it was until . . ."

"Don't you dare say what I think you're about to say," said Roberta.

"Who's your buddy?" Victoria asked.

Bruce looked from Victoria to Roberta, who was looking extremely fresh and attractive after her time on the boat. "I'd rather not say."

Richard leaped down onto the deck after his inspection. "You sure keep her Bristol fashion."

"I care about this boat," said Bruce. "I don't like the idea of some shopworn hussy parking her fat self on my clean boat."

"Shopworn!" sputtered Roberta. "Hussy? Fat! You arrogant pinhead. You think I'd set foot on this worm-eaten dump for one second of my own accord?"

"Stop!" ordered Victoria. "Both of you."

The Ivy Green College Oversight Committee met in Woodbine (Poison Ivy) Hall, convened by the university's provost. They were seated in assorted chairs around a card table in the dining room. Hammermill Jones had taken control of the meeting in the absence of their usual chair.

Petrinia Paulinia Kralich flung a strand of her long white hair over her shoulder. "What are you doing here, Hammermill? I thought you quit." Today Professor Kralich was wearing a pinstriped navy blue suit coat above layers of filmy rust-colored skirts over black leggings, bottomed off with her combat boots.

Hammermill ignored her. "Professor Bigelow arrived this morning around four a.m., but he's in the hospital."

"The hospital? What happened?"

Hammermill shrugged. "He's suffering from shock."

Noah Sutterfield had been sorting through a manila folder plastered with stickers of flags of African nations. He looked up. "How did that happen?"

"He fell into one of the open graves at the edge of the campus," said Hammermill. "Beyond that, we don't know."

"I don't understand why they haven't filled in those graves," said Petrinia. "It's not only dangerous, it's gruesome." She arose in a swirl of skirts and went into the kitchen. Water splashed. The microwave chirped.

Sutterfield closed the folder. "Did I understand you to say Bigelow got here around four? I thought the first boat got in around quarter to seven."

"He came over on the boat that carries the newspapers. The delivery man gave Bigelow a ride from Oak Bluffs."

The microwave chirped again and a moment later Professor Kralich returned, dipping a tea bag into a cup of steaming water. "I heard what you said, Hammermill, but why did Professor Bigelow come over so early?" She pushed the sleeve of the blue coat up exposing a massive watch and studied it. "It's only a little after nine now, and this meeting was scheduled for nine o'clock."

"Who knows what was going through Bigelow's mind?" said Hammermill. "The provost insisted that we meet at the earliest possible moment, and, as we know, Bigelow has a literal mind."

Petrinia squeezed the tea bag and dropped it into the wastepaper basket. "Why is the provost getting involved in our affairs?"

Sutterfield covered a yawn. "He wants to deflect the bad publicity generated by that bad dog that keeps digging up corpses."

"It's not funny, Noah." Petrinia blew on her tea. "How long will Professor Bigelow be in the hospital?"

"Who knows? They'll probably keep him overnight for observation and release him tomorrow," said Hammermill. "It's hardly life threatening to fall into an open pit."

"Grave, not pit," said Petrinia. "How did he get out?"

"The delivery man was heading to West Chop and spotted him cutting through the police tapes," said Hammermill. "The fellow parked and saw him fall." Hammermill selected a letter from the pile of papers in front of him and held it up. "The provost wants us to make a determination on whether or not to continue the university's support of this"—he waved his arm around the shabby room—"this institution."

"It's a college," corrected Petrinia.

"Whatever," said Hammermill. "There's not much we can do until we get the committee back up to strength."

"Someone had better find the killer first," said Sutterfield. "Committee members are losing interest right and left. Harlan Bliss and Journeyman Cash—dead. Dedie Wieler—left the university. The Reverend Bob White—moral issues with the murders. Cosimo Perrini—too sensitive to handle the plethora of corpses." Sutterfield leaned back in his chair. "I'm ready to quit. What about you, Petrinia?"

"Frankly, I think this oversight committee is a sham," said Petrinia. "Thackery Wilson is trying to make education available to Island residents. What's wrong with that? Why should he need an oversight committee?"

Hammermill cleared his throat. "Standards, Petrinia."

"Standards, baloney. Best qualified faculty I've ever heard of. Retired from Ivy League colleges, Nobel Prize winners, Pulitzer Prize winners." She gestured around the dining room. "So what if the buildings are shabby? And what's going on between Bigelow and Wellborn Price?"

Sutterfield laughed. "You mean, you hadn't heard?"

Petrinia sat forward. "Now what?"

"Wellborn Price, who was an associate professor at the time, fathered Bigelow's sister's son. She was his graduate student."

"And Wellborn Price wouldn't marry her?" asked Petrinia.

226

"Her father wouldn't let them marry. He tried to block his tenure application, but Wellborn got tenure anyway."

Hammermill pushed his chair away from the card table, got up, and strolled over to the window. "I don't think we need to go through all of this," he said.

"*I* hadn't heard about it," said Petrinia. "I gather that didn't settle the matter?

"Of course not," said Sutterfield. "A couple of years later, Wellborn was on the tenure committee when our Bigelow applied for tenure." Sutterfield waved a hand in the air. "Tenure denied."

"So that explains why he's harassing Wellborn Price," said Petrinia. "I wondered. What happened to the son?"

"Who knows?" said Sutterfield.

Hammermill returned to his seat. "I make a motion that we adjourn."

"We've come all this way, it seems as though we ought to accomplish something," said Sutterfield.

Hammermill gathered up loose papers and stashed them in his briefcase.

"Has anyone talked to Thackery Wilson recently?" asked Petrinia.

"Can't imagine why we would," said Hammermill, standing up again.

"I think we should call the hospital and find out how Bigelow is," said Petrinia.

"Privacy laws. They won't tell you a thing," said Sutterfield.

"Isn't anyone concerned about him?" Petrinia looked from one to the other.

"Not especially," said Hammermill.

"I need a cup of real coffee," said Sutterfield, heading for the door.

CHAPTER 30

When Victoria ordered the two combatants, Roberta and Bruce, to stop squabbling, they looked at her in astonishment, but stopped.

Richard grinned.

"Professor Chadwick has been missing for more than a week, Bruce," said Victoria. "Clearly, she was taken here by people who knew you were otherwise occupied." She paused. "Who knew your plans?"

He didn't answer.

She asked Roberta, "What do you recall of your capture?"

"I was working on my papers for the journal when someone came to the door, and that's the last I remember."

"Do you recall what the person looked like? Tall or short?"

Roberta paused. A wave lifted the boat and she shifted with the motion. "Tall. Quite a bit taller than me."

"Man or woman?"

Roberta paused again. "It was awfully dark. Man, I'm pretty sure. I was bleary-eyed from editing. Someone may have been behind him. There may have been two people."

Victoria started to get to her feet. The boat rocked and Richard held out his arm. She took it.

"We need to get Roberta back to shore right now," she said. "Bruce, you must talk to the police. Roberta was kidnapped. This is a police matter."

"I don't want the police involved," said Bruce. "My show. My reputation."

"You have no choice. Check out your boat. Then we've got to get back to shore."

Richard jumped down into the whaler and started the motor. He held out a hand for Victoria, who eased herself down into the launch. She glanced up at Roberta. "Do you have anything of yours on board Bruce's boat that you want to take with you?"

Roberta indicated the wrinkled pink sweatshirt she was wearing. "This is it." She thought a moment. "A couple of things I want are below." She went down into the cabin and came back with the journal she'd been keeping. She was wearing a blue down jacket.

"That's my jacket," said Bruce.

"Tough," said Roberta, zipping it up.

O'Malley and Price Henderson pulled up alongside Price's sailboat, and were met by a sobbing, hysterical Jodi.

Price tossed a line to her, but she was incapable of doing anything with it, so O'Malley snuggled his boat against the sailboat and held it there while Price reached up and wrapped the line around a cleat.

"What's the matter, Jodi?" Price asked, clambering aboard. "The boat? No big deal. I'm sure she's okay."

Jodi sobbed and shook her head. Price noticed that her nose stud had fallen out.

"You hurt? Where's Chris, down below?"

Jodi dropped onto the deck, curled up, and put both arms over her head.

O'Malley finished making the two boats fast and climbed aboard the sailboat. "What in hell's her trouble?"

Price knelt next to her. "Jodi? Chris—where's Chris?"

"Da . . . da . . . da . . . dead," she whispered.

"What? Where is he?"

Jodi sobbed. "No . . . no . . . no . . ."

"For Christ's sake," said O'Malley. "Let's get her below and give her a shot of brandy."

They got her to her feet and down the three steps into the cabin, laid her on the settee, and put a blanket over her.

"You got brandy aboard? Whiskey? Spirits of any kind?"

"Rum," said Price, searching through lockers.

"There it is, right there," said O'Malley, reaching above Price's head. "I always did have a nose for finding the stuff."

O'Malley poured a dose into a plastic tumbler, held Jodi's head up, and poured some of the rum into her. "I hope you're not an alky," said O'Malley. "This would be the last thing you need."

Jodi coughed and sputtered. She shook her head as O'Malley tried to get her to drink more. He handed the glass to Price with an inch of rum still in it. "Take it away from me, will you?"

Price took the tumbler. "Jodi, you gotta tell me what's happened."

Jodi gasped out, "Chris fell overboard. He's dead."

"How do you know?"

"I saw him make it to shore. He staggered a few feet and collapsed." Jodi coughed.

"Drink some more of this, Jodi."

She shook her head. "The surf must have washed him out to sea. I'll never see him again."

"Use the radio in my boat, Price," said O'Malley. "Call the communications center."

"Not the Coast Guard?"

"Communications first. He may have made it to shore. After that, call the Coast Guard."

On the way back to the Vineyard Haven harbor, Bruce Steinbicker and Roberta Chadwick sat as far apart as anyone can get on an eighteen-foot boat. Neither spoke.

The sound of the engine made it difficult to talk, anyway. Victoria seated herself on the bench in the sheltered cabin and Richard headed back to the harbormaster's dock.

During the short time they'd been gone, the bright clouds of sunrise had cleared away leaving a brilliant blue sky. The sea surface had only an occasional whitecap.

At the dock, Bruce helped the harbormaster tie up the launch, then held out a hand for Victoria to step ashore.

What a difference a week had made in Roberta's appearance, Victoria thought. It wasn't just dropping four or five pounds, it seemed to be her entire attitude. She was more relaxed than she'd been at their aborted luncheon. The tan was becoming. Her eyes were clear.

On the dock, Roberta turned and embraced Victoria again. "Thank you so much. You have no idea how much you've meant to me."

At Victoria's puzzled look, she continued. "Not only did you rescue me, but during this past week I've thought a lot about what you said."

"What I said?" Victoria repeated, leaning against a dock piling.

"Plagiarism."

"Ah," said Victoria.

A gull flashed by in the brilliant sky. Victoria looked up. Richard stepped up onto the dock. "Any time you need to leave for home, I'll give you a ride, Mrs. Trumbull."

"Thank you," said Victoria.

He left them and began to coil up the tangle of lines that had been tossed onto the dock.

"You were saying, Roberta?" said Victoria.

"I guess tenure isn't all that important. There are other jobs out there," Roberta said. "Anyway, I wanted you to know I listened to you."

Bruce Steinbicker helped Richard tidy up the boat and approached Roberta.

"Excuse me, Professor Chadwick." He cleared his throat. "I believe I owe you an apology." He spoke with the mellow voice so familiar to TV viewers. "I was too hasty. May I buy you lunch at the Black Dog to make amends?"

"Well . . ." Roberta looked down at her faded and grubby clothes.

"As you know, the Black Dog is accustomed to serving sailors. After lunch, I'll be glad to drive you home."

"Thank you. I accept your apology," said Roberta. "I suppose I may have been a bit hasty myself."

"Both of you need to talk to the police, right away," said Victoria. "Now."

"We need to eat lunch first," said Bruce. "The police station is practically next door to the Dog."

They parked in front of the Black Dog Tavern and sat by the wide windows on the porch where they could look out at the harbor and the ferries coming and going.

"Again, let me tell you how sorry I am that I snapped at you," said Bruce, once they'd ordered. "I didn't understand the situation. Someone apparently played a silly practical joke on you."

"Hardly silly," said Roberta, bristling.

"I'm sorry. Putting my foot in my mouth, again. You're quite right. It was a nasty practical joke."

"Not a very funny one," said Roberta, straightening her utensils. "Any idea who the joker might be?"

"No. Certainly not." Bruce toyed with his utensils.

Roberta said, "Someone had access to your boat, right?"

"The harbormaster does."

She gave a short laugh. "The harbormaster didn't kidnap me. Surely you must know who had access to your boat. I'm going to the police." She gestured toward the door. "If you know something I should know and aren't leveling with me . . ."

"No, no, no." Bruce covered his eyes with a hand, his elbow on the table.

"Well? What about it?"

"A guy I know loaned me his guesthouse for a couple of weeks so I could," he paused, "entertain a woman friend."

"Oh?" Roberta tapped her fingers on the table. "Are you married?"

"Yes."

"You don't wear a wedding ring."

No answer.

"Is she?"

No answer.

Roberta laughed again. "I suppose you don't want the media trumpeting it around that Bruce Steinbicker was shacked up with someone else's wife?"

Bruce looked away.

"This guy who loaned you his guesthouse, did you let him use your boat in return?"

"He was going to keep an eye on it for me."

"Right," said Roberta again. "And his idea of keeping an eye on your boat was to kidnap me and hold me prisoner on that boat? Give me a break."

The waiter brought their orders, Roberta's iced tea and hamburger, rare, and Bruce's beer and fish-and-chips.

"Will there be anything else?" asked the waiter.

"Not for me," said Roberta, eyeing the huge hamburger in front of her.

"No, thanks," said Bruce.

After the waiter left, Bruce said, "I don't know the explanation, Roberta." He glanced at her and shrugged.

"After we eat, we're going to the police. Mrs. Trumbull is right." She picked up her knife and cut into the hamburger.

"Please," said Bruce. He hadn't touched his fish-and-chips. "I can't afford the publicity if this gets out."

"What about me?" She gestured at him with the knife. "Think of my life. Do you expect me to just accept the fact that I was a prisoner on your boat for a week?"

"Before we go to the police, let me talk to the guesthouse owner.

234

Find out what he has to say about the whole thing. Then we can go to the police."

She went back to cutting the burger. "You're not listening to me. When I finish my lunch I'm going to the P. O. L . . . ."

"Stop!"

She put down her knife. "So, who *is* this guy?"

"We went to prep school together."

"What's his name?"

"I can't believe he would do something so crazy."

She picked up one of the halves of the hamburger and bit into it. They were both silent while she chewed. He still hadn't touched his food.

She said, "This isn't some cute practical joke, Bruce. Two men drugged me, carried me out to your boat, and left me there with no way to communicate, no way to get off the boat, and a two-week supply of food. Explain that, if you can."

"Wait for a day. Just one day."

"A day?!" Roberta put the burger down. "Are you out of your mind?"

"Half a day, then."

"Be practical, *Mr.* Steinbicker. The police are going to wonder why I waited a half-day to contact them about a kidnapping? I mean, that's serious stuff. What sort of fool do you think I am? What kind of fool are you?"

Bruce sat back. Pushed his plate with its uneaten fish aside. "I can't let this get out to the press."

"I see," said Roberta. "Your fans. Viewers of *Family* something."

The ferry whistled, and they both glanced out the window as it pulled away from the dock, a trail of seagulls coasting on the air astern.

"I've never watched your show. You preach family values, I suppose?"

235

Bruce looked down at his plate. "Give me a half-day."

"To save your neck? So you can warn the practical jokester kidnapper? Come on, Bruce. The police will never believe I let even two minutes pass before notifying them."

"What can I do to persuade you?" said Bruce.

"What?! You want to bribe me?" Roberta threw her napkin on top of her partly eaten hamburger and stood up, toppling the bench she'd been sitting on.

The waiter rushed over. "Is everything all right, Mr. Steinbicker?" He set the bench upright.

"It's fine," said Bruce at the same moment Roberta said, "No, it's not all right. This guy stinks," and she walked up the step into the main dining room and out of the restaurant.

Bruce tossed a hundred-dollar bill onto the table and strode after her. "Roberta!"

He caught up with her outside and grabbed her arm. "I'm taking you home."

"No, you're not. I'm walking myself over to the police station."

"You've got no car, no money. How are you going to get home?"

"The police will give me a ride." She pulled away from him. "Mrs. Trumbull hitchhikes."

He held his hands up, palms out. "Truce."

"Not until you give me the name of your so called friend."

"I'll go back in and get us doggy bags."

"Forget it," said Roberta, heading toward the police station. "I want the guy's name."

"Okay," he said. "Okay. You win. I doubt if you even know him."

She stopped and turned, hands on her hips, her face flushed beneath the tan, her eyes glittering. "Well?"

"He's president of a software company. Name's Chris Wrentham."

Roberta froze. Her face paled. She opened and shut her mouth as if she were gasping for air. "Christopher Wrentham?"

"You know him?" asked Bruce, concerned.

"I can't believe it." She wrapped her arms around her waist as though she were cold.

"Are you okay?"

"Take me home," she whispered.

CHAPTER 31

As Bruce pulled up to Roberta's small house on the outskirts of Oak Bluffs, Mrs. Hamilton, always alert to the goings-on in their secluded neighborhood, bustled over.

"Miss Chadwick, I've been so worried about you."

"I'm glad to be home, Mrs. Hamilton." Roberta eased herself out of Bruce's Porsche. Bruce remained in the driver's seat.

"Where have you been? I was so worried I contacted the police." Mrs. Hamilton planted a concerned look on her face and folded her arms under her ample bosom.

"Oh, no!" said Bruce.

Roberta said, "Thank you, Mrs. Hamilton. Please, if you don't mind, I'd like to have some time to settle in." She edged past Mrs. Hamilton and headed toward the front door.

Bruce got out of the car and shut the door carefully.

"I understand, dear," said Mrs. Hamilton. "Of course you do. And who is this nice young man?"

"Please, Mrs. Hamilton. I'll talk to you later. Give you a call."

"I've fed your poor little cat . . ."

"Thank you, Mrs. Hamilton. I'll explain everything later."

"Why don't I bring you over a tuna noodle casserole? I know how much you like it."

"I do, Mrs. Hamilton, but please, not now. I'll call you. I've got to get into my house."

Bruce leaned against the car and checked his fingernails.

"Your house must be a mess after all this time. I'll be happy to help you clean, you've been gone so long. I hope you had a nice time."

"No, no, no, Mrs. Hamilton. Thank you, but leave me alone for now."

"Your gentleman friend . . . ?" Mrs. Hamilton glanced at Bruce, then stared at him. "Aren't you Bruce Steinbicker? Oh, my word, how I love your show. I watch it all the time."

Bruce smiled. "Thank you."

"Mrs. Hamilton! Please!" said Roberta.

"Would you autograph my copy of *TV Week* for me?"

"I'd be glad to," said Bruce.

"Not now, Mrs. Hamilton. I have to go to the bathroom. Right now. I'll call."

"But, dear . . . ?"

Roberta slipped past her and dodged into the house. After Bruce bestowed a charming smile on the smitten Mrs. Hamilton, he followed.

Roberta collapsed onto her couch and Bruce settled into the armchair at right angles.

She rubbed her forehead with the back of her hand. "My God! That woman!"

"She means well," said Bruce.

"Busybody." Roberta leaned back against the soft cushions. "You said you're staying at Chris Wrentham's guesthouse. He's one of my student advisees. And you said he's taking care of your boat?"

Bruce raised an eyebrow, a gesture his fans Twittered about. "I'm not sure I understand."

"I know *I* don't understand," said Roberta.

"Chris is a longtime friend of mine. Funny guy, real comedian." Bruce smiled. "We were buddies in prep school. Never serious. A

240

big practical joker. Now he owns a software development company and," he looked modest, "I act."

"You loaned him your boat," said Roberta. "Someone held me captive on your boat. Someone planned the whole thing in great detail."

"I didn't lend him my boat." Bruce shook his head. "Couldn't have been Chris."

"It took someone time to stock the boat with two weeks' supply of food, and remove the radio, life jackets, flares—every possible means of communication or escape."

"Jee-zus. I didn't realize they'd stripped my boat."

"Not exactly stripped, since it was stocked with two weeks' worth of food."

"I didn't lend him my boat," Bruce said again. "He loaned me his guesthouse."

"In exchange for your boat?"

"No, of course not. He promised to keep an eye on it."

"Well, he went back on his promise. No one came near your boat the entire time I was stuck on it. Unless," she flung her arms out, "he was involved in kidnapping me."

"He couldn't have been. According to his wife, he's been attending some weeklong conference off Island."

"According to his wife?"

"Since I'm staying in his guesthouse I see her all the time. How in hell am I going to get my equipment back?"

"I'm more concerned with who did it," said Roberta.

"Why would Chris want to kidnap you?"

"I can't imagine. He's a straight-A student, and I was about to publish a paper based on his work."

"He doesn't need a graduate degree," said Bruce. He's got a Ph.D. in computer science and taught at some prestigious university."

"He's working on a master's in sociology."

"What's the subject of his paper?"

"My paper, actually. It's based on his work. It was on the inter-marriage of white settlers and Wampanoags on Martha's Vineyard." Roberta took a deep breath. She'd heard a faint echo of Victoria Trumbull's voice, *Plagiarism.*"

"Interesting subject," said Bruce.

"Unfortunately, because I was imprisoned on your boat, the paper won't be published this year."

"There's always next year," said Bruce.

"Actually, there isn't. My tenure approval depended on that paper and two others I was working on."

"What's so important about tenure?"

Roberta smiled. "That's something I thought about the entire time—the importance of tenure. And you're right. What *is* so important about tenure?"

Bruce's cell phone rang with the theme song from *Family Riot,* his show. He answered.

"Jonah who? How'd you get my number?" Pause. "Yeah. I was staying in his guesthouse." Long pause. "What in hell are you talking about?" Long, long pause. Bruce's face turned red. "Thanks, I guess," he said, and disconnected.

"What was that all about?"

"A woman named Jodi?"

"Oh my God!" gasped Roberta. "What is going on?"

"Chris is in the hospital. Some dog found him washed up on the beach."

"Whaaat?!"

"I've got to go. Are you going to be okay?"

"Mrs. Hamilton will take care of me."

"Heaven forbid," said Bruce. "I'll come back later and explain." He added, with a smile, "We have a lot to talk about. You still want to go to the police?"

When Victoria arrived home shortly after noon, Robert was stacking wood neatly on the woodpile. A truckload of wood had been dumped nearby.

"Good afternoon, Robert."

"How're you doing, Miz Trumbull," he greeted her. "You got a touch of sun."

"I've been out on the water," Victoria said.

He fished his cigarette makings out of various pockets and rolled, patted, licked, and lit one. That critical task finished, he said, "You must've got up pretty early."

"You get up even earlier. Every day."

He went back to wood stacking, the cigarette dangling from his lip.

Victoria continued out to the garden to see what she could find for lunch.

Late tomatoes were still ripening on her staked-up vines. She picked one and found a cucumber under the squash leaves. This had been a good year for her garden.

During lunch, she wrote a few notes for her column and checked her calendar. Another lecture was scheduled for tonight. So far, attending lectures hadn't helped her at all to identify either a killer or a potential victim.

After being out on the water all morning, she didn't really feel like going out again. The thought of a drink in front of the parlor fire with Elizabeth and with McCavity in her lap was much more appealing. But before Elizabeth came home, Victoria took a long, hot bath, dressed in her green plaid suit, and was ready to go.

After the storm of the day before, the evening was cool and dry and the sky was full of stars. While Elizabeth was bringing the car up to the west step, Victoria gathered up her sweater and her cloth bag.

The lecture was at the Chilmark Community Center, a

twenty-minute ride. Victoria settled into her seat, pleased to have a long drive on a pleasant evening in the company of her granddaughter.

"What's tonight's lecture?" asked Elizabeth.

"Frank Hopkins is speaking on the Island's geology."

"There'll be a crowd."

Victoria nodded. "I was so sure a visiting professor would attend one of the lectures, and equally sure the killer would attend, hoping to identify a professor victim."

"At least it's been informative," said Elizabeth. "Is this too much air for you? I can close the window."

"The breeze feels good." Victoria settled into her seat and looked out at the passing lights of houses along the way. She knew the histories of most of them, when they were built and by whom, and who'd lived in them over the years.

Elizabeth interrupted her thoughts. "How many lectures does this make, Gram?"

"Too many. One more, and that will be all. It seemed a good idea when I thought of it. Now, I just don't know."

"Maybe you'll get lucky tonight, Gram."

Perhaps it was a lucky evening. The lecture was well attended. Victoria knew most of the fifty or so people. Mrs. Hamilton, Roberta Chadwick's neighbor was there. So was Robert, her part-time helper, dressed in clean jeans and a white dress shirt. He looked quite presentable, except for his usual two-day growth of beard.

Before they took their seats, Victoria said to him, "Getting up so early, you won't have much time to sleep."

"I nap after I deliver the papers." Robert's voice always sounded weary. "Good speaker." He nodded at Frank, who was approaching the lectern.

The Island's geology was an interesting subject to Victoria, even though she felt Frank didn't know as much about the Island as she did. After all, she'd known him since he was in diapers.

After the talk there were the usual questions. When did the glacier create the Island? (Twenty thousand years ago.) Where did all the varicolored rocks come from? (The northeast, from Connecticut and New Hampshire and even Canada.) Why are Chilmark and Aquinnah so hilly while the center of the Island is so flat? (Up-Island is where the glacier bulldozed rocky moraine and West Tisbury is where sand that was washed out of the moraine was deposited.)

She could have answered those questions. But two men she didn't know asked questions she didn't even understand.

One identified himself as a visiting professor from India. He asked a question about Pleistocene ostracods.

For the enlightenment of a puzzled audience, including Victoria, Frank explained that ostracods are common tiny crablike creatures with shells that look like miniature clams. To the professor, he said, "See me later and I'll give you a reprint on the subject."

The second man was a professor from MIT who was studying the movement of sand along coastal beaches.

After the lecture, Victoria made a point of talking to each of the two professors. Both were visiting the Island, neither had family with him, both planned to be away from home for an extended period. The professor from India was staying at a bed-and-breakfast, the MIT professor was staying at the Mansion House, both in Vineyard Haven.

On their way home, Victoria dozed, lulled by the pleasant drive. The lights of an approaching car flashed past. The dark road continued to unroll ahead of them.

She awoke as they were passing the Allen Sheep Farm. "Sorry, I didn't mean to drop off."

"You've had a long day," Elizabeth said. "Looks as though you identified two possible victims tonight, Gram."

"Possibly," said Victoria. "I'm afraid I've been on a wild-goose chase, hoping to find victims and killer attending a lecture. It's been a waste of time."

"Mrs. Hamilton is relieved that Roberta is safe."

"Roberta can sleep in her own bed tonight."

"Your handyman cleans up pretty well. I never thought I'd see him attending a lecture."

"He's got a good mind," said Victoria. She gazed out the window at the passing darkness. Trees, two-dimensional stage settings flashed past, lit up by Elizabeth's headlights for a brief second. "I think the week on the boat was good for Roberta."

"A sort of desert health spa treatment?"

"More like a retreat. It gave her time to think about what's important."

CHAPTER 32

The next morning the sky was a brilliant autumnal blue, washed clean. The only signs of the storm two days ago were the fallen branches, some quite large, that the wind had torn off the old maple trees.

Victoria had called Casey as soon as she got home from the lecture, and Casey set up a meeting at the state police barracks with Sergeant Smalley and Dr. Killdeer, the forensic scientist.

While she waited for Casey to arrive, Victoria walked around her property with a basket, gathering sticks for kindling and breaking up what branches she could. The rest she carted to the sawbuck, where Robert would cut them.

She was still lugging branches when Casey arrived.

"I'll wash up and be right with you," said Victoria. "I lost track of time."

Joel Killdeer was already at the barracks. Victoria and Casey, Dr. Killdeer, and Sergeant Smalley moved into the conference room and Victoria took her seat at the head of the table.

Trooper Tim Eldredge set a tray of coffee and doughnuts on the table. Smalley poured, passed around mugs, then straightened his yellow pad on top of a thick manila folder.

"We'd like to hear what you have to report, Mrs. Trumbull."

Victoria clasped her hands on the table. "At last night's lecture, two visiting professors identified themselves, one from India and one from MIT. Neither is here with his family, and both are working on projects that will keep them away from home for a while."

Killdeer leaned back in his chair and folded his arms over his chest. "In other words, two ideal victims."

"I didn't spot anyone who looked like our killer."

Smalley picked up his pencil and began to draw what looked like lush tropical vegetation.

Killdeer snapped his gum. "Our killer won't stand out as anyone suspicious, Mrs. T. He'll look just like you or me. Well, not you."

"The professors?" asked Smalley.

Victoria reached into her cloth bag and brought out a business card. "Professor Ranjit Singh is a geology professor at Hyderabad University." She handed the card to Killdeer who looked at it and handed it on to Smalley.

"He's here alone?" asked Smalley.

"Yes. He expects to be on the Island for several weeks before he moves on to Block Island."

Killdeer chewed steadily.

"And the second professor?" asked Smalley.

"He's Professor Seymour Stevenson, on sabbatical from MIT. He's spending several weeks here on the Vineyard and then will work his way down to Florida."

"What about his family?"

"His wife is in Seattle with their daughter and a new grandson." Victoria toyed with her coffee mug, turning it in circles on the conference table. "I'm not sure how much help this has been."

"Fact is," said Killdeer, "you've identified two men who fit the victim profile. Our killer needs to kill again, and kill soon, based on what we've unearthed so far." He chewed for a moment. "Be nice to find him before he does."

Smalley continued to draw his tropical scene. He looked up. "Let's say we've got two potential victims. This raises several questions. How many lone professors in their fifties and sixties are visiting the Island now? Any thoughts on how the killer connects with them?"

"The victims have to eat," said Killdeer. "Given their age and the fact they're alone, they'll eat in restaurants and most likely find a pub where they can socialize. We should check on bars and pubs where there's some kind of evening activity."

"That narrows it down to Oak Bluffs and Edgartown," said Smalley, "the only towns with bars."

"We have to move, and move fast," said Killdeer. "Mrs. T identified two possible victims. Has the murderer targeted them, too?"

"If we're talking about putting a tail on the two," Casey said and shrugged, "we're talking a lot of man hours, and we don't have any to spare. I don't know what to tell you, John."

Smalley went back to his drawing and sketched a coconut hanging from one of the palm trees. He glanced at Killdeer. "How soon is he likely to kill again?"

Killdeer unwrapped a new stick of gum and folded his used gum in the foil wrapper. "My guess is within the next week. He's got to kill, and kill soon."

The others were silent.

Victoria said, "What if we warn the two visitors about the potential danger? That would save manpower."

"Do you know where they're staying?" asked Smalley.

"Both are staying in Vineyard Haven, Professor Stevenson at the Mansion House, Professor Singh at a bed-and-breakfast."

Smalley sketched in a second coconut, falling.

"I'll invite them both to lunch," said Victoria. "I'm sure a warning is all they need."

Smalley stood. "In the meantime, we'll dedicate what manpower we have to watching those two and identifying other potential victims. We need to get busy."

Victoria stood, too. "I wanted to ask about something."

"Yes, Mrs. Trumbull?" said Smalley.

"Walking around the campus, I noticed that the earliest burials were along Main Street. Didn't anyone see the killer disposing of bodies in such a public place?"

"We checked into that. Seven years ago, the Public Works Department opened up a trench to install a sewer line. About when the first body was buried."

"The next wasn't for another year," said Victoria.

"Right, but the ground would have been easy to dig for some time. No stones, no tree roots, no compacted soil."

"The next several were buried almost on the property line between the Ivy Green campus and the Unitarian Church."

"You're right on it, Mrs. Trumbull," said Smalley. "The church was connected to the sewer line about four years ago. The killer had more soft ground for his burials."

"By the time he dug up your outdoor classroom, he was getting more sure of himself," said Killdeer. "Got careless with his last three burials."

After she returned from the state police barracks, Victoria phoned the Mansion House. The professor from India, Ranjit Singh, was staying at a bed-and-breakfast, but Victoria didn't know which one. Perhaps Professor Stevenson would know.

"Professor Stevenson is not answering his phone, ma'am. Would you like to leave a message?"

"Please have him call me right away," Victoria said. "It's important." She gave her phone number.

She didn't want to stray too far from her phone, yet she needed to go out to her garden. This was one of the few times she wished she had a cell phone. Robert would be here soon, and she wanted him to buy gas for the mower and to remind him not to put the grass clippings on the far bin. The compost in that bin was ready to spread on the garden.

She decided the answering machine would pick up the return call from Professor Stevenson, and went out to the vegetable garden to harvest beets. The tops had died down and the roots were the size of lemons, perfect for winter storage.

Robert drove up in the rusted white station wagon he used to pick up the newspapers from the paper boat.

"Sorry I'm late, Mrs. T. Customer complaints."

"What could they possibly complain about?"

Robert sighed and got out of the car. "Rough weather. Some of the papers got wet. They want dry papers."

Victoria always marveled at his voice, which was dejection personified. She imagined that Eeyore, the stuffed donkey in *Winnie-the-Pooh*, might sound like Robert. "Surely they don't blame you?"

Robert shrugged. "Who else are they going to blame?" He opened the back of the car and brought out two battered five-gallon plastic buckets. "Washed up on the beach. Want them?"

"Yes, thank you. I like to use them for compost."

"Figured. I'll put them by the bins."

Victoria instructed him about the grass clippings and gas, and he nodded.

Like many Islanders, he worked at a series of jobs and seemed well educated, and like too many, he had a drinking problem. Some mornings he reeked of the previous night's intake, other mornings he reeked of breath mints. However, he worked hard, didn't talk much, and accepted in a surprisingly gracious way what she was able to pay him.

Victoria finished harvesting the row of beets, snipped off the dried tops, and dropped them into her basket. These would last her well into the winter.

The phone was ringing as she went into the kitchen. She hurried to answer. "Hello!"

"Mrs. Trumbull? Seymour Stevenson returning your call."

"Thank you for calling back." Victoria moved her chair next to the table in the cookroom and sat down with the phone. "We met last night at the geology lecture."

"I remember, of course, Mrs. Trumbull. How can I help you?"

"I'd like to invite you and Professor Singh to lunch. But I don't know where he's staying."

"I do. He's at the Foghorn Inn on Upper Main Street." He paused, and Victoria imagined a fleeting grin. "We two lone academic souls compared notes and had planned to get together tomorrow for lunch."

"Come to my house, then." Victoria gave him directions. "I'll call Professor Singh, but if I can't reach him, would you mind?"

"Of course. Tomorrow at noon. I look forward to getting to know the eminent poet, Victoria Trumbull."

Victoria hung up with a smile.

From Upper Main Street to the far side of Woodbine (Poison Ivy) Hall, from Greenleaf, the side street nearest town to the Unitarian Church, the Ivy Green campus was a shambles. Altogether, eleven bodies had been unearthed, ten located by Brownie, the sniffer dog.

Thackery Wilson surveyed the once peaceful grounds now pitted with nearly a dozen open graves. Victoria stood beside him. Classes had continued, despite the constant sound of shovels and police radios.

Victoria's class was working on a small book of poetry that she intended to have published. Every one of the poems was special, the kind of poetry she loved to read and reread and think about. She was amazed at the depth of feeling these children, her students, could distill into words, universal feelings, not self-centered navel gazing. Despite the disruption of the search for corpses, Brownie's frenetic barking signaling yet another discovery, and voices shouting, her students had concentrated on their work and she was proud of them. A few had worked the theme of sudden death into their poetry. One had written a limerick on a dog, clearly patterned after Brownie. Thackery and she walked along the narrow lanes between open graves.

"Is that it?" asked Thackery, not expecting an answer. "They've checked every square foot of the campus. There's no place else to bury a body."

"There's room in the cellar of Woodbine Hall," said Victoria, then felt ashamed of herself for making light of the situation. "Dr. Killdeer expects the murderer to strike again soon."

"I can't stand much more," said Thackery, wiping his hand across his forehead. "I want it all to be over."

"I don't blame you," said Victoria. She leaned down, picked up a hacked root that she'd almost stumbled over, and tossed it into the grave they were passing on their right. "You must be relieved to have Dr. Price finally approved as a faculty member."

"Such nonsense," muttered Thackery.

"His presence will certainly be a draw."

"I want it to be over," said Thackery.

They had to make a jog to the right to avoid a pit directly ahead of them.

"Once the police are finished here, you'll be able to have the graves filled in and the campus leveled."

"And who'll pay for it?" Thackery kicked a stone into a nearby pit.

"You could have a work party for the entire Island. You could charge so much per hour for the privilege of filling in the graves, like Tom Sawyer whitewashing his aunt's fence. Wonderful publicity for the college, and it will make people feel it's their own college."

"Last thing I want," muttered Thackery.

"You'll probably make the national news."

They'd reached their goal, the grave at the edge of the campus abutting Upper Main Street into which Professor Bigelow had fallen.

"Curious. Why was he cutting across campus in the dark like that?" asked Victoria. "Surely he knew what this looked like." She waved her arm around the giant waffle iron with its six-foot-deep pits.

"I don't want to discuss Bigelow. In case the man files legal action of some kind, I simply want to see where he fell."

"Wasn't it lucky that Robert, the newspaper delivery man found him? He does some gardening work for me."

"The Island's version of a street person. Drink. Down on his uppers," said Thackery. "Bigelow would have gotten himself out eventually."

"I don't know about that," said Victoria. "He was suffering from shock, and shock can kill."

"Insufferable man. Serves him right." Thackery kicked another stone into a grave.

"I can't imagine what could have shocked him," said Victoria.

CHAPTER 33

The two professors parked their green rental car under the Norway maple. Victoria ushered them into the parlor.

"A delightful house, Mrs. Trumbull," said Seymour Stevenson, the MIT professor. "Thanks so much for inviting us for lunch."

"It must be difficult being away from home for such a long period," Victoria said as they seated themselves, Victoria in her wing chair, Professor Stevenson in the rocker, and Professor Ranjit Singh on the stiff couch. "Especially for you, Dr. Singh. Do you have children?"

Professor Singh clasped his hands over his ample stomach. "Oh, yes," he said. "I have three daughters. All are grown and married to fine young men."

"And your wife?"

"She is staying with my youngest daughter, who is about to have her first child." He smiled, showing a gold tooth.

"Your first grandchild?" asked Victoria.

"Oh, no. This will be my fifth."

"And I understand your wife is with your daughter and new grandchild in Seattle, Professor Stevenson."

They talked about grandchildren and Victoria bragged about her own granddaughter for an appropriate amount of time, then she led them to the cookroom and brought out the chicken salad she'd made earlier.

After they'd eaten and talked more about families, about India, about Professor Singh's study of ostracods and Professor Stevenson's study of sand transport, they were on a first-name basis.

Victoria pushed her plate back and stood. "Coffee for you, Ranjit? Seymour?"

"Oh, yes," said Professor Singh. "If it's no trouble."

"Love some," said Professor Stevenson, also standing. "Can I help?"

"You can bring in the mugs and sugar and cream . . ."

"Glad to."

When the coffee was poured, sugared, and creamed, Victoria said, "I had a special reason for inviting you."

"Oh, certainly." Professor Singh set his coffee mug down. "Whatever I can do to help, Mrs. Trumbull, that is, Victoria. It will be my pleasure."

"A special reason?" asked Professor Stevenson.

"We are concerned about a series of murders on the Island," said Victoria, "the work of a serial killer."

"How unfortunate. How horrible," said Professor Singh, leaning forward.

"The first seems to date back seven years," said Victoria, "and the most recent was in mid-August."

"What is your involvement, Victoria?" asked Professor Stevenson.

"I found the first body." Victoria glanced out of the window at the church spire in the distant town.

"Really!" exclaimed Professor Singh. "How very distressing. How appalling."

"How many victims have there been?" asked Stevenson.

"The groundkeeper's dog, Brownie, found ten more bodies after the first that I found."

Professor Singh held up his pudgy hands. "Terrible. Just terrible."

Professor Stevenson asked, "Have the victims been identified?"

"All but two," said Victoria. "They were tenured professors at various colleges and universities."

Both men were silent.

"The police believe the killer may be a frustrated scholar who was denied tenure," said Victoria.

Professor Stevenson stroked his chin. "The tenure process can be stressful."

"The killer wishes to even the score," said Professor Singh, nodding. "I see."

"We're concerned that any visiting professor far from home may be in danger."

"You think, Victoria, that we should be aware of a too friendly stranger?" asked Professor Singh.

"I do," said Victoria.

"This is most interesting, Victoria," said Professor Stevenson. "Last night a man at the Tidal Rip invited me to go surfcasting with him early Friday morning."

"Who was he?" asked Victoria.

"He was well-known, I'd say. At least at the Tidal Rip. The bartender drew him a draft beer before he asked. Everyone called him Rabbit."

" 'Rabbit'?" asked Victoria.

"I didn't ask him how he got that name."

"How did he happen to invite you to go fishing?"

"He sat next to me at the bar, asked if I was visiting the Island. I said I was. We got to talking. Nice guy. Seemed well educated. I told him about my research on coastal beaches. He said he'd bet I was a fisherman. I told him I love fishing, but I didn't bring gear with me. He promised to lend me a surf rod and reel."

"When are you going?"

"He's picking me up around three in the morning."

"Fishing is a route throughout the world to fast friendships," said Professor Singh.

Victoria nodded.

"Ranjit's right. Fishing leads to good friendships. I'm sure his invitation is completely innocent, but I'll keep on the alert." Professor Stevenson looked at his watch. "I'm afraid I have an appointment with the outgoing tide, Victoria. Thank you so much. This has been a delightful break. I appreciate the warning."

"As do I," said Professor Singh, getting up and bowing to Victoria. "I will most certainly heed your advice."

Victoria went with them to the door and watched them get into the green Ford. She hurried back into the house and called Casey.

"The name Rabbit means nothing to me," she said. "But someone needs to follow Professor Stevenson and whoever meets him at the hotel Friday morning."

"I'll tell Smalley what you said. It could be nothing. A visiting professor gets invited to go fishing. Happens all the time. You think that raises a red flag?"

"Dr. Killdeer says pressure is building up in the killer and he must kill again. Soon," Victoria said. "He's preying on tenured professors and I've found one who's been invited to go out in the middle of the night with a complete stranger. Yes, that raises a red flag."

"Did you warn the professors?"

"I did."

"That should be enough. They're grown men."

"So were the other eleven victims."

"I'll call Smalley, but he's short of manpower, too."

After Victoria hung up, she paced back and forth, thinking. If she were the killer, she would do exactly what this man named Rabbit did. Befriend a stranger at a bar, learn that he's a college professor away from home, invite him to go fishing at night. The killer might simply ask his victim if he wants to see the graves at the college, quickly wrap a rope around his neck, and push him into the grave.

Who could she get to help her with a stakeout?

———

Howland Atherton dropped by later that afternoon.

Victoria greeted him warmly.

"I'm taking Bowser and Rover to the vet's for their shots and thought I'd say hello."

"Do you have time for coffee?" she asked.

"I'll make time."

She started a fresh pot, and they seated themselves at their usual places at the cookroom table.

"I haven't seen you for several days," said Victoria while they waited for the coffee to brew. "Do you have news I can use for this week's column?"

"I do." Howland was wearing his baggy gray sweater and tan slacks. He pulled off his sweater and flung it over the chair at the end of the table. "The dogs found a man washed up on the beach this morning."

"Dead?" Victoria asked.

"Not quite. He's at the hospital now. He seems in fairly good shape except he doesn't know his name or where he came from. He's a redhead with a bad sunburn."

"Is he a fisherman swept off his boat in the storm?"

"He doesn't look like a fisherman," said Howland. "His hands aren't calloused. He was wearing expensive sportswear and a good wool jacket. He may have come off a yacht."

"That storm hit suddenly. Elizabeth and I barely made it to the Vineyard Haven harbor."

"What were you doing out in it?"

Victoria told him about her adventure and the follow-up rescue of Roberta Chadwick.

"How did she end up on the boat?"

"I have no idea."

The coffee finished with a last few gurgles. Howland got up and returned with two steaming mugs.

"What about the castaway you found?" asked Victoria.

"Hope was on duty when we got him to the hospital and she said his amnesia is probably temporary. He's suffering from exposure and dehydration. She thinks he'll be fine."

"What a strange experience that must be," said Victoria, "to awaken in the hospital and not know who you are or how you got there."

At the hospital, Hope, Victoria's grandniece, pulled aside the curtain surrounding the redheaded castaway. He'd been rehydrated and the sloughed-off skin of his face had been cleaned off. He turned out to be quite nice looking.

"How's the patient?" Hope asked. "Need anything?"

"Just want to know who I am."

"It'll come back. Don't push it." She thrust a thermometer into his mouth, checked his pulse, took his blood pressure, and wrote something on her clipboard.

"I remember being on a boat," he mumbled around the thermometer.

"We figured as much." She removed the thermometer and recorded his temperature. "A fishing boat?"

"A sailboat. I was up at the bow. I slipped and remember falling." He sat up and winced. "How long have I been here?"

"Only a few hours. The ambulance brought you in this morning, and it's a little after two now."

"When can I be discharged?" He lay back down again.

"As far as your physical condition, you'd probably be kept for observation but we can't let you go until we can identify you."

"Thanks. That sounds weird. 'Identify you.' Makes me feel like a dead body."

"You almost were," said Hope. "Get some rest now. Dinner's at five-thirty and the meals here are pretty good."

———

On the sailboat, O'Malley was trying to get through to the communications center on his handheld radio.

"You're breaking up, sir. All I hear is 'body.'"

"Lambert's Cove!" O'Malley shouted into his cell phone, as if that would make the reception clearer.

"Body off Lambert's Cove."

"Yes!" shouted O'Malley.

"Unidentified man found at Paul's Point, sir."

"Dead?" asked O'Malley.

"Can't hear you, sir."

"Hell!" shouted O'Malley. "Is he dead or alive?"

"No information, sir. He was taken to the hospital. Your name, sir?"

O'Malley disconnected. "Someone found a man on the beach at Paul's Point and took him to the hospital."

"I've got to see what those characters did to my boat," said Price. "They got the anchor line fouled in the prop."

Jodi was hunched over in the cockpit, mumbling.

"We'd better get her to shore," said O'Malley. "Your boat can wait."

Price scowled. "Those idiots."

"Who are you talking about? Your friend may be dead and Jodi's a basket case. Come on, help her into my boat. We'll get back to my place and try to figure out what's going on."

As Howland was leaving, Victoria asked, "Do you have any plans for this evening?"

Howland paused at the door. "What do you have in mind?"

"A stakeout."

Howland laughed. "I've got to get to the vet's. I'll stop by on my way back and we can discuss this stakeout."

———

Price and O'Malley, between them, took turns carrying Jodi up the path from the boathouse. At the top of the cliff they set her down, and, one on either side, walked her to the house.

"You don't need to do this," mumbled Jodi, her voice broken and scarcely audible. "I can walk."

"No, you can't," said O'Malley.

They marched her into the living room, laid her on the couch, O'Malley put a blanket over her, and Price brought out the bottle of Scotch.

"One of us should stay with her," said O'Malley. "The other needs to go to the hospital to identify the man who washed up on the beach, dead or alive."

"I'll go," said Price. "If it's Chris, I can identify him." He nodded toward Jodi. "Sorry to lay this on you."

"One of these days, you'll have to tell me what this is all about," said O'Malley. "Take my car. The keys are in the ignition."

After Price left, O'Malley poured a half-glass of Scotch. He poured it slowly and sniffed its fragrance, held the glass up to the light and let the sun shine through the golden liquid. He lifted it to his lips. Before it touched them he pushed the glass away and set it down firmly on the kitchen counter. He took a deep breath.

He picked up the glass again and took it into the living room, where Jodi was sitting up.

For a brief moment, he watched her sip.

"I'm sorry," she whispered. "Thanks."

He turned away. "I'm fixing an omelet. Think you can eat something?"

"I guess I'm hungry." She set the glass down, scarcely touched. "I've got to talk to Jonah, and I dread it."

"Boyfriend?"

"Husband. He's taking care of our boys."

O'Malley didn't even get as far as the kitchen. "You were on a sailboat for a week with those two guys?" He sat down in the chair

262

next to the fireplace and raised his eyebrows. "What did Jonah think about that?"

"Oh, God!" She pressed her hands over her eyes. "What can I say!"

"You're welcome to use my phone to call Jonah. You'd better let him know you're safe."

Jodi tossed the blanket off and swiveled around, bare feet on the floor.

"Would it help to talk to me? I'll bet you a hundred bucks I've been through worse scrapes than what you've got yourself into." He fished out his wallet, withdrew a dollar bill, and placed it on the coffee table under her glass.

She smiled.

O'Malley stretched, loosening his back muscles. "You need to tell someone, and it might as well be me."

She glanced away, smile gone.

"Think about it while I'm making the omelet. I'll keep your secrets safe. After you tell me, you can decide what to say to Jonah." He grinned. "Maybe you'll win the bet."

CHAPTER 34

Price took some time figuring out the eight gears on the convertible, but once he was on the dirt road leading away from O'Malley's place with the top down and the wind brushing the trees on either side, his spirits lifted.

It was hard to think of Chris as dead. One instant you were living and thinking about breakfast, the next you were dead. For him to have been swept overboard, knocked around on the rocks, flung onto the shore, and survive, would have to be a miracle.

Price turned onto the paved Lambert's Cove road. He had a brief moment of appreciation of the changing colors, the rich reds and rusts of beetlebung and oak, the orange and yellow of sassafras, the scarlet of poison ivy.

After that brief moment, he thought again of Chris, the wild man with a wacky sense of humor.

I've spent too much time searching for the dead, Price mused. A dead father, now a dead friend.

He'd been so excited when he'd heard about Professor Price. Was he so desperate for a father figure? Setting himself up for yet another disappointment? It was time to give up. The kidnapping debacle had shaken him badly. The idea had been stupid. Was it going to end with Chris dead and Jodi gone crazy?

He moved his hands high up on the steering wheel of this incredible car. What gear was he in, third? Fourth?

How had Professor Chadwick weathered the storm? He slapped his hands on the wheel. Prison. He was going to prison. Their research papers had seemed important a week ago. How important were they now?

He shifted down through gears to pass around a truckload of firewood.

A mile or so later he turned from the Lambert's Cove road onto State Road, followed it through Vineyard Haven, across the Lagoon Pond bridge into Oak Bluffs, and turned into the new hospital's parking lot.

He looked down at himself. Pretty scruffy. He took a deep breath and strode through the main entrance.

"May I help you?" A pretty woman wearing an elaborate hat was at the reception desk, probably the age of his mother. She smiled, and her face lit up.

"I'm inquiring about a man who was brought in this morning, apparently fell off a boat," Price began.

She looked questioningly at him.

"I think I may know who he is." Price stopped, not knowing what to say. He finally blurted out, "Is he okay?"

"We're not supposed to tell anything about a patient's condition. Privacy laws, you know."

"Well . . ." Price shifted uncomfortably.

"Must be a full moon tonight," the receptionist said with a laugh. "We always get weird stuff on the full moon."

"Oh?" said Price.

"This morning they brought in some elderly gentleman who fell into a grave and thinks he's dead, and a little while later they bring in this man some dogs found washed up on the shore."

"Is he dead?" Price asked.

"I don't know. Did you want to see him?"

"If I can."

"I'll check with Nurse Hope." She swiveled her chair around to make the call. After a brief conversation, she said, "Hope will be here in just a moment."

In a short while he heard the squeak of rubber soles moving swiftly down the corridor, and a clear voice said, "Hi, there! Need help?"

Hope was a tall, slender woman with long, dark hair, large dark eyes, and a mischievous expression that seemed to be permanent. She was wearing a blue scrub suit, a shirt with V-neck and long pants.

Price cleared his throat and said, "I heard that a man is here in the hospital who was washed up on the beach."

"That's true," said Hope.

Price shifted uneasily. "A friend of mine, Chris Wrentham, fell off a sailboat during yesterday's storm, and we think he may have ended up on Paul's Point."

"You know we can't give you any information on our patients," said Hope.

"I know. Privacy laws. Can you tell me, is he alive?"

"He's alive," said Hope.

"May I see him?"

"Afraid not. At least, not yet," said Hope, folding her arms over her chest. "He doesn't know who he is."

"I may be able to identify him," said Price.

"Sorry about that. We want his memory to return before he has visitors."

"I understand the privacy rules, but maybe you can help. My friend is a redhead with a bad sunburn."

Hope smiled. "I've seen a man around here answering that description."

"Thanks. Thanks a million!" Price suddenly felt lighter, freer. "Let me give you my phone number." The receptionist handed him a pad. He scribbled his cell number on it and handed it to Hope. "I don't expect you to call me, but if he gets his memory back?"

"I'll see that he gets it," said Hope.

Price went out of the wide front doors into a brighter world. The man could only be Chris and he was alive.

The man was sleeping soundly. Hope turned on the light over his bed and he awoke with a start. "Where in hell . . . Oh, yeah." He sat up.

"Dinner's on the way," said Hope. "Do you want to use the toilet, get cleaned up?"

He rubbed his eyes. "Okay if I get up?

"Of course. There's nothing wrong with you. At least, not that I can see." She wrapped the blood pressure sleeve around his arm. "You had a pretty good nap. How are you feeling?"

"Okay, I guess. Sore. I remember hitting the beach and crawling out of the surf."

"Good plan, that."

"I'm Chris," he said suddenly. "My name's Christopher," he added. "Christopher Wren, the architect!" He must have seen her expression because he laughed. "I'm kidding. I'm Chris Wrentham. That's who I am. I've remembered, thank God!" Hope unwound the blood pressure sleeve, Chris slid off the bed, grabbed Hope in a bear hug, and danced her around. "It's awful to not know who you are."

"Good," said Hope, pushing him away. "Remember anything else? Do you live here on the Island?"

He frowned.

"Never mind. Don't forget that you need to use the toilet."

There was the sound of a cart being wheeled down the hall. It stopped by his door.

"Here's your dinner. You're in luck. Steak."

Hope hurried to the nurses' station and looked up Christopher Wrentham in the phone book. A listing in Vineyard Haven. She put in a call to Doc Jeffers.

"Our patient remembers crawling out of the surf and his name, and he lives on Island," she said. "Want me to call the home number?"

"Does he recollect anything before that?"

"Not yet. He's having dinner now."

Doc Jeffers paused. "Any calls asking about him?"

"A man came in this morning," said Hope. "He was looking for a friend who fell off a sailboat, a redhead with sunburn."

"Sounds like our patient."

"I told him no visitors yet, Doc."

"Right. We'd better get more information from the patient before making any calls," said Doc Jeffers. "I'll stop by in a half hour. We're keeping him overnight?"

"We are," said Hope, and disconnected, wondering what the story behind her patient's present plight could be.

On the way back, Price had trouble keeping the convertible under the 45 mph speed limit. He sang a lusty sea chantey bellowing out the chorus that ended, "Oh for a life on the rolling sea!" at the top of his lungs, stretching out the "rolling" through three gears as he slowed before the turn into O'Malley's road. He was on the third rendition of the chantey by the time he skidded to a stop next to O'Malley's garage. He vaulted out of the convertible and raced into the house.

"Jodi!" he shouted as he opened the kitchen door.

The smell of Scotch hit him, and he smiled, thinking how low Jodi had been when he left, how O'Malley was nursing her with two or three, well, maybe four, fingers of Scotch, and how this news—Chris risen from the dead—was going to perk her up.

But when he moved into the living room he saw why the Scotch smell was so strong. The empty Macallan bottle was lying on its side on the coffee table next to two empty glasses. Jodi was asleep on the couch, snoring. A box of tissues was on the floor, crumpled used tissues dropped around it. O'Malley was sprawled in the chair that had been next to the fireplace and was now pulled up close to the Scotch bottle.

O'Malley looked up, eyes unfocused. "How're you doin', Price, my man?"

269

Price, prepared to blurt out the good news that Chris was alive, hesitated.

"Well, well, my man. I had my firsh drink in five years, seven months, three days, and . . ." He peered at his empty wrist. "Can't tell hours."

"My God!" said Price.

O'Malley pointed vaguely at the bookcase. "Behind the *Chicago Manual of Schtyle,* er, *Style.* Got more Macallan. The Macallan, that is."

"I'm so sorry!" Price exclaimed.

"Nothin' to be sorry about. We've been celebrating the late lamented Christopher Wren. A wake," said O'Malley. "Only she's asleep. Go ahead, hep yourself."

"Jodi?" Price asked.

"She tol' me all about the great caper." O'Malley looked serious. "Then she called her ol' man."

"She called Jonah?"

"Told *him* all about it."

"What did he say?"

"She passed out after a couple swallows. Had to finish it for her." A sly grin. "Can't waste good single malt Scotch, y'know."

"What did Jonah say?"

"Said he was gonna come pick her up."

CHAPTER 35

Bigelow, still feeling a bit shaky, fumbled along the corridor to the solarium, where he found himself an easy chair and settled into it. The hospital intended to keep him overnight for observation. Probably just as well. Have dinner and a night's sleep. Then return home on the paper boat early the next morning. Have to make arrangements to be discharged early. He'd get the delivery man who'd fished him out of the grave to give him a lift. He picked up a magazine from the table by his chair. He could see the print if he held it close to his nose. A fashion magazine. He dropped it back on the table with disgust. He had to find his glasses. That meant going back to the so-called campus. That meant ticks. He shuddered. He'd have to get someone to go down into that grave and search for the glasses.

"Mind if I join you?" A voice out of the myopic fog.

"Please," said Bigelow. "Forgive me, but I've lost my glasses and all I can see is that you're quite tall and you're a redhead. What are you in here for?"

"It's a long story, but the short of it is, I fell off a boat and some dogs found me washed up on the beach. Still trying to get my memory back, but at least I know my name." He held out a hand. "Chris Wrentham."

Bigelow held out his own and they shook. "Professor Phillip Bigelow."

Chris pulled up a chair close to Bigelow's and sat.

There was a hum of conversation coming from the other side of the sunny room, where a robed and slippered wheelchair-bound patient and several members of her family had gathered.

"Professor, eh? Where do you teach?" asked Chris.

"Cape Cod University."

"Interesting," said Chris, not recalling that he was taking a graduate course in sociology there. "Your field?"

"Military history." Bigelow went into some detail about the courses he taught.

Chris listened attentively.

Bigelow finally came to the end of his discourse and asked, "Do you live on the Island or are you visiting?"

Chris scratched his forehead, where the sunburned skin itched. "I don't know where I live. They tell me my memory will come back. In the meantime, it's frustrating."

"I don't suppose you recall what you do for a living?"

"Bits and pieces," replied Chris. "Software development rings a bell, but damned if I know whether I'm the head of a Fortune 500 company or some flunky who shreds records."

"I'm sure it's the former," said Bigelow with rare tact. He glanced up. "Is someone heading this way? I hear footsteps."

Chris turned to look. "Hope. My nurse."

"Yes, mine, too. Excellent woman."

"Visitors' day for you two," said Hope. "My great aunt, Victoria Trumbull, is here with the head of Ivy Green College and one of his professors to see you, Professor Bigelow."

"That would be Thackery Wilson," said Bigelow, "along with Professor Trumbull. And the other professor?"

"I didn't get his name. Okay if I show them in? Auntie Vic brought one of her poetry books for you."

"I can hardly appreciate it until I find my glasses," grumbled Bigelow. "Show them in. I'll talk to them."

Hope turned to Chris. "There's a Mr. Henderson to see you. You okay with that?"

Chris shrugged. "Sure. I guess. His name doesn't ring a bell, but maybe he'll jog my memory."

Hope left, and shortly after, Victoria arrived, followed closely by Thackery and Professor Wellborn Price.

Thackery was acting like a kid dragged away from his baseball cards to Sunday school. His face was a scowl set off by thick horn-rimmed glasses. His fringe of hair curled untidily around his scalp.

Dr. Wellborn Price was dressed in his usual plaid shirt and jeans and was wearing a happy smile.

Chris went to fetch more chairs.

Professor Bigelow stood and held out his hand to the nearest fuzzy shape.

Victoria grasped it. "I was horrified to hear of your fall, Professor Bigelow. What a frightening experience. Are you all right?"

"I was badly shaken, as you can imagine," said Bigelow. "I seem to have recovered, though."

Chris pushed over three more armchairs.

Victoria glanced up. "Chris Wrentham! What a surprise to see you here. We thought you were attending a conference off Island."

Chris shrugged. "I should know your name, but I've lost my memory, temporarily, I understand."

"How did that happen? That is, if you know?"

"Fell off a boat and washed ashore."

"Good heavens, you're the man Howland's dogs found this morning. What were you doing on a boat?"

Chris shrugged again.

"You have a good strong constitution," Victoria said. "You'll be back to normal in no time." She turned away and murmured, "What *was* he doing on a boat? How curious."

Chris went back for a fourth chair and Victoria looked down at the book in her lap. "Professor Bigelow, I thought you might like this book of mine." She handed it to him.

"Thank you," said Bigelow, holding the book up close to his nose to read the title. He set it down. "Is that Thackery Wilson with you, Professor Trumbull? I didn't get the name of the other man."

"Wellborn Price," said Wellborn. He'd seated himself and was grinning at Bigelow, who obviously couldn't see his expression.

Bigelow opened his mouth and shut it again, his face pale.

"Understand you had a grave experience," said Wellborn, and laughed.

"Hardly something to laugh about," snorted Bigelow. "You haven't changed."

"Still alive, Bigelow, old boy, despite reports to the contrary." Wellborn laughed again.

Nurse Hope reappeared. "Mr. Wrentham, your Mr. Henderson is here."

Price strode into the room. Chris stood up, a blank expression on his face.

"Chris, my man! How're you doing?"

Victoria turned at his voice. "Price! Another surprise. When did you get back?"

Wellborn, too, stood abruptly and stared at Price, who, with his pale hair and bright blue eyes, was the spitting image of Wellborn as a young man.

"Back?" asked Price, not noticing Wellborn.

"From the conference?" asked Victoria, feeling somewhat unsure of herself at this point.

"Oh, back!" said Price.

"Price?" asked Bigelow, moving his head to face this new visitor. "Price Henderson?"

Wellborn, white hair and bright blue eyes, stood frozen.

"The same," said Price. "Who are you?"

"I am Professor Phillip Bigelow." He cleared his throat. "Professor of military history at Cape Cod University. Unusual first name, Price. A family name?"

"Sort of." Price was clearly uneasy under this scrutiny.

Victoria sat back, hands in her lap, and watched the scene unfold.

"My sister had a son named Price," said Bigelow.

Wellborn groaned, and Price glanced over at him, then did a double take. "I didn't get your name, sir."

"I'm Wellborn Price." He paused, clasped his arms under his chest, and closed his eyes briefly. "I teach economics at Ivy Green College." He opened his eyes again and smiled. "Thanks to our Professor Bigelow, here."

Price continued to stare at the familiar face. "I've signed up for your course." He, too, paused. "Sir."

"Price!" exclaimed Chris suddenly, running his hands over his hair. "It's coming back. I know you! Your sailboat. Jodi."

"Jodi?" Victoria glanced away from the unfolding scene and sat up straight. "What about Jodi?"

"Maybe we should continue the conversation outside?" said Price, looking away from Wellborn.

"Jodi was supposed to be attending the same meeting Chris and you were attending. And so was Roberta Chadwick," said Victoria.

"Roberta Chadwick?" said Bigelow, peering from one blurred speaker to another. "What about Roberta Chadwick?"

"She's my advisor." Chris beamed. "It's coming back! It's all coming back in a rush!" He twisted around. "Hope! Where's Hope?"

A man in the group on the other side of the solarium called out, "Press that button on the side of his chair, and she'll come right away."

"Thanks!" Price glanced away from the image of himself in twenty years and called back, "I hope we're not disturbing you."

"Not at all," said the man. "If you got any juice leftover from dinner, we can party. We brought a bottle of vodka." He held up a frosted-looking bottle.

"Sounds good." Chris scratched his forehead. "Come on over."

Price pressed the button on the side of Chris's chair.

"What about Jodi?" asked Victoria, glancing from Chris to Price.

"I don't exactly recall who she is," said Chris. "But it's coming back. Just the name so far. Sexy, I think."

"Roberta Chadwick was reported missing," Bigelow said.

"We found her," said Victoria.

"Found her?" asked Price, sitting forward. "Where did you find her?"

The group on the other side separated into three segments. One man wheeled the robed and slippered patient, another man carried two Cronig's grocery bags full of something, and three women, all giggling, followed along.

"Thought we'd join you," the wheeler said. "This is our mom, Audrey. Alzheimer's."

"I've got the booze," said the bag carrier. "And, ta dah! Potato chips and dip."

"We brought napkins," said the women's contingent. "I think Hope can find us some of that pineapple juice, or whatever."

"Someone call?" said Hope, appearing. She stopped abruptly. "What do you think you're doing?"

"Party!" cried out Mom from her wheelchair.

Chris enveloped Hope in yet another bear hug. "I've remembered Jodi—hubba, hubba."

Hope extricated herself and pointed to the bag-carrying, bottle-wielding group. "You will leave, immediately. Out!" She pointed to the door.

Murmurs of protest.

"Party?" asked Mom.

"Auntie Vic, what is going on?"

"I have only a sketchy idea," said Victoria. "Chris Wrentham, Price Henderson, and Jodi Paloni were supposed to be attending a conference off Island with Roberta Chadwick."

"Roberta Chadwick!" said Chris. "No wonder that name sounded familiar. It's all coming back."

276

Price glanced again at Wellborn and said to the others, "We really need to continue this discussion outside."

Hope, fists on her hips, watched as the family gathered up scattered belongings and began their exodus from the solarium.

"If the rest of you will excuse me," she said, getting down to business, "I have to take Mr. Wrentham's and Professor Bigelow's blood pressure and temperature."

"Party?" asked Mom as they wheeled her away.

CHAPTER 36

Joel Killdeer, the forensic scientist, was in Woodbine Hall, going over reports and making notes. He scratched his head, put his pen down, leaned back in his chair, crossed his arms, and stared at the cracked window. He chewed his gum with a steady, grim rhythm.

Brownie was curled up at his feet on a plush doggie bed bought especially for him at Good Dog Goods.

Tim, the state trooper who'd been assigned to help Killdeer, looked up from his own paperwork. "You okay, boss?"

"Our man should have made a move before now."

Brownie sighed, opened his eyes, looked up, and shut them again.

"Maybe the garage corpse was his final victim. That was the only one never buried."

"Nope," said Killdeer. "He's going to kill again. He'll keep killing until we catch him. This bastard's meticulous about timing. Look at this." He set his chair down and shoved the papers he'd been working on toward Tim.

Tim picked up the papers. "What am I looking at?"

"We've got the timeline down pretty close. Look here." Killdeer pointed his pen at a series of numbers. "First death was one we dated back to seven years ago. Second death, five years ago. Then four, three, two-and-a-half. See? He's got to get his killing fix more often."

Brownie got to his feet, stretched, yawned, walked over to the front door, and stood there, staring at it.

"What makes a guy turn like that?" asked Tim. "I mean, I can understand how a guy gets into a fight in a bar and knifes someone in a rage, but killing like this? Like it's an obsession or something?"

"Serial killers apparently are genetically disposed to become psychopaths. A psychopath becomes a serial killer through a combination of lousy upbringing, frustration, and stress." Killdeer took the papers back from Tim. "The reason they're so difficult to catch is their victims seem to be picked at random, but in the killer's mind, he's being logical. Killer wants to rid the world of blue-eyed blondes, or prostitutes, or, like our man, college professors." He slapped the papers with the back of his hand. "Victim six, two years ago. Victim seven, one-and-a-half years ago. Then one year, then nine months. The poison ivy victim killed six months ago, the garage victim almost three months ago."

"Next one should be, like, now," said Tim.

"What I'm telling you, man."

"He's running out of time," said Tim.

"He's not. *We* are. He'll kill, kill, kill until he's stopped."

Brownie looked over his shoulder and whined. Killdeer stood. He went through Thackery Wilson's living room office to the front door and let Brownie out.

"He's supposed to have his leash on," Tim called out.

"Laws don't apply to our boy," said Killdeer, watching Brownie sniff a tree trunk.

Thackery had moved his work to Catbriar Hall, where Victoria held her classes. Killdeer was using the entire first floor as his forensics office.

He closed the door and rubbed his fingers up the oiled wood of the frame, across the decorative stained-glass inset of purple grapes and green leaves, along the twisted metal vine. "Such beauty," he said. "Made for just an ordinary home. Don't see stuff like this today."

"Sir?" asked Tim.

"Nothing," replied Killdeer.

"Come on, Brownie," said Killdeer, after Tim had left for the day. "We've got a job to do. Need to sniff out a corpse before it becomes a corpse."

Brownie looked up with sad eyes and wagged his tail.

"Hear me, dog?"

Tail thumped.

"All-night vigil. Might take a few all-nighters."

Brownie arose from his bed, stretched, yawned, and scratched himself.

"He's gotta strike soon. C'mon, boy." Killdeer gathered up a flashlight and blanket and went out into the gloom. As he closed the door behind him he touched the stained glass, which glowed in the last light of day.

"I can't believe you talked me into this, Victoria," said Howland as he walked with her out to his car. Except for his white station wagon, which seemed to have gathered up the starlight, the evening was dense black velvet, and chilly.

"There's a chance we can catch the killer tonight," said Victoria, shifting her cloth bag into her left hand.

"I don't like that 'we.' I want nothing to do with this caper. Have you told the police what you're doing?"

"Of course. Casey gave me a cell phone and showed me how to use it if I need backup."

"Great," said Howland. "The killer slips a noose around my neck and you're fumbling in your bag for a cell phone."

"Don't be ridiculous," said Victoria.

An icy dew had settled on the grass and on the car's windshield. The Milky Way was a bright gauzy scarf flung across the sky from horizon to horizon.

Victoria settled into the passenger seat.

"Explain to me what you have in mind," said Howland, after

he'd turned onto the Edgartown Road. "You were a bit sketchy this afternoon."

"First of all," Victoria said, "I have no intention of confronting the killer."

"Good," said Howland.

"I intend to watch the Mansion House, see who picks up Professor Stevenson at three o'clock, and follow them. They have to go right past the Ivy Green campus. A perfect setup for the killer."

"Suppose they do stop at the campus," said Howland, as he turned onto Old County Road.

"I'll call Casey," said Victoria.

"Not the state police?"

Victoria sat up straight. "I'm going through channels."

"If you call the police, Victoria, the police will race up Main Street, sirens wailing, surround your professor and his new friend, and discover the friend was simply showing the professor the place where eleven professors had been buried. The Island's latest sight-seeing attraction."

Victoria dug into her cloth bag for her hat and set it on her head. "You're right, of course. I've thought of that. We wait until the killer makes his move."

An ancient white station wagon pulled up in front of the Mansion House, and in the dim light shining from the hotel, Victoria could see surf rods on the roof carriers. Professor Stevenson scrambled down the steps of the hotel and climbed into the passenger seat, and the car took off heading up Main Street.

Howland had parked in an angled slot across the street from the hotel.

"We don't want to be too obvious," said Victoria.

Howland glanced at her in amusement. "You forget. I've been on a few stakeouts as DEA agent."

"Yes, of course." Victoria settled into the passenger seat and

Howland followed the station wagon, almost a twin to the one he was driving.

The car with the surf rods turned left onto Greenleaf Street, which bounded the Ivy Green campus on the town side.

"Just what I suspected," said Victoria.

"I'll go around the block and park in the Ivy Green faculty lot," said Howland. "We can walk from there to wherever Stevenson and this guy named Rabbit go."

The heater in the station wagon hadn't conquered the early morning chill, and to Professor Stevenson, the car seemed colder than the outside air after the warm hotel lobby. He shivered.

Rabbit greeted him. "Morning, Professor. You going to be warm enough?"

"I'll be fine."

After that, neither Rabbit nor Stevenson spoke for a few minutes. During the night a light frost had touched the dewy grass, and the car's headlights reflected from myriad stiff blades. An owl flew low and silently across the road.

"I hear the bluefish are running," Stevenson said.

"Right," said Rabbit. "Derby's on this month."

"I suppose it brings in a lot of anglers?"

"All over the world," said Rabbit. "So you're on Island doing research?"

"I'm spending a year studying coastal sand transport from here to Florida."

"Where do you teach?" asked Rabbit.

"MIT. I'm on sabbatical this year, doing my own research." Stevenson was well aware of Victoria Trumbull's warning. But Rabbit seemed like a pretty ordinary guy, at least, so far. "How'd you get the name 'Rabbit'?"

Rabbit laughed. "I was a sprinter in college and my name is Jack, so it morphed into Jack Rabbit."

A skunk wandered into the road and Rabbit braked hard. "Don't want to tangle with them," he said as four baby skunks tottered across behind their mother.

"Where'd you go to college?" asked Stevenson, when the skunks had reached the other side of the road.

"Harvard." He pronounced it "Hah-vud."

Stevenson laughed. "What's your field?"

"Astrophysics. Got a Ph.D."

"I'm impressed," said Stevenson. "Astrophysics and you're working as a carpenter?"

"You needn't be impressed. This Island has the most highly educated workforce in the world. Ph.D.'s all over the place working as landscapers, fishermen, farmers, carpenters, painters, you name it." Rabbit waved a hand at the trees arching over the road. "We want to live here and we don't much care whether we use those degrees or not." He checked the rearview mirror. "Someone else is up and about. Another crazy fisherman."

"Did you ever teach?" asked Stevenson, feeling a first twinge of anxiety. The serial killer had been a college professor at some time, Mrs. Trumbull had assured him.

"I taught for a while, got fed up with academic politics and the petty power struggles and quit. Carpentry is a lot less stressful. No one to bite your back."

"Tell me," said Stevenson.

Rabbit slowed the car. "We're about to pass our latest attraction, the site of mass burials. Care to take a side trip and see where they've dug up eleven bodies?"

"I heard about that." Stevenson felt a touch of fear.

"College professors," said Rabbit. "All eleven victims were college professors."

"So I heard." Stevenson's voice was tight. "And they haven't caught the killer yet."

"Nope. They probably won't until he kills again."

Stevenson said nothing.

They turned left onto Greenleaf Street. Rabbit pulled over to the side of the road and parked.

"Place is really dark," said Stevenson.

"The Island doesn't have much light pollution. Get to see the stars that way."

"Let's forget the sightseeing," said Stevenson. "I don't want to miss a minute of fishing."

"Scared?" asked Rabbit. He reached across Stevenson and opened the glove compartment. "Flashlight in here somewhere. Remember how it was when you were a kid listening to ghost stories? This is the grown-up version. Real scary stuff."

"Uh . . ." said Stevenson.

"It'll be fun. Won't be another chance like this."

"I appreciate your giving me a lift from the hospital at this hour of the morning," Bigelow said to the newspaper delivery man.

"No problem," said Robert. "No big deal." He took one hand off the wheel, and with the other, found cigarette papers in the well between the seats. One-handed, he detached a paper, filled it with tobacco, rolled a cigarette, licked the edge of the paper, and sealed it by pressing it against his chin.

Bigelow watched in awe.

Still one-handed, Robert stuck the cigarette onto his lower lip, produced a kitchen match from a shirt pocket, swiped his thumbnail against the tip to ignite it, and lit his cigarette, steering all the while left-handed. He transferred the steering responsibility to his left knee, opened the window, and tossed out the spent match. He started to close the window.

"I like the fresh air," said Bigelow.

"It's fresh, all right. Frost last night." Both hands back on the wheel, the cigarette dangling from his lip, he said, "Shouldn't take long to find your glasses."

Bigelow said, "We'll need a ladder. I suppose we can find it in one of the buildings."

"I saw a lawn chair around someplace."

Bigelow watched the cigarette ash grow and drop onto Robert's shirt. "Pity the grounds are such a shambles. It was an attractive property."

"Aeration does it good," said Robert. The cigarette rode up and down on his lip when he spoke.

Bigelow glanced at him. "What do you mean?"

Robert looked down at his greasy sweatshirt and swiped off the ash. "Taught forestry management for a few years."

"You taught?" asked Bigelow. "College level?"

"Graduate level."

"Tenured?" asked Bigelow.

"Don't talk to me about tenure," said Robert.

"What happened?"

"You mean, why did I get fired?" Robert turned watery eyes on Bigelow, who could just make them out in the dashboard light.

"Well, yes."

Robert held an imaginary bottle to his lips.

"Sorry about that."

"Don't be. I hated that rat race."

"How are we doing for time?" asked Bigelow.

"We've got time."

"Did you bring a flashlight?"

Robert reached down into the well and produced one.

"I don't want to go back down into that grave," said Bigelow with a shudder.

"Can't say that I blame you."

The cigarette had burned down to a nubbin. Robert squashed out the ember with his thumb and forefinger and tossed the butt out the window.

They rode the rest of the way up the dark and deserted Main

286

Street in silence, and Robert pulled over to the side. "Won't get a ticket this time of day."

"I certainly hope not," said Bigelow, getting out of the passenger side.

Brownie, sleeping with his head on Killdeer's thigh, woke with a start, the hair on his back lifted. Killdeer put a hand on the dog's neck and stroked him.

"Okay, buddy?" He started to get up, but his thigh, where Brownie's head had rested, was numb and his leg buckled. He fell back with a crash.

"Damn." He rubbed feeling back into the leg.

Brownie growled a deep-throated rumble.

"Hush up, boy! What do you sense?" Killdeer looked around and saw the faint glow of a flashlight. Man and dog moved silently toward the light along the narrow strip of ground between mounds of dirt and open graves. Killdeer stopped. Brownie clearly wanted to go forward.

"Hold it," whispered Killdeer, crouching on a wide spot. "We wait here."

Victoria led the way to a wide mossy place within a thicket that had been undisturbed in the search for cadavers. She gazed up at the familiar constellations, Orion, the hunter. Cassiopeia. The Pleiades. The Big Dipper, its pointer stars pointing to the North Star. The navigating star, her grandfather told her.

Howland nudged her, and she looked away from the bright stars. Her eyes, adjusted to the dark, picked out the glimmer of a flashlight.

"Let's move closer," he said. "Can you find the way?"

"Easily. I know the campus well," said Victoria.

They moved close enough to hear low voices. Victoria recognized Stevenson's.

"I warned him," she whispered. "He didn't listen."

"Who's he with?" whispered Howland.

"Robert, my landscaper."

"I thought you said 'Rabbit.'"

"'Robert' with a Boston accent is 'Rabbit,'" Victoria whispered. "I never suspected him until this evening. I recognized his car."

"His car looks like a hundred other Island cars. Looks exactly like mine."

"I know cars," whispered Victoria. "It's Robert's."

"Creepy," Stevenson murmured. "Let's get out of here."

"Perfect time to view this place," said Rabbit, swinging the flashlight around in an arc, illuminating mounds of dirt and deep black pits.

"I want to get to the fishing spot."

"There's time," said Rabbit.

"This is dangerous. Why aren't the graves filled in?"

"They want to catch the killer first," said Rabbit.

"Seems like an opportunity for the killer to bury more victims without having to dig the graves."

Rabbit shone the flashlight into the nearest grave. "One shove and down you go. Bring someone here on a night of fishing, smack him on the head, and topple him in. Just like that." He snapped off the light, and the night was darker than the darkest imagined darkness.

Stevenson backed away from the grave.

Rabbit laughed.

"We've got to make our move," whispered Victoria.

"Wait," said Howland.

"You'll have to lead," said Bigelow to Robert.

"No problem."

"Can you find the grave?"

"I was there when you fell in."

They walked from where they'd parked across the narrow sidewalk, and through the undergrowth at the edge of the campus. Robert held up the yellow crime scene tape and they ducked under. They walked a few more feet.

"I'm concerned about ticks," said Bigelow.

Robert said nothing. He stopped and shone the light at one of the open graves. "Here we are."

"What about the chair?"

"Wait here," said Robert. "I have to take the light to find it."

"There are ticks here," said Bigelow.

"Don't worry about ticks. They're everywhere."

Bigelow said, "I don't want to miss the boat."

"There's another light," whispered Victoria.

"Damnation."

"We'll have to check both of them. You take this close one," said Victoria. "I know the path and you don't."

"The police have a buddy system for a good reason," said Howland. "We stick together."

"One must be a sightseer," said Victoria.

"Why in hell would anyone come sightseeing at three-thirty in the morning?"

"Fishermen," said Victoria. "They're insane when the fish are running, but they're lunatics during the derby."

Lights flickered on either side of them.

"Professor Bigelow is to go back on the paper boat this morning. He lost his glasses when he fell into the grave. Robert was to pick him up. That means . . ." she stopped.

Howland said, "Who's the Rabbit with Stevenson?"

———

Killdeer spotted the second light at the same time Victoria did and had the same baffled reaction. Two killers? Two sightseers at three-thirty a.m.? Fishing derby crazies?

Brownie kept up a low, steady growl. He headed toward one of the lights. Killdeer's hair rose on his arms. He trusted Brownie. One of the lights must belong to the killer.

When Rabbit snapped off the flashlight, Stevenson spotted the second light. Someone must have parked along Main Street and come through the underbrush.

"What do you make of that?" he asked Rabbit.

"Another fisherman. This place attracts more crazies than the Lizzie Borden place. People are ghouls."

"Let's get out of here," said Stevenson.

"We'll sneak up on them, give them a thrill."

"Come on, Rabbit. I want out." Stevenson started toward the car and realized that, without the light, he was likely to fall into one of the open graves. He stopped.

"You scared?" asked Rabbit in a low voice.

"Damned right, I'm scared."

"Be a sport." Rabbit turned the flashlight off again.

"If someone sneaked up on me right now," Stevenson whispered, "I'd damned well have a heart attack."

Rabbit laughed. "You got a weak heart?"

Robert hadn't gone far with the light before Bigelow called out, "Come back! Hurry!"

"I haven't found the chair," Robert called back.

"Forget it!" Bigelow screamed.

"Are you okay?" Robert shouted.

"Hurry!"

"Did you hear that?" whispered Victoria.

They'd been standing, Victoria leaning on her lilac wood stick, Howland with his feet apart, arms folded, uncertain which way to go, when they heard Bigelow call out.

"Couldn't help but hear," Howland answered.

Victoria started off with Howland holding the flashlight. She could see what must be Robert's flashlight moving erratically as he dodged between graves.

"What's your trouble?" Robert called.

"Something's crawling on me. I can't see! Get it off!"

"Oh, for God's sake," said Robert. "Probably a tick."

"I hate ticks! Get it off!"

"Did you hear that?" said Stevenson.

"You kidding?" answered Rabbit. "Wake the dead with that yelling back and forth."

"Can't quite make out what they're yelling about."

"May be in trouble. Let's get over there."

"Damn! You're determined to keep me here."

"Someone needs help," said Rabbit. "Stay here if you want. I'm going."

"No way am I staying here. One wrong step . . ."

Rabbit headed toward the voices, Stevenson behind.

"Let me have the light," said Bigelow.

"No way." Robert swung the flashlight behind him.

Bigelow caught his arm and snatched the light out of it. He shone it down, where he'd pulled his trouser leg up, exposing his bony shin. "There!"

Robert moved in behind him. "Where?"

Bigelow swung around, slammed the flashlight over Robert's head, and shoved him into the grave. He crouched on the ground and was clawing handfuls of dirt from the nearest mound when Victoria reached him.

"Stop!" she commanded, lifting her stick.

"Watch it, Victoria!" Howland moved in with the light.

Bigelow looked up, his hands full of dirt.

Victoria brought down her stick with a powerful whack on his wrists. Bigelow dropped the earth and reached for her, his hands dripping muddy dirt, when Brownie attacked with a mighty growl.

Killdeer and Rabbit held Bigelow, who shouted obscenities at them. Howland and Stevenson hauled the stunned Robert out of the grave. Victoria called Casey on the cell phone, and within a few minutes the state police arrived followed soon after by Casey.

CHAPTER 37

Linda, Thackery's assistant, was out sick again. The news of her sister Roberta's imprisonment and release had sent her to her bed with a sick headache.

Victoria volunteered to help in Linda's absence.

She was on the phone when Wellborn Price came into the office.

"I'm sorry," Victoria was saying, "we have no comment at this time." She set the phone down and it rang again.

Wellborn slapped a bundle of letters and magazines on the desk in front of Victoria. "I picked up the mail."

"Ivy Green College . . . I'm sorry, no comment at this time."

"Sounds like this is where I first came in," said Wellborn. There was a knock on the door and Price Henderson entered.

They shook hands, then Price threw his arms around Wellborn Price and they hugged each other until Victoria thought she heard bones cracking.

"Hey, Dad, old man!"

"Hey, kid. Answer the phone, will you? Mrs. Trumbull and I want to talk."

"Yes, sir."

The phone rang. Price picked it up.

Thackery strode into the office, wheeled Linda's chair over, and sat down. "Mrs. Trumbull, I don't know how we can thank you enough. You saved that delivery man."

"I had help," said Victoria.

"Much as I couldn't stand Bigelow, I never imagined him as a serial killer."

"Combination of genes, rigid upbringing, bad choices, and stress he couldn't handle," said Wellborn.

Victoria was slitting envelopes. "Bruce Steinbicker didn't want Roberta to press charges, and when she learned her students were behind her kidnapping and why, she decided not to." Victoria held up an envelope. "Here's a letter for you, Thackery, from Ocean Engineering, Inc." She handed him the opened envelope. "That's where Dedie Wieler works."

"Who's she?" asked Wellborn.

"She was a faculty member on the oversight committee. She . . . what's the matter, Thackery?"

"This." Thackery held the letter out to her. "This is the matter."

Victoria read the letter and looked up. "A five-million-dollar grant to Ivy Green College to train ocean engineers?"

"Plus any required courses," said Thackery. "Five million dollars. You realize what that means?"

The front door opened and Walter entered. "Where's Thackery?"

Thackery put the letter down, took off his glasses, rubbed his eyes, and put his glasses back on. "What is it, Walter?"

"I want my dog."

The phone rang and Price answered. "No comment."

"What are you talking about?" asked Thackery.

"That officious cop took my dog."

"Dr. Killdeer?" asked Victoria. "He took Brownie?"

Walter stuck out his lower lip. "He took Brownie and left me a fifty-thousand-dollar check."

"What!?" said Thackery.

"I don't want the money. I want my dog," said Walter.

"Oh, my!" said Victoria. The phone rang again.